FIREWORKS AT PENNYCRESS INN

SARAH HOPE

B

Boldwood

First published in Great Britain in 2025 by Boldwood Books Ltd.

Copyright © Sarah Hope, 2025

Cover Design by Head Design Ltd.

Cover Images: Head Design Ltd. and Shutterstock

A CIP catalogue record for this book is available from the British Library.

Paperback ISBN 978-1-83617-466-0

Large Print ISBN 978-1-83617-465-3

Hardback ISBN 978-1-83617-464-6

Trade Paperback ISBN 978-1-80656-059-2

Ebook ISBN 978-1-83617-467-7

Kindle ISBN 978-1-83617-468-4

Audio CD ISBN 978-1-83617-459-2

MP3 CD ISBN 978-1-83617-460-8

Digital audio download ISBN 978-1-83617-461-5

This book is printed on certified sustainable paper. Boldwood Books is dedicated to putting sustainability at the heart of our business. For more information please visit https://www.boldwoodbooks.com/about-us/sustainability/

Boldwood Books Ltd, 23 Bowerdean Street, London, SW6 3TN

www.boldwoodbooks.com

For my children,
Let's change our stars
xXx

1

Polly Burrows pulled the sleeve of her chunky jumper over her hand before using it to wipe the condensation from the window of the taxi. 'Are we almost there?'

'Almost, miss. Just another mile or so.' The taxi driver glanced at her as she sat in the back seat, his broad grin revealing a missing front tooth.

'Great.' Smiling, she watched the treeline to their left give way to fields and squashed the desire to squeal. The excitement bubbling beneath the surface she'd felt ever since Mr Bob had promised her this job, and the impending promotion it would lead to threatened to overspill.

'You look happy there, miss. Not that I blame you. It's lovely around these parts. Mine and the wife's happy place, it is. Can't beat the Cotswolds for a romantic getaway, can you?' The taxi driver looked in his rear-view mirror.

Shaking her head slightly, it took Polly a few seconds to catch up with the conversation. A romantic getaway? Now, that's something she wouldn't know the first thing about. Not that she was about to admit it, especially to someone she'd only met fifteen minutes ago at Stratford-upon-Avon's train station. 'No, it definitely can't be beaten... for a romantic getaway.'

'So, who's the lucky fellow?'

Shifting uncomfortably on the back seat, Polly tried to avert her eyes from catching his gaze in the rear-view mirror. 'The trip is for a new job.'

'Ooh, I see. Well, congratulations. Career first, romance later. That's all the rage these days with you young lot, isn't it?' The man chuckled to himself as his focus shifted back onto the road.

'Something like that.' Polly pulled her mobile from her flower-print cloth tote bag, desperately hoping the conversation was over. She'd spent enough time trying to justify her decision not to accept her friend's offers of setting her up on blind dates with their mates, colleagues or the delivery guy from the local pizza restaurant, she sure didn't need a random stranger telling her lies about how fabulous it was to be in a relationship. Been there, done that, got the T-shirt and the never-worn wedding dress to boot.

Nope, all daft notions of a fairy-tale ending were way, way back in her past. Her future, on the other hand, was bright. After years of volunteering in the Education and Outreach department for the Cotswold Wildlife and Wilderness Trust, she'd finally been given the job as an outreach and education officer and Mr Bob, who managed the programme across the trust, had all but promised she'd be given the promotion to project manager at Meadowfield Nature Reserve as soon as the current holder of the role retired in three months' time.

'Here we are, Meadowfield.' The taxi driver tapped his knuckles against the side window.

Looking up from her mobile, Polly slipped it back into her bag and looked out of the window. Small cottages, hugging the narrow pavements, had replaced the fields, their yellow Cotswold brickwork crowned by old, thatched roofs.

'Just a couple more minutes and we'll be at Pennycress Inn.' The taxi slowed as the car in front turned into a side street.

'Great.' This was it – Meadowfield! Her new home for the next three months until she secured the promotion and was able to apply for a mortgage to buy somewhere either in the village of Meadowfield itself, or else close by. And three months was plenty of time for her childhood home, her grandparents' flat, to sell too.

The taxi slowed to a stop in front of a large Cotswold-stone building, its garden brimming with the colours of autumn. The leaves on the trees had begun to change from yellow to copper and the border burst with the oranges and reds of chrysanthemums in full bloom. The broken pathway meandering towards the lavender-coloured front door added a particular charm to the property that newly laid slabs would not have.

Turning in his seat, the taxi driver whistled. 'What a lovely place. I think I may have just found the next spot for me and the wife's next trip.'

'It is beautiful.' Polly had always dreamt about living in a cottage. Not that she'd ever be able to afford a place as grand as this. She'd be lucky if she could get enough from the sale of her grandparents' small two-bed flat back home to be able to afford a bedsit in a place as idyllic as Meadowfield. Although, perhaps when she got the promotion...

'And would you look at that?' The taxi driver wound his window down and pointed upwards. 'See the animal on top of the thatched roof? What's that meant to be? I haven't got my glasses.'

'Er... I'm pretty sure it's a cat. Why haven't...' Thinking better of asking why he hadn't been wearing his glasses while driving, she shook her head. She wasn't sure she wanted to know his answer. Besides, he'd got her here in one piece and he'd already told her when he'd first picked her up that she was his last fare of the day.

'I'll help you with your bags.' The driver jumped out of the front seat before making his way around the back of the car.

Slipping her tote bag over her shoulder, Polly opened the door and stepped outside. Pausing, she looked towards Pennycress Inn in front of her. She was early – too early to check in – but if she could just leave her suitcase and bags somewhere, she could wander into the centre of the village and explore a little, get her bearings before heading to the nature reserve tomorrow and starting her new job.

2

Dragging her old green suitcase up the step to the quaint lavender-painted door, Polly pressed the doorbell before glancing behind and watching the taxi disappearing down the road.

After a few minutes, the door opened and a woman appeared, her hair escaping from a messy bun and framing her flushed face. The tips of glittery pink fairy wings were visible above her shoulders and as she greeted Polly, she brandished a silver wand. 'Hi, oh, you must be Polly Burrows? Is that right?'

Polly blinked before glancing at the little sign next to the front door again. Yes, it definitely read Pennycress Inn, so she was in the right place. She just hadn't been expecting to be welcomed by a life-size fairy. She cleared her throat. 'Hi, yes, that's me. I'm afraid I'm a little early, but I wondered if there was anywhere I could store my luggage for a few hours before I can check in, please?'

'Yes, of course.' Swinging the door open wide, the woman waved her wand towards Polly's suitcase. 'I'll get that for you. Come on in.'

'Thanks.' Stepping inside, Polly looked around the large hallway. The dark oak floorboards were complemented by gorgeous, flowered wallpaper and a large decorative staircase wound its way upwards next to the reception area.

Pulling the suitcase inside, the woman closed the door before turning to Polly. 'I'm so sorry. I can't remember if I introduced myself or not. I'm Laura and welcome to Pennycress Inn.'

'Thanks. It's beautiful in here.' Following her towards the large oak reception desk tucked beneath the ornate staircase, Polly jumped aside as two children ran from the door to her right before disappearing into the room opposite.

'Careful!' Laura called after them.

'I'm going to turn them into frogs!' A small girl raced after them, holding an overly bright wand with the words 'Happy Birthday' emblazoned in the centre of the star-shaped head.

That explained Laura's fancy dress outfit. Polly must have walked in on a children's birthday party.

'Slow down, Willow! We don't want you tripping on your birthday, do we?' Laura grimaced.

Coming to an abrupt halt, the small girl, Willow, turned and looked across at Laura. 'Sorry.'

'That's okay.' Laura glanced towards the door the girl had run out from as a woman followed her through into the hallway.

'Come on, Fairy Princess Willow, Laura's right. You can't be running around the inn like this. Let's go and play musical statues. I have prizes.' The woman held up a bag brimming with small toys.

'Ooh, prizes!' Lowering her wand, Willow approached the woman. 'Can you make sure I win, Mummy? It is my birthday.'

Shaking her head, the woman laughed before turning to Laura and Polly. 'I'm so sorry. I'll try to contain the chaos.'

'Oh, don't worry. I've arrived early, so pretend I'm not actually here.' Polly smiled. By the looks of things, the inn doubled as a base for children's parties and the last thing she wanted to do was to curb any enjoyment when it was her fault she'd decided to get to Meadowfield so early.

'You may just regret saying that.' The woman laughed.

'That's true.' Laura looked at Polly. 'Is it okay if I call you Polly?'

'Yes, of course.' Polly grinned. She had a feeling she was going to enjoy staying here.

'Thanks.' Laura continued and waved her wand between Polly and the other woman. 'Polly, this is Jill. She's the genius who brings the inn's gardens to life, whatever the season. Jill, this is Polly, who will be staying with us for three months. That's right, isn't it?'

Polly nodded. 'Yes. All being well, at least.'

'Lovely to meet you, Polly. And welcome to Meadowfield.' Stepping forward, Jill took Polly's hand in hers as her daughter, Willow, made an attempt to snatch the bag of prizes. 'I promise you it's not normally like this. Pennycress is usually a peaceful place to stay.'

'Don't worry. I used to be a primary school teacher, so this is nothing.' Polly waved her hand to encompass Willow, the music and shrieks wafting from the other rooms.

'Haha, Jill's right. I mean, we do cater for children's parties and other celebrations, but we keep those strictly for during the day.' Laura smiled.

'Come on, Willow. Let's give Laura and our guest a bit of that peace we're talking about.' Lifting the bag of prizes just out of reach above Willow's head, Jill glanced back at Polly. 'See you around.'

'Okay.' Willow crossed her arms, almost batting herself in the face with her large wand as she did so, and watched her mum disappear through the doorway. Then, a mischievous glint in her eye, Willow pointed her wand at Laura and Polly in turn. 'And I turn you into frogs!'

'Ribbit, ribbit.' Laughing, Laura shook her head as Willow chased after her mum. As the music was turned up, Laura walked across to the door and quietly closed it. 'Sorry.'

'Honestly, it's no problem. It's good to hear the children enjoying themselves.' Polly smiled. The children hadn't been the reason she'd left teaching. It had been the politics and the never-ending tasks thrown at her to add to the never-ending to-do list, and the fact the senior leadership team had appeared to care more about the same set of data being inputted into five different formats rather than allowing her to use her time to actually plan and resource lessons she'd be presenting to the children. 'Sorry again for being so early. I'll get out of your hair as soon as I've sorted my bags.'

'Not a problem and you're very welcome to check in early. Your room is ready and waiting.' Tucking her wand beneath her arm, Laura walked behind the counter. 'You're here for work, right?'

'Yes, that's it.' Polly grinned. It was Monday tomorrow, the start of a brand-new week and the beginning of the rest of her life. 'I'm starting a new job just outside of Meadowfield in the morning.'

'Oh, you must be excited?' Laura dipped behind the counter, the tips of her wings just visible above the oak surface. Standing back up, she held a key in her hand.

'And you've forgotten something... Another reason why this job is going to be great for you.'

'What? What have I forgotten?' Polly wracked her brain. 'You mean because I don't have to deal with our wonderful headteacher any longer or because, hopefully, any children I meet through my new job will actually be interested in what I have to say rather than me trying to entice them to learn about a million and one things they'll never have to encounter again once they've grown up?'

'Haha, that's rubbish. I use Pythagoras' theorem every single day of my life.'

'Sure you do.' Shaking her head, Polly grinned. Stacey might have always been a mathematics buff, but she, Polly, most definitely was not and that was one subject she wouldn't miss teaching. 'You do remember it's not actually on the curriculum until secondary school, right?'

'I know. I may be slightly exaggerating.' Stacey laughed. 'Anyway, the beautiful and intricate subject of maths aside, there's still something else you're forgetting.'

'The beautiful...' Polly snorted. 'You can keep your maths, Stacey. I'll take the flora and fauna of the nature reserve over brackets and indices any day of the week. But enlighten me. What am I forgetting?'

'Zac Sinclair.' Stacey paused before adding with a dramatic flair. 'Your arch-nemesis. The one person you'll be glad to be free of now you're no longer volunteering at the trust's HQ.'

Polly shuddered. Two words, that was all they were, but two words and the name of the man who was a master at getting under her skin, the king of sarcasm and making her feel as though she were two inches tall. The very man who had belittled her volunteering role at the trust time and time again, mostly just to get ahead himself. A man who had seemingly had everything passed to him on a silver plate: his job, his money, heck, probably even his good looks... Nope, nope, he wasn't even good-looking. Not with that arched eyebrow of his and the way his lips curled in that permanent sneer. Plus, the way he spoke, talking to everyone besides her with all the charm of a man on a first date but all the intention of a measly slug. Yuck.

'Polly? Are you still with me? Or have you been swallowed up by the daydream of you and Zac Sinclair's wedding and subsequent eighty-four children?'

'What? Eurgh. You're really gross, Stacey. Do you know that?' Polly pulled the phone away from her ear and looked suspiciously at the screen, where Stacey's name stared back at her. How did she do this? How did she read her with such accuracy? Yes, they'd worked together at the same school and in the same year group for twelve years, had shared a flat for seven of those before Stacey had moved in with her partner, Freddie, and Polly had briefly moved in with her ex-fiancé before then moving back into her childhood home to take care of her grandma, but that didn't explain how Stacey knew her so well. Polly couldn't read her. She shrugged. Spy camera? Secret microphone? Or maybe Stacey was just a better judge of character than she was and Polly an open book.

'Uh-huh.' Stacey's giggle erupted down the phone before she spoke again, her tone becoming a staged seriousness. 'And methinks you doth protest too much.'

'No. Just no. Zac Sinclair has made my life a living misery for the past four months. I most certainly will not be missing him.' Polly pushed herself off the windowsill and turned to look back outside, where the thin, stringy branches of the willow tree were being pulled in all directions by the wind. It was almost as though the tree could sense this conversation was heading into tricky territory and was trying to warn her. 'In fact, if I'd had a moment to think about things, I should have thrown a party just to celebrate the fact he's now out of my life for good.'

As soon as Stacey's guffaw met Polly's ear, she regretted ever letting the word 'party' escape her lips. Why had she said that? Had she secretly wanted to mull over this topic for the thousandth time? Nope, she did not. She silently cursed the willow tree for not making the warning a little more obvious.

'I knew it! That fateful night is still on your mind,' Stacey said between fits of laughter.

'Stop it. It is not. You know I wish it had never happened.' Polly traced the pad of her forefinger across her lips. Her leaving party, a night she'd supposed to have spent celebrating the end of her old teaching career and the beginning of a new one at Meadowfield Nature Reserve, the job she'd be starting tomorrow. And she knew exactly what Stacey was referring to. That two-second snog she and Zac had shared. Four whole months ago. A moment of drunken madness that she'd regretted ever since. And the moment things had changed between her and Zac. She'd noticed the difference the first time she'd seen him after the party, that first day back at the trust headquarters where she'd continued to volunteer until her new position here in Meadowfield began. He'd been different with her, aloof, sarcastic, all the damning characteristics she now described him as having, whereas before she'd been shown the charming, friendly side of his personality, the side he portrayed to others. 'Besides, you're making it sound as though it was something more than it was. It was just a kiss. A measly, tiny, short-lived kiss.'

'Uh-huh.'

'It was and you know it.' Yes, it had been nice and, yes, even though she'd rather pull her teeth out than admit it, that evening, in that moment, she'd let herself think there might just be more to it than there had been. But Stacey would be the last person she'd admit that to.

'Aw, I'm sure he'll be missing you just as much as you'll miss him,' Stacey continued, her voice laced with sarcasm.

'And what's that supposed to mean?' She'd never outwardly retaliated to his indifference. And she'd never spoken to him about the kiss they'd shared either. They were both adults and she'd got the message he wasn't interested loud and clear.

Yes, she'd said a few choice words in her head when he'd said something to suck up to the management – not that he needed to, not with his parents being huge benefactors to the trust, up until a year ago anyway when that had stopped for some reason, perhaps because they felt with their son working there they were still contributing without dipping into their bottomless pockets – but she'd always maintained her professional, friendly persona around everyone she'd worked with, whether or not she'd liked them. A skill she'd perfected whilst teaching at Daisy Chain Primary and answering to Mrs Jedd, the headteacher.

'Nothing. Just that...' The phone line became muffled before Stacey's voice returned. 'Sorry, I'm going to have to run. Freddie's back and he's a bit worse for wear. I believe a long liquid lunch has been had.'

'No worries. Speak to you soon.'

'Yes! Ring me tomorrow. I want to hear all about your first day at the office.' Stacey paused before whispering loudly, 'I'll leave you with two words before I go though – Leaving Party!'

'Don't...'

Too late. The phone line was silent. Stacey had gone.

Taking a deep breath, Polly pushed all thoughts of Zac Sinclair from her mind. He was in her past and she was now focusing on her future.

Polly threw her mobile onto the bed, the device bouncing on the spongy mattress. Now, that looked good. She'd have just five minutes, maybe ten, before she went out exploring. After all, what with saying goodbye for now to her little home and the train and taxi ride, it had been a long, emotional and exhausting day.

Throwing herself down next to her mobile, she sank into the puffy duvet and closed her eyes, the faint tune of 'Happy Birthday' from the children's party below lulling her to sleep.

4

Letting the glass door of the large visitor centre positioned on the edge of Meadowfield Nature Reserve close behind her, Polly slipped off her coat and pulled at the hem of her pale blue shirt. She hadn't known what to wear. As a volunteer, she'd always rocked up in jeans and an old jumper, but now she was an employee she wanted to make the right impression.

Polly looked around. The vast foyer was largely unused by the looks of things, more a sad corridor leading to the cluster of visitor toilets at the far end. Someone had tacked tired-looking photographs of the reserve to the walls a couple of feet apart, the curling edges of the information guides beneath told dreary stories of its history. It didn't look particularly engaging to her, someone who was interested in conservation, so she could only hazard a guess that the normal day-to-day visitor strode right past, ignoring them at best and not even noticing them at worst, on their way to relieve themselves after the picnic lunch they'd brought with them.

Or maybe not. She glanced back out of the large windows surrounding the double doors as rain lashed against the glass. There'd be no picnics here for a while. Not with this weather.

Looking around, she noticed two doors leading off the foyer, one labelled 'classroom', the other 'offices'. That's where she'd be going, then. To the offices. Now she was here, all the excitement which had been building up to this day had suddenly disappeared and instead been replaced with cold fear.

What if she didn't fit in? She wasn't local, after all. What if her new colleagues didn't believe she could do a decent job because she didn't know the area? Being local would definitely be an advantage in a role like this.

Or what if they just didn't think she was likeable? Even Stacey had once admitted it had taken a while to warm to her. Polly had tried hard over the years to be more assertive, less shy, but she knew she still had a long way to go. She knew people still came to the conclusion that she was stand-offish, even though that was the furthest from the truth. Apart from with Stacey and a handful of old school friends, she'd never felt anything like confident with her peers.

Turning back towards the door, she took a deep breath, hoping the sight of the trees circling the car park, the rain and the general ambience of the nature reserve would go some way to steadying her nerves. Today was a big deal. She couldn't pretend it wasn't. After all, if her new colleagues didn't like her, didn't gel with her, or came to the conclusion that she was incompetent, then the promotion might just be less of a given than Mr Bob had promised her. But she was here now. She was on the first step of her new journey, and she was damn well going to do her best to make a good impression.

Fixing a smile to her face, Polly turned back around and made her way towards the office door before rapping her knuckles against the wood.

'Hello?' A man sporting a dark green short-sleeved polo shirt despite the chill in the air, a brush of a white beard and the greenest eyes she'd ever seen pulled the door open and stood in the doorway, his large frame almost reaching from one side of the doorframe to the other.

'Hi, Declan, is it? I'm Polly Burrows, I'm your new recruit.' Trying to feign an air of confidence, Polly stuck her hand out, grateful when the older man took it. At least he was wearing a name badge with his title of project manager written beneath. It was a good start that she didn't have to flounder and try to work out if he was her new boss or not. He was.

'Polly! Fantastic to meet you! Come on through. We're all excited to have you join our small team. We're small but mighty, ay?' After closing the door again, Declan held his arms out wide to encompass the room, the one person sitting at her desk turning and grinning at him.

'Oh yes. We are. Or that's what we tell ourselves.' Pushing her wheeled chair back, a woman with jet-black hair stood up and walked towards them.

'Hi, Polly. I'm Vicki. I'm the program assistant around here, so any admin jobs you need doing, just shout.'

'Great, thanks.' Shaking Vicki's hand, Polly frowned as something bubbled beneath the sleeve of the woman's dark green sweatshirt. 'Have you got something in your sleeve? It's moving.'

'Haha, that'll be Rolo.' Vicki held open the cuff of her sleeve as a small, brown rat poked his nose out.

'It's a rat!' Polly swallowed. She wasn't sure what she'd been expecting, but it definitely hadn't been that.

'Vicki here volunteers at a wildlife rescue centre in her spare time. Not sure how she does it, but she's always bringing in some sort of creature or another, aren't you, Vicki?' Declan gently stroked the rat's nose before it disappeared back up her sleeve.

'I do. This little one is only a baby. He was abandoned by his mother, so he's being hand-reared.' Vicki laughed as Rolo continued to make his way up her arm before peeping out of her collar. 'He's such a sweet character.'

'That's what you say about all the waifs and strays you bring in,' Declan chided.

'Well, they are.' Vicki shrugged before turning back to Polly and flicked her hair dramatically as she grinned. 'As I said, I'm Queen of the Admin, although there is only one of me for the entire team, but I'll do my best to support you where I can.'

'Great, thanks.' Polly smiled as Vicki turned and flourished her arm towards her desk in the corner, an array of photographs of various animals crammed across the surface, with minimal space left for her laptop, which peeped amongst the clusters of frames.

Turning back, Vicki pointed towards two empty desks sitting side by side at the far end of the large room. 'Over there are Dennis and Art. They're out at the moment, but Art is the outreach and education officer and David the community engagement officer. They'll be back at lunch, so you'll catch them then.'

Polly blinked. Had she heard that right? Had Vicki said Art was the outreach and education officer? Did that mean there were going to be two of them? She'd been told her job was to fill a gap and, given the nature reserve wasn't particularly large, she'd assumed she'd be the only one. Unless Art was here to show her the ropes and would then be leaving? Yes, that seemed likely.

'The ranger, Harold, will be pottering about somewhere,' Vicki continued, not once letting her cheery smile slip.

'Sorry, can I just check that you said Art was an outreach and education officer?' Polly glanced back towards the desks at the far end of the office as if half expecting him to appear on command.

'Yes, that's right.' Vicki nodded before leading the way towards the other end of the office, where two more empty desks sat. 'And this is your desk right here. Well, either of them, to be honest. You're the first newbie to arrive so you can have first dibs.'

Polly glanced between the two empty desks and Art's desk. Wouldn't it make more sense for her and Art to sit together? It seemed slightly daft to have the two of them located at opposite ends of the office if he was going to be training her up.

'Which would you like? I'd choose quickly if I were you, your colleague might arrive at any point and then you'll be left with no choice.' Vicki laughed, her delicate voice taking on the sound of a hyena.

'Oh, umm.' Polly shrugged before placing her handbag on the desk closest to where she was standing. Both desks were centred in the middle of a large window overlooking the nature reserve, although it looked as though the view from the other desk would be hindered slightly by a large shed-like structure. She felt a little bad for taking the desk with the best view, but she figured she'd worked long and hard for this opportunity and given up a ton of stuff too. Besides, as Vicki had said, she was here first.

'Good choice.' Vicki grinned before pointing towards an open door revealing a small kitchen leading off from the end of the office. 'I'll let you get settled in. Would you like a coffee?'

'Oh, I'd love one, please.' Polly smiled. She wasn't too sure she actually had room for a drink after the delicious breakfast of cinnamon-sprinkled French toast and filter coffee she'd enjoyed at the inn this morning, but she didn't want to offend her new colleague.

'Great. I'm parched. I ran out of the door without even attempting to make one this morning. Milk? Sugar?'

'Milk, one sugar, please.'

'Coming right up.' Vicki began to walk towards the kitchen before calling back over her shoulder. 'Declan, you want a cuppa?'

As he answered, Polly wheeled her chair out from beneath the desk before sitting down. Swinging it gently from side to side, she grinned. She could get used to this comfort. It certainly beat sitting on hard miniature plastic chairs in the classroom.

Pulling herself towards her desk, she rested her elbows on the pine surface and cupped her chin in her hands. The view was stunning. From here she could see a narrow gravel pathway winding its way towards a little bridge over a stream to lead the way into the midst of the nature reserve. Trees hugged the pathway, birds fluttering from branch to branch as though on some secret mission or other.

Perfect. It may have taken five years of dedication, five years of juggling teaching with volunteering, but it had been worth it. She was out of the classroom but still able to work in her field of expertise and passion – teaching. What could be more perfect than mixing educating with nature?

Yep. She had her dream job – outreach and education officer. She might be new to the nature reserve and Meadowfield itself, but she wasn't new to her position and what would be expected of her, she'd volunteered for five years assisting in the role. She could do this, and she couldn't wait to get started.

Tearing her eyes from the idyllic view, she began to unpack her tote bag. She hadn't really known what would be provided and what wouldn't, so she'd bought a new notebook and pen set for the occasion, just to have something she could take notes in before getting to grips with where stock was kept and before she got the laptop the trust would provide. She'd also brought the photo frame holding an image of her and her grandparents. The one which had taken pride of place on her desk in the classroom for twelve years and would now take pride of place on her desk here.

Three months of being dedicated to the job in hand and she'd be promoted to project manager, which is what she needed if she were to be able to make ends meet and settle in this part of the Cotswolds.

Next, she pulled her mobile from her bag and grinned as she spotted a missed call from the estate agent. This might be just the news she'd been waiting for! Her grandparents' flat, which she'd been struggling to sell for months now, ever since she'd been offered this job, might just have had an offer. She hadn't heard about any viewings, but she'd been out all day Saturday and, of course, travelling here to Meadowfield yesterday, so perhaps David, the estate agent, had shown someone round on Saturday. She'd given the agency the key after all.

Everything was coming together. After months of uncertainty and living off savings, things were on the road to aligning.

'Here you go, Polly. One coffee with sugar and milk.' Vicki slid a large green mug onto her desk before hitching her thumb behind her. 'You're being summoned to the meeting room. I think the other newbie has finally arrived and Declan wants to speak to you both.'

'Oh great. Thanks for this.' Nodding towards the mug, Polly slipped her mobile back into her bag and stood up. She'd ring the estate agent back when she had a spare moment. Picking up her heavy mug, she headed towards another door next to the small kitchen, which she hadn't actually noticed until Vicki had pointed it out.

5

With the large mug in one hand, Polly tapped on the door with the other, and lifted the mug to her lips. She frowned as a dribble of coffee ran over the rim and settled down the front of her shirt. Taking a quick sip, Polly lowered the mug again and brushed at the droplets of coffee, the brown liquid forming a smudge which closely imitated one of those ink pictures promising to reveal secret childhood trauma or such you see on some social media quizzes. Typical.

'Come in.' Declan's cheerful voice sounded through the thin door.

After a final attempt at soaking up the coffee stain with a tissue from her pocket, Polly shoved the tissue back and opened the door. A large, very well-used pine table sat in the middle of a white-walled plain room which was barely bigger than the table itself. Squashed at one end stood a sizeable flip-board and a tiny table housing a kettle and jug of water in the corner. Declan was sitting at the far side of the table, papers in front of him and a grin spread across his face, whilst a man was sitting with his back towards her, presumably the other new addition to the team.

'That's it, pull up a chair. I'd like you to meet our other new team member.' Declan indicated the chair next to the man.

As Polly approached the table, the man stood up and slowly turned around. When she saw his face, she halted. Her pulse quickened and her stomach churned, threatening to exhume the lovely breakfast she'd gobbled down a couple of hours ago. Of all the people...

'Polly Burrows.' He uttered her name almost before he'd turned with his hand held midway in the air, ready to offer a handshake. Pausing for a millisecond before realising she wasn't holding hers out, the man lowered it as his steely blue eyes narrowed.

'Zac Sinclair.' She spat the words through her clenched jaw, her grip tightening on the handle of the mug. This couldn't be happening. The one person she'd been glad to see the back of... no, the one person she'd been overjoyed to be leaving behind her, was here. And he was joining the team.

'You two know each other?' Declan slapped his forehead jovially. 'Of course you do. You were both working at headquarters.'

'I was working; Miss Burrows was volunteering.' The coldness seeping into Zac's voice was unmistakable as he sat back down, minus the handshake.

'Yes, yes – well, we're all the same here at the trust – workers, volunteers, we're all colleagues.' Declan indicated the chair next to Zac again.

Polly slipped into it and placed her mug carefully on the table before shifting the chair along, as far away from Zac as she could without appearing rude. With her heart racing, she clasped her hands around the mug, hoping the warmth of the coffee would calm her. It didn't matter if he was here. It was still her new start, the beginning of her career with the trust and she wasn't about to let his presence put a dampener on that. Lifting the mug to her lips, she took a long, shuddery breath, hoping no one would see how off-kilter his presence had made her.

'I would like to formally welcome you both to the team.' Declan shuffled the pile of papers in front of him before pulling two out and sliding them across the table towards Polly and Zac. 'Now, I know you've both already signed contracts for a temporary position here, but these are to outline your allocated positions and job descriptions, so if you wouldn't mind signing these, we can then get on with the other nitty-gritty admin stuff before Harold takes you for a tour of our wonderful reserve.'

'Thanks.' Taking the contract, Polly looked down and blinked, willing her eyes to focus instead of being tempted to glance in Zac's direction. Temporary? She didn't remember Mr Bob telling her it was temporary. And she was sure the contract she'd already signed hadn't stated anything to that effect. She shrugged. He must mean temporary until the promotion. That made sense.

'I hate to be this guy, but there's a typo. I'm here for the role of communications and marketing officer, not fundraising and development.' Zac turned his contract around and pushed it back across the table towards Declan.

He hated to be that guy. Polly swallowed a snigger. In the two years she'd known and tolerated Zac's presence, she'd learned one thing about him and that was that he always wanted to be that guy. There was nothing he loved more than to point out someone else's mistake – and take advantage of it any way he could.

She looked down at her contract. No, she wasn't being fair, she was letting her feelings about the kiss and the subsequent events cloud her. He was thorough, yes, but he didn't really enjoy getting one up on someone, even if it had felt that way since the night of the party.

'No, no mistake. We have had a recent shuffle around here at the reserve, and we have that position covered already.' Declan slid the paper back across the table as he smiled kindly.

Zac tapped the contract with the tip of his pen. 'That's not the position I applied for.'

'Oh, I'm sorry, but I'm afraid that's the position we have to fill. I think there must have been a misunderstanding in communication between us and HQ.'

Stealing a glance at Zac, Polly picked up her mug in an attempt to hide the small twitch of her lips as she struggled not to smile. *Ha, serves you right, Zachary Sinclair. Maybe you can leave now?*

'But fundraising isn't my specialism. I've worked in marketing for corporate organisations for years. That's what I do.' Leaning forward in his chair, Zac frowned.

Holding his hands out, palms up, Declan raised his eyebrows. 'I apologise for any misunderstanding. You're both here to be our fundraising and development gurus. We're having a little trouble with funds at the moment and need fresh eyes...'

Both here to be fundraising and development gurus? *Both?* Her and Zac? Zac and her? What? No.

Lowering the heavy mug with a bang, Polly watched in dismay as the now tepid liquid rolled down the edge of the ceramic before pooling on the pine table and making its way towards the paper in front of her. Swallowing, she cleared her throat, her voice coming out as a squeak. 'I was told I would be working in outreach and education.'

Looking from Polly to Zac and back again, Declan pulled the contracts back towards him, waving hers in the air in an attempt to dispel the coffee. Taking his glasses from their spot tucked beneath his beard in the collar of his polo shirt, he placed them at the end of his nose and looked at the contracts again. Tapping his finger against the paper, he then looked back up. 'I fear there must have been quite the communication error if you were both informed of the wrong job titles. We do have Art and Dennis who, although relatively new to their current roles, are working very well as outreach and education, and communications and marketing officers. I couldn't possibly ask them to shuffle around again.'

Polly glanced towards Zac, who ran his fingers through his dark glossy hair before slumping back in his chair. Wasn't he going to question Declan's decision? Insist he retract the job offer and instead offer them both – ha, or him – the role which had been promised?

Polly cleared her throat. 'I'm not sure if you know my employment history. I was a teacher and have volunteered in the outreach and education sector of the trust for the past five years.'

Declan nodded. 'Yes, Mr Bob passed across both of your CVs. Most excellent, both of them, but it doesn't change the fact that the positions we have available are for fundraising and development officers. Two of them. Now, I can see what a shock this must be to you both, particularly when you had been promised entirely different roles, but, in all honesty, I think this could work to our advantage and yours.'

'How so?' Zac shook his head, disbelief etched across his features.

Leaning forward, Declan smiled. 'Because you're precisely what we need, both of you. This nature reserve is quite frankly on its knees with regard to funds. We have a wealth of wildlife; we have enrichment opportunities and rewilding projects ready to go. The only thing we lack is funding.'

'But we've already established that's not in either of our backgrounds.' Zac straightened his back.

'Precisely. Over the years we've had experienced fundraisers come and go, but there's one thing they lacked, and I just think you both might be able to provide it.' Declan wagged his finger at them.

'What is it?' Polly frowned.

'A fresh pair of eyes.' Declan pointed his finger first at Polly and then at Zac. 'Or, in this case, two fresh pairs of eyes. You're coming into the job with no expectations. You're not going to spout to me that this or that fundraising tactic worked at a reserve down in Devon or up in Cumbria and so will work here. We've been there, tried that. Meadowfield Nature Reserve will be a clean slate to you.'

'I...' Polly stuttered before falling silent again. Her head was whirring. How was she supposed to take on a job which she had zero experience in? Especially for the trust – the trust which had taken a chance on her, the trust which she wanted to do her best by?

'And another thing, we've been burnt. We've had people come and go quicker than a yo-yo. We need people with passion who understand how these things work at a place like ours. Yes, we're not huge, we're not offering anything particularly exciting here at Meadowfield Nature Reserve, but what we are offering – a sanctuary for both wildlife and locals alike – is special. We need people to come in and see what we're missing. To see what those past employees couldn't see, to see the little things, the things that got overlooked.'

'Right.' Polly nodded, still unsure quite what it was he was trying to say. What was she supposed to do? The closest she'd ever come to fundraising was selling raffle tickets behind a stall at the school summer fête. She couldn't be responsible for raising the amount of money the nature reserve needed to function. She just didn't have the experience. And if she did take the chance and agree to the new role then she'd be jeopardising the promotion, but if she didn't take it there wouldn't even be a promotion opportunity for her... It all felt wrong.

'Of course, I understand if all of this' – Declan held his arms aloft, encompassing the small meeting room and the reserve through the window behind him – 'is out of your comfort zone.'

'I'll take it.' Reaching across the table, Zac snatched the contract back and signed it before glancing across at Polly and raising an eyebrow.

Huh, he didn't think she was capable. That's why he had that smug look on his face. Well, she'd show him. She'd show him she could do this. She grinned as she held her hand out for the contract. It was only for three months, after all. Three months of pretending she had a clue what she was doing and then she'd be promoted and move into the role of project manager and, with her experience as Key Stage One lead, she knew she was more than capable of doing that job. That would show him. Yes, there may have been a miscommunication with the job roles, but Declan was definitely retiring, so his position would need filling. 'I'd love to take the job.'

'Good, good.' Waiting for them to sign and then taking the contracts back, Declan grinned from ear to ear, completely oblivious to the fact that moments before Polly had been questioning whether to take it or not. Pushing his chair back, Declan held out a hand, first to Polly and then to Zac. 'In that case, welcome aboard.'

'Thanks.' Shaking Declan's hand, Polly tried to keep her expression neutral rather than let on how she was really feeling about the whole misunderstanding. Three months. That was all she had to give to the fundraising job and then Declan would be retiring and, as long as she proved herself, she'd be able to step into his role as project manager. Yes, three months. She could cope with that. She'd do a ton of research into fundraising when she got back to Pennycress Inn, find out what would actually be expected of her and make sure she was prepared.

'Looking forward to the new challenge.' Zac nodded.

Trust him to suddenly be 'looking forward' to the change of job role. Bringing her hands into her lap, she clenched her fists. Yes, it might only be three months but that would be three whole months of working closely with Zac. Three whole months of sitting side-by-side at their desks. Three whole months...

'Great! Well, if you'd both like to wait here, I'll go and see if I can track down our ranger, Harold. He's the expert on the reserve and will be able to show you around.' Leaning down, Declan shuffled the papers before jabbing his finger to the tiny table in the corner of the room. 'Help yourself to refreshments while you wait.'

'Thank you.' Sitting back down, Zac ran his fingers down his striped tie before lying it flat against his starched white shirt.

Lowering herself back into her seat as well, Polly pulled her mug towards her again as the door clicked shut behind her, announcing Declan's departure. She stole a glance at Zac as she brought her mug to her lips, the cold coffee tasting a little more bitter than it had done previously. They were in this together then? Both of them had just had the rug pulled out from beneath their feet. Both of them had just had surprise jobs thrown at them. Placing her mug down, she cleared her throat. 'Well, that was a surprise, wasn't it?'

'Uh-huh.' Without giving her so much as a look, Zac nodded, his gaze seemingly glued to the view out of the window.

Right. Nothing had changed then. Zac was still cold to her. She let her mind wander back to when he'd first started volunteering at the trust and she'd helped him settle in, pointed him in the right direction when he'd been looking for resources, had even advised him on a couple of things. He'd been normal. Nice. He'd appreciated the help even though she'd been a volunteer and he had taken a job there. He'd treated her like an equal and respected the time and work she put into the trust. Not for the first time, she thought that the kiss hadn't been worth the sacrifice of losing the charming Zac she'd fallen into an easy friendship with. And so dramatically as well.

'Coffee?' Standing up, Zac made his way towards the refreshment table.

'Umm, no thanks.' Polly nodded towards her mug. That was the first time in months he'd offered her a drink. She missed that. She missed the way they'd always got along. Maybe one day she'd get used to this uncomfortable dance they now did together. She shifted position, crossing her legs.

Huffing, Zac shook the oat milk carton before pouring it into his cracked mug.

No, the shift hadn't happened the exact moment of the kiss. It had happened the day after, but not straight away, not until halfway through the day in fact. She remembered because she'd been going to give an assembly on the subject of the Cotswold Wildlife and Wilderness Trust at her old school, the one she'd just left. Having left a week before the end of the summer term due to staff changeovers, she'd been nervous because she didn't want to make a fool of herself in front of her old colleagues. She hadn't wanted them to question her decision to quit teaching to work at the trust and then think she was rubbish at the whole outreach and education role she was taking on.

When she'd left the reserve to go and give the assembly, Zac had wished her luck, given her one of his awkward half-hugs, but when she'd returned, brimming with confidence because it had gone so well, she'd been met by this steely demeanour that was currently trying to squeeze as much oat milk from the near empty carton into his mug as he could. And that's the way things had stayed between them for the next four months. The strange thing was his attitude hadn't changed with all the team. Just her. And she had no idea why.

An awkward silence enveloped them as Zac sat down. Trying to block all thoughts of what he used to be like, Polly was relieved when the door behind her opened and Harold the ranger bustled in.

6

'Honestly, I just don't know what to do.' Taking a final look out of the window at Pennycress's beautiful back garden below, the fairy lights woven through the branches of the willow tree illuminating the lawn in the dim moonlight of the evening, Polly drew the curtains and sat on the edge of the bed, her mobile firmly clasped to her ear. 'I mean, can you believe it? First the role completely changes and then in walks Zac Sinclair. My dream position is quickly turning into the nightmare from hell.'

'Oh, come on, don't be dramatic,' Stacey admonished. 'You still have a job in the wildlife trust. Yes, the actual role might not be what you were expecting, but fundraising? That sounds fun!' The crackling of plastic made its way down the line before her friend spoke again, her voice muffled, as though her mouth was full. 'You never know, you might have hidden talents to bag millions for the reserve.'

'Haha, I think I'd be happy to just meet the target.' Polly laughed. She'd known Stacey would take some of the nerves away. 'Are you eating on the line with me?'

'Oh yes, I'd apologise, but you have two choices, to put up with me talking with my mouth full or else hear me retching with starvation.'

Polly slumped her shoulders. 'You missed lunch again?'

'What's lunch? I missed breakfast because I had to get in early to get myself organised for assembly and then at lunchtime, I had lunch duty for the first half as we're not one, but two dinner ladies down, and then had to deal with a bust-up in Year Six as the supply teacher refused.'

'Yikes. Fun times.'

'So, you know, if you want to come back to teaching, we have positions available.' Stacey finished chewing and took a huge gulp, most likely of coffee. 'Please come back. I don't even have anyone to complain to anymore because your replacement is fresh out of uni and still in the honeymoon period.'

'Oh, you love it really.' Stacey had always had a passion for teaching, a passion that, even after twelve years, hadn't waned like Polly's had.

'Umm, I do. But I miss you.'

'I miss you too, but I can't come back. As much as I loved actually being in the classroom and teaching the kids, all the rest of it...' Polly shrugged. 'You know – the paperwork, the pointless meetings where I'd just sit and think how irrelevant the topic was to our year group, the marking, the assessments, the—'

'Not to mention the elephant in the room. Or, more aptly, the elephant trying to block the phone line.' Stacey sighed. 'He's put in his resignation, you know.'

Polly lay back onto the bed, the puffy duvet almost engulfing her. She took a deep breath in before she replied, the lavender-scented fabric conditioner reminding her of her grandparents' house. 'Don't even—'

'Benjamin Joines—'

Slapping her free hand over her eyes, Polly groaned. 'I told you not to say his name.'

'No, you didn't, but I knew what you were going to say.' Stacey laughed before her voice grew serious again. 'Honestly, Pol, you shouldn't have let him force you out. I can only imagine how it must have felt seeing him day in, day out, but look, he's leaving now. He's moving to Castlewold Primary.'

'I take it that's as headteacher?' Her ex had always been career-motivated, hungry for promotion. More so than Polly, and that had eventually come between them. She swallowed as an image of him came to mind. When Ben had been promoted to deputy headteacher, he'd lorded it over her, patronising her and chiding her, telling her she should have more ambition, more drive. But the truth was, if she'd stayed in teaching, being promoted would have been the last thing she'd wanted. When she'd worked full time, she'd struggled enough trying to keep on top of everything. She hadn't wanted to add to her workload, and besides, her favourite part of the job had been teaching the children in her care. She hadn't wanted to be pulled away from the classroom to focus on paperwork.

'Yep. Headteacher. So now he's out of the picture. Why don't you come back?' Stacey began chewing again.

'Nope, you'll still see him. Castlewold Primary is still part of the same academy trust. He'll still be at all the academy meetings, the career development courses...' Taking a deep breath, Polly gripped hold of the mahogany bedside table and pulled herself to sitting. 'Besides, my love for teaching has gone. I don't want to do that anymore.'

Stacey sighed heavily. 'Answer me one question then?'

Polly rolled her eyes. She knew what she was going to ask her. It would be the same question her friend had asked her about a million times before. And that wasn't an exaggeration. 'I know what you're going to ask me. Would I still have left teaching if Ben and I hadn't broken up?'

'Well?'

'I'll give the exact same answer I always give to your exact same question: yes.'

'I don't believe you.'

Polly picked up the small bronze alarm clock next to her. She'd have to ask the inn's owner, Laura, if she minded moving it out of her room. There was no way she'd be able to sleep with that ticking in her ear. The only reason she had last night was because she must have been so shattered that she'd fallen straight to sleep as soon as her head had hit the pillow. She blamed her grandmother for filling the flat with loudly ticking clocks when she was growing up. 'Well, the truth is the only thing I can give you.'

'Umm...'

'It's the truth. Besides, we've been split five years now.' Polly placed the clock under the pillow. She couldn't cope with both Stacey's interrogation and the relentless ticking.

Stacey carried on, ignoring the little detail of the time passed between Polly's heart being broken into a thousand pieces and today. 'I'm your best mate. We've known each other twelve years now, ever since the first day you walked through the gates of Daisy Chain Primary School. We've been together through the highs and lows of every relationship either of us has had since...'

'Ha, the one jerk you encountered before you met, Freddie, the love of your life, you mean?'

'Yes, okay. I admit I've been lucky, but still, me and you, we've been best mates through all of your heartbreaks and lucky escapes, but the one with Ben was different. It really hit you and you've let it – him – take over your life.'

'I have not!' Polly placed her hand over the pillow, cocooning the clock in a soft cavern. Stacey was right, her break-up with Ben had been brutal – she'd been merrily planning their wedding without realising her fiancé was having second thoughts and had been discussing all their problems with their head-teacher before ending the relationship the day she'd brought home her wedding dress, but that wasn't the point. She hadn't left teaching because of him. Not really. 'The break-up made me realise I wanted something different out of life. It made me want to try a different avenue.'

'Polly...'

'It's true. Yes, Ben did change me, but he didn't take my love of teaching away from me, he just made me look at life a little differently.' Polly looked towards the window, wishing she hadn't closed the curtains. 'Yes, if he hadn't broken off the wedding, if he hadn't insisted on staying in our home until it had sold, then I might never have got involved with volunteering at the trust just to escape the impossible atmosphere in the house, but I did, and I'm glad I did. Plus, it let me spend the last few years caring for Grandma in her own home. And now, I need this change. More than ever, Stacey.'

'Okay.' Stacey's voice changed from exasperation to kindness. 'I hear you and I won't question your reasoning again.'

'Thank you. Sorry if I sounded super grumpy. It's just been a real day of it.' Polly sighed. She'd been so looking forward to her first day in her new job and to have the role changed at the last minute and then for it to be topped off with Zac Sinclair's surprise appearance, she just wanted to hole up for a bit. But she wouldn't. She had research to do, preparation to start on.

'About that, don't let Zac get under your skin. Tolerate him for the three months and then when you're promoted you can jolly well sack him on the spot.'

Polly's lips twitched, the image of her standing there and shaking a finger in Zac's direction as she hollered, 'You're fired' in her best Alan Sugar impression, bringing a smile to her face. 'I'm not sure it quite works like that, but I'll keep it in mind.'

'There you go then.' Stacey took a deep breath. 'Right, I'm going to force the rest of this warm and likely salmonella-riddled chicken sandwich down my throat and crack on with marking, you go and grab a cuppa and research the heck out of what a fundraising agent or whatever is so you can wow the boss tomorrow.'

'Officer. Fundraising and development officer,' Polly corrected.

'Yeah that. You've got this, Pols.'

'Thanks.' Ending the call, Polly held the phone to her chest. After years of having her friend right there by her side, she missed Stacey and the guaranteed positivity she brought to any situation. Taking the offending noise machine from under the pillow, Polly stood up and grabbed her laptop. She'd get a cup of tea and sit in the gorgeous sitting room downstairs for a couple of hours and make use of the time she had before bed.

7

'Polly?'

Looking up from the laptop screen, Polly smiled as Laura appeared in the doorway.

'I've just taken a fruit cake out of the oven. Do you fancy a slice whilst it's still warm?'

'Ooh, that would be lovely, please.'

'Great, I'll bring some through.' Laura grinned before leaving.

Shifting her laptop, Polly curled her legs up onto the comfy Chesterfield sofa and looked around the sitting room. The open fire had been lit and the dancing flames were emitting both a cosy warmth as well as a comforting light show against the stoned hearth. Laura and Nicola, who worked at Pennycress Inn, as well as Laura's fiancé Jackson, had made her feel so welcome, and Laura and Jackson had even insisted she share their dinner with them so as to avoid a walk out in the rain to the shops. She couldn't have asked for a better place to spend the next few months.

She slapped her forehead. She'd forgotten to ring the estate agents back. She checked the time: six forty-five. Would they still be open this late? When she'd agreed for them to sell her grandparents' flat which had been her childhood home as well as where she'd lived for the past five years since splitting up from Ben, they'd spoken about the possibility of evening viewings to help get the buyers in. She picked up her mobile from the large coffee table in front of her. It was worth a go. Scrolling through, she pressed the Call button.

'Grundy and Smith estate agents. How can I help you?' David, the estate agent who she had signed up with, answered.

'Hi, David. It's Polly Burrows. I'm sorry it's so late, but I'm just ringing you back. Sorry I missed your call earlier.'

'Polly! No worries. I've just finished a viewing, so popped back into the office to check on something, anyway. I'm glad you've returned my call.'

'Oh, a viewing at my place? That's good. How did it go?' Maybe her luck for the day was changing.

'Ah, no, not on your place, I'm afraid. Although there is something I'd like to discuss with you.' David paused.

'Okay.' Balancing her laptop on the arm of the sofa, Polly stood up and made her way across to the fireplace, watching the flames as they engulfed the rocks of coal. She forced herself to ask the question she dreaded the answer to before holding her breath. 'Do you have any more viewings booked in for the flat?'

'I'm afraid not, no. And, as you know, we spoke about the price last time we met, and I think we need to have another discussion about it.'

Polly reached her fingers to her necklace, running her forefinger and thumb along the golden chain before gripping the blue stone pendant. 'We've already lowered it. Twice.'

'I know, but there's just not much market for a flat in that area of town. Particularly in the...' David cleared his throat. 'Particularly with the unique décor it presents.'

'Umm.' Closing her eyes, she ran the pad of her finger across the gold encasing the back of the large pendant, tracing over the cursive engraving of 'Edwina and Edward', her grandparents. The grandparents who took her in and brought her up after the tragic house fire which had cost her parents' lives and almost her own.

Her grandad had decorated that flat and her grandmother had filled it with love, the aroma of baking and an array of cherished possessions. Polly knew what David had been about to say, he'd been about to say 'the state it was in' before he'd carefully reselected his words. She knew the décor was hugely outdated. Avocado bathroom suites had gone out of fashion at about the same time as pink woodchip wallpaper, but she hadn't been able to bring herself to change a thing when her grandmother had passed away last year and she'd inherited it. She hadn't wanted to. She'd needed to feel at home, to feel safe and secure, cocooned in memories of her grandparents.

'Another ten, fifteen thousand, and it will sound like a steal. An investor is sure to snap it up at that price and it'll be worth the time and money they'd need to pay for renovations before it's sold or rented out,' David continued.

'But... I just can't. We've dropped such a lot from the original asking price as it is.'

'It's been on the market for four months. If we leave it to languish, nobody will look twice at it because it's been on so long.' Polly could hear tapping down the phone, likely his pen against the desk. 'Look, there is another option.'

'There is?' She nodded. All wasn't lost.

'We can pull it and relist it in a couple of months' time. You can even do a bit of redecorating. Nothing much. I wouldn't suggest you spend an enormous amount on the place, but even a fresh coat of paint and a clear-out will improve the photos, draw people in.'

Polly swallowed. Yes, she knew she had to sell. She'd listed it as soon as she'd found out about this job. Okay, as soon as she'd found out about the original position she'd been offered, but painting over her grandad's hard work? She wasn't sure she could. She dreaded the day she had to go back and pack up her grandparents' possessions as it was, she wasn't sure if she could bring that date forward before it was even sold. Looking down, she watched as a lump of coal, red from the heat, shifted and rolled towards the edge of the bronze grate. 'I don't know.'

'I'll give you a few days to think on it. If you can let me know come the weekend, then we can either lower the price again or get some fresh photographs taken after a bit of a refresh. How does that sound?' David's voice was kind despite what he was suggesting.

'Yes, thanks. We'll do that.' Ending the call, Polly picked up a frame from the mantelpiece. It looked as though it was an illustration of Pennycress Inn, but from years ago, maybe decades. The willow tree in the front garden was a lot smaller for one thing and...

The whimsical tune of the doorbell filtered through from the hallway. Pennycress Inn must have been someone's special home once, before Laura and Jackson began running the place. The original owners, too, must have felt torn, must have felt the same dread and strange numbness as she did at the prospect of selling her grandparents' flat, her childhood home, her sanctuary, but she supposed if she was really going to move here, then she'd need to sell. Not that the money she gained from the flat would secure anything for her around here, but once she was formally offered the promotion, she'd be able to get a mortgage.

Yes, selling her grandparents' flat was a stepping stone to where she wanted to be in life. And she knew how much they'd have approved. Her grandma had always made Polly promise 'to get rid of the place and buy herself something nice' when she went and Polly just needed to take that leap and follow her wishes.

'I'll just show you around before taking you up to your room.' Laura's voice wafted in from the hallway. '...And here is the guests' sitting room.'

'Lovely. Very cosy.' The deep, familiar voice shattered the peaceful atmosphere in the room.

With her hands shaking, Polly placed the picture frame back on the mantelpiece, the metal of the frame clanking against a bronze candlestick. Moving it a millimetre and hoping it wouldn't fall, Polly turned. Sure enough, standing there in the doorway holding the same pretentious briefcase he'd laid on his desk hours earlier, was Zac Sinclair. The last person she'd want to spend any time with, let alone be cooped up in a bed and breakfast with, however lovely the inn itself, and the owners, were. 'Zac.'

'Oh, you two know each other?' Beaming, Laura looked from Zac to Polly and back again.

'We're colleagues,' Zac muttered as he glanced around the large room.

'Fantastic. It's always nice having someone you know in a new town or village, isn't it?' Laura continued, seemingly oblivious to the sudden chill in the air. 'When I first moved to Meadowfield last year and discovered that Jackson was living next door, it meant a lot to have someone I knew living here, too.'

'Oh, you only got together last year? I assumed you'd been together forever.' Polly turned her attention to Laura. From the little she'd seen of Laura and Jackson, she'd never have guessed their relationship was so recent.

'Ah, yes. He was – still is – my brother's best friend, so I grew up with him.' Laura laughed. 'Oh, and when I say it was fantastic to have him here, that doesn't mean initially. Jeez, initially I'd just wanted to have a new start, you know? But, still, things worked out for the best. I just had to let myself see it.'

Polly nodded. She was pleased things had worked out well for them. This situation with Zac though, she was damn sure nothing good would come of it.

Laura glanced behind her as the doorbell chimed again. 'Sorry, I'll just run and see who that is. Let you both catch up before I show you to your room, Zac.'

'There's no need...' Zac's voice trailed off as Laura disappeared. Sighing, he placed his briefcase on the floor by his feet and pulled out his mobile from his jacket pocket.

Shifting on her feet, Polly stole a glance in his direction. The one tuft of dark hair which always stubbornly refused to be tamed stuck up from the middle of his parting, hinting that he might just be human beneath the steely surface after all. She stifled a laugh, not that this situation – or any of what had happened today – was anything to be laughed at, but simply at the mere suggestion Zac could be human. Or have feelings. Any feelings which weren't egocentric. Now, that was wrong. That little tuft of hair was giving the wrong vibes to anyone who happened upon him. She reminded herself that wasn't true. Not until four months ago when he'd left the office human and walked back in the next day with the personality of a robot, preserved just for her.

She rolled her eyes. Well, didn't she feel special.

Needing to do something, to stop staring at him, she picked up the picture frame again. He wasn't happy. Whatever he was looking at on his mobile, whoever he was messaging, wasn't pleasing him. Forcing herself to focus on the delicate willow branches in the picture, Polly sighed. That much was true, the thought about his personality changing overnight. With anyone else, he was still the charming, friendly Zac she'd been introduced to five years ago. To her, though, the mask had slipped, and he wasn't making any effort whatsoever to replace it.

With the picture frame still in her hand, Polly turned to him. She needed to break this stifling silence before it choked her. And she had questions to ask. All day, she'd been trying to find the time. No, that wasn't right. She'd been trying to find the words to ask what she wanted. Taking a deep breath, she blurted out her first question; the words tumbling from her mouth. 'Why are you here?'

Slowly, he looked up from his mobile, his expression strongly hinting that he'd forgotten she was standing there, a mere few feet away from him. 'I'm staying here.'

Feeling a curl coming loose and settling on her nose. Blowing it away, she shook her head. 'No, why are you here, as in working at Meadowfield Nature Reserve?'

'The same reason you are, I assume. To do my job.'

Biting down on her bottom lip, she refrained from telling him what an eejit she thought he was being. 'Right. I just didn't realise you were transferring. I didn't think anyone else from HQ was.'

Zac shrugged slowly, his face briefly clouding before he set his expression back to neutral.

'Why didn't you say anything?' she persisted.

'I didn't realise it was a secret.'

'Right.' Well, it had been. Or at least she'd not been told. Maybe this was just another tactic of his to make her feel awkward, showing up to her new job without giving her any prior warning.

'I'm here to examine how the reserve works before I take the promotion.' Zac looked back down at his phone.

'The promotion?' Polly stuttered. What was he saying? There was another promotion going at the reserve? Had Mr Bob planned this? He'd planned for both of them to come here and be promoted? 'What to?'

Glancing back up at her, Zac met her eyes, irritation clear in his expression. 'To project manager, of course.'

Project manager? What was he talking about? That was her promotion. She'd been promised it. 'Wait, no…'

'Sorry about that.' Stepping back into the room, Laura placed a large brown box on the sofa closest to the door. 'Are you ready, Zac?'

Slipping his mobile into his pocket, Zac smiled at Laura, his charm returning, before picking up his briefcase and following her.

With the sitting room now empty, Polly replaced the picture frame and sank onto the sofa. Zac thought he had been transferred here to be promoted to project manager. Nobody had told him it was her job? That it had been promised to her? Pinching the bridge of her nose, she looked down at the patterned rug covering the oak floorboards. She'd have to tell him. She'd have to let him know that the job had basically already been allocated. Well, that was going to be a fun conversation. And with them both staying here, too.

Just her luck.

8

'I will. I'll just tell him.' Standing in front of the full-length mirror in her room, Polly smoothed the creases from the dark green sweatshirt Declan had given her to wear, the now familiar Meadowfield Nature Reserve logo emblazoned across the chest. She knew she should have ironed it last night when she'd realised just how creased it was after taking it out of its packaging. Instead, she'd decided on the method of hanging it up in the bathroom whilst she had a shower this morning, hoping the creases would fall out. So much for that little trick.

'You'd better. It'll only be worse when he finds out for himself.' Stacey's voice rose from where Polly had placed her phone on the desk next to her make-up bag.

Polly scoffed. 'Yep, now that's a room I wouldn't like to be in when he's told.'

'It's only fair to him. Imagine it was the other way around. If you'd been led to assume you were getting the job and he'd been told he was. You'd want him to give you warning, wouldn't you? A chance to get used to the idea without it just being thrown at you last minute.' Stacey's voice grew muffled as a loud scraping noise filtered down the line.

'Stacey? Are you still there?' Giving up on the idea of smoothing out the creases from her sweatshirt, Polly picked up her hairbrush.

'Yes, sorry. Just needed to move these desks around. It's like playing musical chairs in the classroom at the moment. Whoever I sit people next to, all they want to do is chat about where they're going for Bonfire Night or what they've asked Santa to bring them for Christmas.'

'Yuck, the C word already? It's not even November.'

'I know, but all the adverts are out on TV already. Besides, the supermarkets have been selling tubs of Roses and Quality Street for months now.'

'True.' Polly sighed. Christmas had always been her favourite time of the year when it came to teaching. Preparing for the Nativity, making Christmas cards, just the general buzz and energy throughout the school.

'Anyway, back to your problem with the gorgeous Zac.'

'Stop it.' She'd told her friend Zac was gorgeous once. One time when she'd first met him, and still Stacey wouldn't let her forget. And, of course, the kiss had only added to this particular tease-factor. 'This is serious. How am I supposed to tell him? He hates me as it is.'

'Umm, I think you're just going to have to come out with it. Just tell him when you see him next and get it over and done with.'

'I guess you're right.'

'Look, he probably just knows that the boss, Dylan, or whoever, is retiring soon and has decided to apply, that's all. He'll be more annoyed if he puts the effort into going for the job and then finds out.'

'Declan,' Polly corrected her as she forced the brush through her damp hair before watching her wayward curls spring back to life. 'Yes, you're right. I'll tell him when I see him next.'

'As soon as you see him. The moment you walk into that office, you tell him. Unless you see him running around the inn with a bath towel wrapped around his middle or something.' Stacey giggled. 'Okay, maybe that wouldn't be appropriate timing.'

Rolling her eyes, Polly shook her head. 'All the rooms are en suite, I think I'll be quite safe from that sight, thanks.'

'That's a shame. Right, I'd better get going. I've got prep to do before a staff meeting at eight.'

'Okay. Have fun.' Now that was something she didn't miss. The staff meetings or the prep.

'Oh, I'm sure I will,' Stacey answered dryly before hanging up.

With the room once again plunged into silence, Polly gave up taming her hair and instead drew it up into her signature messy bun before grabbing her mobile and heading to breakfast.

* * *

As she walked towards the kitchen door, Polly could hear chatter and laughter through the delicious aroma of eggs, bacon and French toast. Her stomach growled as she pushed open the door, quickly scanning the room and breathing a sigh of relief that Zac was absent. In fact, there was only an older couple already seated so far.

'Morning, Polly. How did you sleep?' Walking over to her, Laura indicated a table by the window. 'Do you want to sit over here? Make the most of the sunshine before those dark clouds descend?'

'That sounds like a good idea. Thanks.' Following her, Polly then slipped into a chair, the weak morning sunlight trying its best to infiltrate the kitchen. 'Oh, and I slept really well, thanks. The bed is super comfy.'

Laura grinned as she passed her a menu. 'I'm glad. And you like the room? You can see yourself being okay there for the next three months?'

'Absolutely. The room is beautiful.' Polly smiled back. It wasn't the room, or the inn, that was bothering her about staying, it was who she had to share the inn with. If he wasn't here, then she'd quite happily spend the next three years sleeping on the comfiest bed she'd ever had the pleasure of dozing on, enjoying Jackson's delicious breakfasts and not having to lift a finger. What more could she ask for?

'Aw, that's good. I must admit, I love having long-term guests. It's nice to have the chance to get to know people.'

Polly nodded.

'Anyway, I'll stop nattering and get you a drink while you decide what to order. What would you like? Tea? Coffee? Juice? Both? All three?' Laura laughed. 'Or we do have pumpkin spice lattes on the menu. A Jackson speciality for the autumn.'

'A pumpkin spice latte sounds perfect.' She could do with the caffeine and the warmth of the pumpkin spice. If it hadn't been the comfort of the bed lulling her to sleep, she probably wouldn't have got the few hours' sleep she did have. Every time she'd closed her eyes, all she could think about was Zac being here, sleeping in the same inn, working at the same reserve. Heck, they almost shared a desk they were positioned that close!

Yikes, and there he was. Polly watched as he sauntered into the kitchen, pausing by the oven as he chatted and chuckled with Jackson before Laura walked him through the kitchen, menu in hand. He'd ironed his sweatshirt then. Of course he had. Mr Perfect.

Turning, she looked out of the window behind her just in time to see a robin hop along the banister encircling the decking. She smiled as she remembered the saying her grandma had always repeated whenever she saw one, 'When robins appear, loved ones are near'. Was this her grandma's way of telling her she wouldn't be disappointed if Polly did redecorate the flat?

'Sorry, Polly, you look deep in thought, but I wondered if you two would like to be seated together for breakfast?' Laura grinned.

Looking from Laura to Zac, who looked as horrified as she felt about the prospect, Polly nodded slowly. What else could she do? Refuse? Tell Laura exactly what she thought of Zac Sinclair and the fact it made her feel sick just thinking about him staying under the same roof as her, let alone having to force food down her throat in his presence? And all before her first coffee of the day? 'That would be nice.'

'Great. Make yourself comfortable then, Zac. Take a look at the menu while I fetch the coffees.' Once Zac had reluctantly seated himself opposite Polly, Laura passed him a menu before walking away.

'Good morning.' Zac pulled a newspaper from beneath his arm and shook it out in front of him, covering half the table.

'Likewise.' Bringing her hand to her head, Polly twisted a curl around her finger, Stacey's words echoing in her mind. She should tell him now. Get it over and done with before they left for the office.

'Here you go.' Returning, Laura placed two large mugs on the table. 'Have you decided on breakfast or do you need a couple more minutes?'

Zac held his hand out, allowing Polly to answer first.

What was he doing? Pretending he was a gentleman? Shame she knew otherwise. 'I'll have the French toast again, please.'

'Perfect. Good choice. And how about you, Zac?'

'I'll just have toast.' Zac flashed a smile before turning back to his paper.

'No problem.'

As she watched Laura walk away again, Polly placed her hands on her knees, willing them to stop shaking. She really didn't want to do this. What-ever she thought of this man sitting in front of her, and despite what she believed about him, he was still a person, a person with feelings – presumably – who had transferred to Meadowfield in the hope of bagging a promotion. One he wasn't going to get. 'About that promotion...'

'What about it?' Zac flicked over a page, his eyes still trained on the newspaper.

'I... umm... I don't know how to say this, but...'

'But what? You don't think you can work beneath me?' Zac shrugged without lifting his head. 'That's your choice.'

Raising her eyebrows, Polly flared her nostrils. If that was his attitude, maybe she shouldn't feel bad for him after all. Maybe he deserved to be brought down a peg or two. 'There's no point applying. Mr Bob has already promised it to me. That's why I've been given this job, to get to know the team.'

That caught his attention. Slowly, he closed the newspaper, folding it to the size of an A4 sheet of paper before meeting her eyes. 'No, that's not quite accu-rate, is it? Mr Bob said the promotion will go to the best candidate, and given that I have far more experience than you in a paid position and—'

'What?' Shifting in her chair, Polly cleared her throat, willing her voice to sound calmer than she felt. 'No, you must be mistaken. He specifically told me it would be mine.'

Leaning back in his chair, Zac took his phone from his pocket and placed it on the table between them. 'Let's get this cleared up, shall we?'

'I think that's probably best.' Polly nodded. She wasn't thrilled about seeing his reaction to what Mr Bob was going to say, but then at least he'd know. Zac must have got confused. Unless he was just playing games with her? Some-thing she wouldn't exactly put past him.

Zac scrolled through his phone until Mr Bob's name filled the screen. 'Ready?'

'Of course.' Polly nodded. The quicker this misunderstanding was resolved, the better.

9

Hitting the Call button, Zac leaned back in his chair, confidently holding his hands behind his head.

'Ah, Zachary Sinclair. However may I help you?' Mr Bob's familiar jovial tone wafted down the phone.

Glancing behind him towards the other diners, Zac lowered the volume before greeting him. 'Morning, Mr Bob. I have Polly Burrows with me. You're on speaker.'

'Morning, Polly. How are you both enjoying the inn? Beautiful, isn't it? Mrs Bob and I visited last year for our anniversary. Stunning building in a great location...'

'Yes, it's nice. Thanks for arranging it.' Zac cut him off. 'That's not the reason I'm calling, though. There seems to be a slight mix-up on the job front we want to clear up.'

Clasping her hands together, Polly leaned forward. Perhaps he wasn't making it up. Zac seemed pretty agitated himself. Perhaps he really had thought he was coming here with the chance of getting the promotion? But if it was a mistake...

'Yes, yes. I know exactly what you're going to say, but to set the record straight, I didn't have a clue either. I didn't realise the job roles would change. I got you both the jobs I thought you'd be best suited to in good faith. Declan always was one to pull the rug out from beneath the feet.' Mr Bob's voice faltered before he spoke again. 'He's not there with you now, is he? With me on speaker?'

'He's not.'

'Good, good. He's a decent man, has the best of intentions but is well known for being a bit of a maverick where the—'

'Sorry to interrupt you, Mr Bob, but we've got to head into the office in a few minutes. The job roles were a bit of a surprise, yes, but that's not the reason we're calling.'

'Right, right, of course. Time to start work soon, ay? What is it I can help you two with?'

Zac cleared his throat, clearly uncomfortable with where the conversation needed to go.

Lifting her hands to the table, still clasped, Polly spoke up. 'Mr Bob, there seems to have been a bit of a misunderstanding with regard to the promotion you promised me.'

'And the fact you told us we were both in the running.' Zac shot her a look.

'You seem to have promised us both the promotion to project manager, but I think there'll only be one job opening when Declan retires, is that right?' *Please break the news to Zac that he's misunderstood.*

'Yes, yes. One promotion. That's right.'

'Like I said...' Zac narrowed his eyes as he pulled at the cuff of his sweatshirt sleeve.

'As Zac said, either of you will be in the running for the promotion, of course! The best person for the job. That's why you're both there.'

'Thank you.' Zac nodded curtly.

Polly watched him grab the phone and bring it to his ear. Without thinking, she leaned across the table and tapped Zac's phone, indicating to him to put it back in the middle of the table so they could both hear Mr Bob's answer. How could Zac be right? And why hadn't she been privy to this conversation?

'...So you see...'

'Sorry, Mr Bob. I didn't hear what you'd said.' Polly narrowed her eyes at Zac. 'Can you repeat it, please?'

'Of course, Polly. I was just saying that the promotion will go to the best candidate. And to be completely honest, things have worked out even better than I had anticipated. With you both being given new job roles, you'll both be at the same starting point and therefore the competition will be much fairer than first anticipated.'

'This isn't a competition, Mr Bob. This is my life. I need this promotion.' Polly swallowed as a lump formed in her throat. She needed it. She had to have it. He'd promised it to her. 'When you assured me of the promotion you didn't say anything about any other candidates, you made out that it would be mine. That it was expected.'

'I'm sorry, Polly. That wasn't my intention. Not at all. Are you certain I didn't mention you were both candidates? I'm sure—'

'You did to me.' Zac's voice was low as he ran his palm across his face.

'Well, if I didn't to you, Polly, then I offer my sincerest apologies,' Mr Bob continued. 'Of course, I'm sure you'll both be aware that the trust legally has to advertise the position externally too, but, of course, you'll both have the advantage over any potential outside candidates as you'll have been working there for a few months before then.'

'Right. Thanks. We'd better go.' Stabbing the pad of his index finger against the phone screen, Zac ended the call.

Bringing the mug of pumpkin spice latte to her lips, Polly took a sip, forcing it down. She felt as though her whole world had been torn apart. Her dreams shattered and the promise of a better future felled. What was she supposed to do now? Yes, she'd been volunteering at the Cotswold Wildlife and Wilderness Trust longer than Zac had been employed. But he'd been employed and worked full-time, whereas, apart from the last few months, she'd had to fit in volunteering around her teaching job. He had more experience. Plain and simple. The trust... No wonder he didn't seem bothered by the fact she was his competition.

'I need to go.' Pushing his untouched mug away towards the salt and pepper shakers at the end of the table, Zac stood up.

'Zac, are you leaving already? Don't you want your breakfast?' Laura bustled towards their table, carrying two plates in her hands.

'No, sorry. Something's come up.' He held his mobile aloft before striding out of the kitchen.

'Did I take too long?' Laura frowned as she watched the kitchen door close behind him.

'No.' Polly shook her head. 'It was a work thing.'

'Oh, right.' Nodding, Laura laid Polly's plate in front of her. 'Are you okay? You look awfully pale.'

Picking up her knife and fork, Polly hovered them above her French toast. It smelt divine; it looked divine, and she could almost taste the cinnamonny sweetness already, but she wasn't sure she could stomach eating it. Not after that conversation.

'Sorry, I'm being nosey, aren't I?' Laura gave a quick smile. 'Ignore me.'

'No, no. Not at all.' Polly placed her cutlery back down and brought her elbows to the table, cupping her chin in her hands. 'I got some rubbish news about work, that's all.'

'Oh, I'm sorry to hear that.' Lowering herself to the chair Zac had vacated moments earlier, Laura indicated Polly's sweatshirt. 'What is it you do? I'm guessing you work at the nature reserve?'

Glancing down at the trust's oak tree emblem stitched in navy on her sweatshirt, Polly nodded. 'Yes, I came here for the job of outreach and education officer and instead was given a role in fundraising and development. Not quite what I was expecting.'

'Ah, I imagine that was a bit of a shock! Are you still taking the job?' Laura picked up a slice of Zac's discarded toast and bit into it, crumbs falling back to the plate.

'Yes. I don't really have a choice. I quit my teaching job to take this one.' Polly nodded. 'Besides, it's been a dream of mine for years to work for the trust. But it's not just that. I was promised a promotion, only it's not as clear-cut as I'd been led to believe.'

Wiping her mouth with the back of her hand, Laura frowned. 'It's not?'

'No. There's another internal candidate. And then it'll be advertised to the general public too.' Polly looked down as the realisation hit her. She wasn't going to get the promotion, was she? Zac had more relevant experience than her. He was charming – to everyone but her – and he was one of those people who always got what they wanted. He drove the expensive car, wore the tailored suits, and with his parents' history with the trust... The job was his. It was bound to be. So why had Mr Bob even suggested it to her? Why would he have been so cruel as to get her hopes up? To make the process appear 'fair'?

'Aw, that's rubbish.' Reaching over the table, Laura rubbed Polly's arm. 'There's nothing to say you can't get it, though.'

Scrunching up her nose, Polly shrugged. 'I think there probably is. I think

I'm just the person to make it look like a fair competition. I don't stand a chance.'

'Sure you do. You wouldn't have been put in the position to apply for it if your old boss or whoever it was who got you this job didn't believe in you.'

'I don't know. I was a volunteer, this is my first proper job at the trust, whereas the other candidate has been working there already.' She didn't like to mention it was Zac who was the other candidate. Somehow, she felt she could deal with living under the same roof as him if no one here knew about the sudden rivalry that had been placed upon them.

'Volunteers are worth their weight in gold. Don't dismiss your chances because this is your first paid job with them. Someone has seen something special in you, and they believe you can do this.' Laura leaned back in her chair. 'From where I'm sitting, the only person who doesn't believe in you is yourself.'

Picking up her fork, Polly stabbed at a piece of French toast. Maybe Laura was right. Polly had known Mr Bob for five years now, and he'd been nothing but kind to her. It wasn't like him to play games. He wouldn't mess with her life. Yes, he could be scatty and forgetful, to the point of probably thinking he had mentioned Zac coming here to Polly, but not malicious. 'Maybe.'

'Nope. Not maybe. Definitely. I know I've only just met you, but bosses don't put in a good word for their employees if they don't think they have every chance of getting the job. It's not in their best interests.'

Nodding slowly, Polly took a shuddering breath in. 'You don't think I should give up?'

'Absolutely not! You want this promotion, don't you?'

'I need this promotion.'

'Then go for it. If you do your very best, then you won't be left thinking "what if".' Laura took another bite of Zac's toast.

'That's true.' Laura was right. Polly had two choices. She could roll over, do the job she'd been given for these three months while she had free accommodation before quitting and going back to her grandparents' flat and taking on another teaching job, or she could fight. She could fight for the future she craved; she could fight for her dreams. It would be tough, and she might not succeed. Heck, she probably wouldn't, but at least she could tell herself that she'd tried.

Glancing behind her as the kitchen door opened, Laura stood up, Zac's now empty plate in her hand. 'I'd better go and seat the newcomers. Think about what I said though, won't you?'

'I will. Thank you.' Polly nodded and picked up her cutlery again, this time actually cutting a square of French toast and popping it in her mouth. If she'd learned one thing from her grandparents, it was to try her best, and that's what she'd do.

Watch out, Zac Sinclair. He may have the family backing, the money and the legacy behind him, but that didn't mean she was going to hand over the chance of the promotion and leave quietly.

10

Placing a fresh mug of coffee on her desk, Polly pulled out the wheelie chair and sat down before glancing across at Zac's desk. Where was he? He'd left Pennycress Inn almost half an hour before she had and yet he'd clearly not come straight into work. And he had a car. She'd had to navigate the bus timetable before almost missing the last bus before starting time. He had no excuse.

She shrugged as she picked up her mug and looked at the view in front of her. A small group of runners jogged along the winding path before the one at the back paused and peered behind her. What was she looking at? Leaning forward, Polly strained her neck to the left, searching for whatever the runner was gazing at. Two moments later, another runner hobbled along towards her, clutching her side.

Ah, stitch. And that was why Polly didn't run. She remembered only too well the excruciating pain of a stitch from cross-country at school. Nope. Never again. They could keep their running, thank you very much.

'Morning.' Zac's voice filled the office and Polly twisted in her chair. She frowned. It seemed his demeanour had turned a whole one eighty since the awkward conversation during breakfast. Gone was the slightly aloof Zac and here was an animated one, smiling and carrying two cup holders full of cardboard coffee takeout cups.

'Ooh, have you really just bought us all coffee?' Vicki rushed across the office towards him. 'I could get used to this.'

'I have indeed. A mixture of pumpkin spice lattes and gingerbread ones too.' Zac held the trays aloft slightly before placing them down on the counter in the small kitchen area.

As Declan, Art and Dennis flocked towards him, Polly turned back towards the window. So this was how he was going to play this. He was going to buy himself into that promotion. She shook her head. What was she supposed to do? She wasn't going to be promoted. Zac would. She could feel her breath quickening as she began thinking about everything – the flat, the fact she couldn't stay at Pennycress Inn all paid for forever, finding her own home on this wage. And that was if she was lucky. That was if Zac deemed her worthy to stay on the team when he took over Declan's role. And he wouldn't. He hated her. Never had more than two words to say to her. He'd fire her.

She couldn't do this. She couldn't sit here listening to everyone cooing over Zac and his super obvious attempt at buying affection, at buying his promotion. She tugged at the collar of her sweatshirt, which suddenly felt as though it were attempting to strangle her. She had to get out.

Standing up, she grabbed her notebook and pen and headed towards the door, navigating her way around the people clustered around Zac and his magic lattes.

'Here's yours, Polly.' Extricating himself from the gathered group, Zac stepped into Polly's path and shoved a takeaway cup beneath her nose.

Glancing around, she realised Declan was watching the exchange as he sipped his latte. Plastering a sweet smile on her face, Polly gushed. 'Wow, for me? Thank you.'

'You're very welcome. Can't have my roomie going thirsty, can I?' Zac passed her the cup.

Taking it, Polly caught his eye. What was that look? Triumph? Fear? She couldn't work it out, but, in that instant, she knew for certain that she'd been right. He'd brought drinks to try to get everyone on his side. 'Thank you.'

Backing away again, she watched as Zac was quickly absorbed back into the conversation going on around him before she turned and headed outside.

Stepping into the tired foyer of the visitor centre, Polly dropped the full cup of pumpkin spice latte in the bin, and sidestepped around another runner before pulling open the heavy door and walking outside. The cold autumn air hit her, a welcome distraction from the scene she'd just left behind. She needed to get away from Zac's schmoozing.

* * *

Making her way back into the visitor centre half an hour later, Polly paused just outside the door to the office and scrubbed at the mud on the knees of her jeans. So much for clearing her head. All she'd done was trip over in front of the runners. Whilst walking. Yep, they'd been jogging past, the first few without even a droplet of sweat clinging to their brows and there'd she been, walking – no, strolling – and she'd managed to fall over her own feet. And as if that hadn't been embarrassing enough, one of the runners had sped towards her and checked she was okay. No wonder they hadn't asked her to join their running team. They probably thought she needed more practice walking first.

Well, she'd blame Zac for that. All she'd been able to think about was the promotion and how precarious her once well-thought-out plan to move to this part of the Cotswolds had become. The last five years of stretching herself thin, of limping by as a single person on a part-time wage and splitting herself between doing the best for the children in her class as well as attempting to secure a job at the trust, and this is where it had got her – running out on her duties to clear her head and embarrassing herself in front of the regular reserve runners. Thanks, Zac.

She felt the swoosh of the door open behind her before hearing Zac's familiar voice. 'Took a tumble?'

Straightening her back, Polly felt a fierce glow of embarrassment sear across her skin. Of course it was him. Of course. 'Er, just a little.'

Zac paused, still gripping the door handle, heat escaping the warm foyer of the visitor centre. 'You, umm, need anything?'

Blinking, Polly stuttered, 'N-no. Thank you.'

'Right.' With the slightest frown, Zac waited until she'd entered the building before letting the door swing shut.

Putting her hands on her hips, Polly watched him through the glass door as he walked towards the ranger's cabin. Had he just been nice? Okay, not nice, but normal? She was certain she'd seen a flicker of normality flash across his features. Jeez, if he kept this up, she might mistakenly think he'd reverted back to the human he used to be.

Nope. Shaking her head, she stood in front of the radiator, about the only thing the foyer had going for it. With the heat warming her palms, she tried to focus. She didn't have a clue what she was doing here. Not now she knew Zac was in line for the promotion too.

Standing there, she watched as he walked up to the ranger, who had just emerged from the trees. What was he up to?

'Ah, Polly. There you are.'

Turning, she looked towards Declan, who was standing in the half-open doorway to the office. 'Hi, sorry, I was just...' She indicated the reserve beyond the glass doors. Did she need to explain herself?

'Acclimatising yourself?' Declan smiled.

'Yes, that's right.' Nodding, Polly wiped her muddy hands down the front of her jeans before following him back into the office. 'Is everything okay?'

'Yes, of course.' As they walked into the office, Declan waved his hand in the direction of the meeting room. 'Shall we?'

Following him into the room, she noticed a stack of papers in the middle of the large table – maps and photographs by the looks of things.

'Sit down, sit down. Coffee? Tea? Water?' Declan pointed to the tiny table of refreshments in the corner of the room.

'No, I'm fine. Thanks.' She swallowed, her mouth dry, as she sat down. Why did she have the distinct feeling this meeting wasn't going to be good? She glanced at Declan, who was hopping from foot to foot before finally walking to the opposite side of the table and sitting down. He wasn't the relaxed man he'd been yesterday, this morning even. Was she going to lose her job? Was that it? Was he going to fire her? That would explain the way he was acting. He looked nervous and she couldn't imagine he was used to firing anybody, and if he was, then he didn't give off an air of enjoyment about it. Gripping her hands on the arms of the chair, she shifted her seat closer to the table.

'Right, something has come to my attention, which I feel I must address. I've already spoken to Zac and so it seems only fair that I inform you at this moment in time too.' Reaching for the half-empty glass in front of him, Declan took a swig of water.

'Okay.' Was he really going to fire her? Could he fire her? Mr Bob had secured the job for her. He'd even made it possible for her to stay at Pennycress Inn. Was Declan about to undo all of that, undo all of her hard work and dedication to the trust over the years?

'Having spoken at length to Zac and then to Robert...'

'Robert?' Who was Robert?

'Sorry, I think you know him as Mr Bob.'

Polly nodded. Of course, Bob, Robert. Why had she never put the two together? Clasping her hands in her lap, she waited for Declan to continue.

'Zachary brought to my attention that you have both had hints that you might stand to take over as project manager when I retire. To your under-standing, is that correct?'

'Yes, it is.' Although Mr Bob had certainly not 'hinted' at the fact, his promise had been clear and precise.

'I see.' Declan stroked his beard before picking up his pen. 'I thought as much. It's true that neither Art, Dennis nor Vicki have any interest in the position...'

'But you don't think I stand a chance of getting the promotion?' Polly could hear her voice rasping. What was she going to do? She'd already used all of her savings when she'd gone part-time in order to volunteer and pursue a career at the trust, and she'd taken a pay cut for this job. She had nothing left, nothing to fall back on. Nothing. And even if she managed to keep this job, she simply wouldn't be able to buy her own place if she didn't get the higher wage the promotion offered. Heck, she likely wouldn't be able to rent her own place either, not with how high the rents were locally. She'd have to flat-share or else go back to teaching.

Laying his hands against the surface of the table, Declan shook his head. 'That's not what I'm suggesting. Not at all. From what I know of you and Zachary's backgrounds, you both stand in good stead. But that is where lies the problem.'

'Why?' So she did stand a chance? Or was he about to say neither of them would be able to apply? That it would be somehow unfair, immoral?

'Because it's ultimately my decision who takes over caring for this beautiful place.' He waved his arms around, encompassing the meeting room and the reserve beyond the window. 'The only solution I can think of is to make you both a proposition, a proposal to make this the fairest solution, if you will.'

'Oh?'

'I've already spoken to Zachary and, what I'm about to say to you, I have said to him. I'll make this proposal and then I want you to take the rest of the day to mull it over and get back to me with a decision tomorrow.' Declan tapped the end of his pen against the notebook in front of him.

'And what is that proposal?'

'I promise not to make any decisions until the end of the three months. You'll both do the best you can at your jobs, and we'll see who is better prepared by the end of the time.' Declan leaned back in his chair. 'As fundraising and development officers, it should be pretty easy to measure both of your success rates. But, of course, I won't only be looking at the amount of new funds you bring in but also your general contribution to the office and, most importantly, to the reserve itself. For both of you.'

This couldn't be happening. It couldn't be. 'But I was promised the job of outreach and education officer. I haven't worked in fundraising before. I don't know what I'm doing.' She spread her hands out on the table in front of her, palms up. Her ability could be measured on the outcome of a job she'd never done before. How was that fair?

'I understand. But Zachary is in the same position as you are. Neither of you have prior experience of the role. I'm afraid I just can't think of another way to do it. The only way I can possibly choose one of you over the other is by merit. You've both come to this team highly rated by Robert.' He lifted his glass to his lips before lowering it again. 'Now, as I've said, take the rest of the day to have a think and, by all means, if you come up with a better solution to our little dilemma, then please let me know.'

'Okay.' Polly squeaked out a reply. Trying her best to appear more composed than she felt. 'I will do.'

'Good. Right, I'd best get on.' Declan stood up and made his way to the door before holding it open for her.

Passing in front of him, Polly forced herself to ask the question she wasn't sure she wanted to know the answer to. 'And I'm guessing the position will be advertised too?'

'That's right. I'm afraid my hands are tied in that respect.'

'Of course.'

As Polly made her way back to her desk, she felt as though she could feel everyone's eyes on her. They must all know about the misunderstanding, about Mr Bob promising both her and Zac a decent shot at the promotion. Art, Dennis and Vicki must know. Slipping into her wheelie chair, she was grateful

Zac was still outside. She wasn't sure she was ready to face him quite yet. Not now he'd suddenly gone from being the irritable man she had to sit next to, to being her work rival.

'Ah, Polly. I'm sorry, I clean forgot to give these to you.' Declan placed a large stack of papers in front of her. 'You'll find everything you need to know about Meadowfield Nature Reserve here. Maps, information about its past, and previous fundraising events. Well, those in the past five years, anyway.'

'Great. Thank you.' Polly pulled the stack towards her. So much for trying to come up with a fairer way to decide who got the promotion. Looking through this lot would take her well into the evening.

11

Leaning back in her chair, Polly yawned. She'd been looking through the information Declan had given her for hours. And still there was no sign of Zac. Whatever he was doing with Harold, the ranger, was taking him forever.

'Hey, Polly, are you going out for lunch?' Vicki called to her as she walked across the office.

Polly turned in her chair. She hadn't even realised it was lunchtime already. Although now Vicki had mentioned the word, her stomach growled beneath her sweatshirt. 'No, I don't think so. I want to make a bit of a dent in looking through this stuff.'

'Can I ask you a favour then, please?'

'Of course. What's up?' Polly smiled. Even though this was only her second day, it was nice to feel needed and included.

'Would you be able to look after Rolo while I pop to the sandwich shop with Art and Dennis, please? He'll just sleep.' Vicki scooped the small rat from her shoulder and held him in her cupped hands.

Polly looked at the creature. He wasn't much bigger than the class hamster she'd used to look after. 'Yes, of course.'

'Thanks, you want anything?'

'No, I'm good, thanks. I've got my lunch.' Polly curled up the hem of her sweatshirt before taking the small rat from Vicki and carefully placing him in the pouch she'd just created.

'Okay, cool. Thanks again.' Kissing her fingertips, Vicki lightly pressed them against the rat's fur. 'Be good, little Rolo.'

Polly waited until the click of the office door sounded before spinning slowly around. The office was empty. Declan had left to meet his wife for lunch half an hour ago and now, with Art, Dennis and Vicki gone, the only person unaccounted for was Zac. Umm, hopefully he'd stay out, too. Carefully checking Rolo was secure in the makeshift nest of her sweatshirt, she leaned down and pulled her mobile from her bag before scrolling through to Stacey's name. With any luck, Stacey wouldn't be covering lunchtime duty or detention, or anything, and would be free for a chat.

She picked up on the first ring. 'Hey, Pols.'

'Wow, that was quick!' Polly laughed quietly, careful not to disturb Rolo, who had settled and was peacefully sleeping, seemingly oblivious to the change in his location.

'Ah, what can I say, there's only so many ways to describe autumn in a poem and only so much patience I have in correcting the spelling of the word hedgehog.' Stacey sighed as the sound of a book being closed echoed down the line.

'Teaching poetry was always my favourite part of the autumn syllabus.' Polly smiled as she stroked Rolo's nose. 'How are things with you?'

'Oh, you know. The same. We're short-staffed, overstretched and Mrs Jedd is on the warpath for me to count calculators and hundred squares in the stockroom again. Good job I've not got anything better to do, isn't it?' The sarcasm rolled off Stacey's tongue.

'Ah, I don't envy you. The responsibility and never-ending tasks of being a subject leader.' Polly grimaced.

'It's fine. I'm sure I'll have time this evening between telling Eden's parents she needs to stop eating glue sticks, marking sixty books and finding enough bottles of poster paint that haven't dried out for tomorrow's art class.' Stacey took a gulp, presumably of the lunch she was shovelling down her throat between tasks. 'Anyway, I need updates.'

'Oh, it's fine. I can't complain.' After being reminded of Stacey's workload, Polly couldn't really start moaning about her life.

'Uh-huh and I'm the King of England. Tell me. Spill the beans. I need something else to focus on and I need the next instalment of life with Zac Sinclair. Go on, let me live vicariously through you before lunch is over.'

Scrunching her nose up, Polly looked across to Zac's desk, with just his laptop perfectly centred on it and not even a hint of humanity – not a photo frame or even a pen or empty mug. She picked up the photo frame she'd placed on her desk the moment she'd arrived and swallowed as she took in the image of her grandparents smiling back at her, herself as a small child holding hands between them. Did Zac's lack of 'stuff' go further to prove that he thought he had this promotion in the bag? That he was ready to desk-hop with a moment's notice? Or was she just being paranoid?

Placing the frame back in its position, she focused on Stacey again. 'Okay, I'll spill the beans, but unless you want to be part of a horror story or some thriller where I'll be forced to drive Zac into the middle of the desert and abandon him, then you definitely don't want to be living my life.'

'Go on, what's happened now? I take it that he hasn't turned to you and admitted he has deep feelings of lust for you, then?'

'Lust?' Polly snorted. 'The only thing Zac Sinclair feels about me is likely hatred. Not only did we both end up here in Meadowfield together in job roles neither of us has ever done before, but you know that promotion?'

'The one you've been promised?'

'Supposedly, but nope, Zac has been promised the exact same thing, so now we're pitted against each other in some sort of office-based Hunger Games to see who can bring in the most funding and secure the promotion.' Polly sank back in the chair with a force she wouldn't have if she'd remembered Rolo was in her lap. Holding her breath, she peeked at him, thankfully still snuggled in the fold of her sweatshirt.

'You're kidding?'

'Do I sound like I'm kidding?' Polly sighed. 'It's like a nightmare. I've given up everything for this position and now I'll end up skint and stuck in this job forever. I mean, I love working here – or I will when I get to grips with my actual role. Hopefully. But that's not the point, I'm never going to get my new start here, am I? Without that promotion, I'll never be able to get my own place and settle down.'

'You never know, you might get more for your grandparents' flat than you think. It's close to the town centre, the perfect location for someone who works there. Plus, landlords will jump at it.'

'But they haven't, have they? The estate agent has already told me I'm going to have to lower the asking price again and redecorate, too.' With her elbow on the table, Polly lowered her chin to her hand. When were things going to go right for her? She'd been so excited to get this job. Her path had been laid out in front of her and then Zac had walked in and turned her world upside down. She was sinking, and she didn't know if she could pull herself out again. 'This job was supposed to be the new start I needed after Grandma passed away. I needed this.'

'I know, Pols.' Stacey's voice was full of concern. 'I know you needed it, but try to think of the positives. You have this job. Yes, the promotion is no longer as guaranteed as it was, but you have as much chance of getting it as Zac has. You've given up and you can't do that. You need to show them the Polly I know and love. Show them how fierce you can be.'

Polly gave a small, quiet laugh. 'I've never been fierce.'

'No? That's not the vibes I've got off you. All you went through when you were just a kid, losing your parents as you did, moving in with your grandparents, later caring for them whilst you juggled full-time teaching. I don't know how you did it, Pols. I can barely get the job done and I haven't got any responsibilities apart from Freddie and he can look after himself. Then you were teaching part-time while volunteering for years. You are fierce. And you're not going to roll over and give up. You want this promotion. You deserve it, after all you've done for the trust as a volunteer. Go get it.'

'Umm, it's not quite as easy as that, is it?'

'Stop.' The word vibrated in Polly's eardrum.

'What?'

'This. All of this. You've been given this amazing opportunity and you're just going to let it bypass you because you don't believe in yourself. Well, I'm sorry, Polly, but that's a you problem. Everyone else believes in you. You've just got to show up and live up to their expectations.'

Polly looked down as Rolo squirmed in his sleep, his long tail flicking out from beneath the fabric. 'What about Zac? It's hardly the clean slate I expected.'

'No, but stuff happens, and you've just got to adapt. Yes, it must be a bit awkward having to work with him after your leaving party and how he's acted towards you since – but you want my advice? Either put it behind you, pretend it never happened and treat him like any other colleague or else talk to him and clear the air. See what his problem is with you and tell him to get over it.'

'Wow, that'll be a fun conversation.' Polly shook her head. There was no way she'd be talking to him about that.

'Okay, then put it to the back of your mind. Treat him as you would anyone else and watch him come around to your charms.'

'Haha, I can't treat him like anyone else when he freezes me out of everything.' Polly's heart sank as she heard the telltale ring of the school bell in Stacey's background, signalling the end of lunch and the end of the conversation.

'Look, I've got to go, but don't give up. Keep going. Zac is just a rat and people will see that. You've got this.'

Tucking Rolo's tail back into the warmth of the fabric, Polly smiled. 'No, Zac isn't a rat. Rats are cute.'

'Yuck, rats bite and give you rabies.'

'You don't get rabies in this country.' Polly laughed softly as Rolo's tail escaped the comfy cocoon again.

'Okay, whatever it is, that other disease thing.' Stacey's voice was interrupted by the noise of her stacking books and the scraping of her chair against the floor.

'Weil's disease?' Polly shrugged. Stacey had always had an aversion to small rodents, whether they were tame or otherwise.

'See, told you. Zac is a rat. Ha, that almost rhymes. I might take a note and plan a lesson around Zac the Rat.' Stacey laughed as the loud chatter and laughter of children erupted into the classroom. 'Really got to go. Love you, Pols.'

'Love you too.' Polly grinned as she ended the call. Stacey was right. She shouldn't just give up. Yes, this hadn't been quite the opportunity she'd been led to believe it would be, but it was an opportunity all the same and she would only be harming herself if she gave up without a fight.

12

'Do you fancy another coffee, Polly?' Nicola called from across the kitchen.

'Yes, please.' Polly barely glanced up from the sheet of paper she was scribbling on. After spending the afternoon in the office with just Zac, Polly had been glad when five o'clock had hit and she'd been able to fight her way out of the strained atmosphere. Art, Dennis and Vicki had spent the majority of the afternoon in a meeting with Declan and the reserve ranger, Harold, leaving Polly alone with Zac. And despite her spending the whole afternoon desperately trying to think of fundraising ideas, she'd drawn a blank. All she'd been able to think about was Zac's close proximity and the fact he was there to take her promotion. Plus, it hadn't helped that he'd spent the entire time tapping away productively on his laptop, leaving Polly feeling as though she didn't stand a chance.

Now, though, she needed to make up the time and with Nicola working on a new social media campaign for the inn on the table next to her and supplying her with endless mugs of coffee, the ideas were finally flowing.

'Here you go.' Standing next to Polly's table, Nicola paused.

'Thanks. Let me just...' Polly placed the sheet of paper in front of her onto the stack to her right. She had seven sheets now, that was a total of seven fundraising ideas. Now all she had to do was to delve a little more into them and work out if any were viable or not. She smiled as Nicola placed the mug down onto the now clear spot of table. 'How's the campaign planning going?'

'Good, thanks. I've just finished, so I'll have a celebratory mug of coffee before heading home. I've been creating social media posts to put on the village community page about our upcoming Bonfire Night celebrations.'

'Oh, are you hosting the bonfire here?' Polly automatically glanced through the window into the garden. It looked big enough.

'No, but we're going to be handing out sparklers and selling mulled cider and toffee apples for the villagers walking past this way.' Nicola grinned. 'The plan is to have a collection of leaflets and information about what the inn has to offer on hand. You know, such things as the fact we host birthday parties and family gatherings.'

'That sounds a good idea.' Polly smiled. 'Anything with mulled cider is bound to be a success.'

'Hopefully! I'm glad I've got everything prepared as Bonfire Night is speeding towards us now autumn's here.'

'That's great. You'll have the evening to relax then.'

Nicola laughed as she slipped onto the chair opposite her. 'I doubt that. I moved in with my partner, Charlie, a few months ago and he lives on a farm, so there's always work to be done, but I like it. Plus, my little diva of a cat, Trixie, keeps me on my toes.'

'Oh wow, a farm. That must be fun?' Polly brought the mug to her lips, the aroma of the sweet coffee hitting her nostrils.

'Farm life is certainly different from what I'm used to, but I love it. Charlie only inherited it from his uncle last year, so it's been a huge learning curve for both of us, but he's really taken to it.'

'Super early days then?' After hearing tales of her grandma growing up on a farm, riding horses and driving tractors, Polly had always romanticised the idea.

'Yes, definitely.' Nicola grinned as she waved her hand across the table, taking in the papers, pens and highlighters scattered across the surface. 'How's this all going?'

'Good, I think.' Polly frowned. 'I mean, my brain is finally coming up with ideas on how to raise money for the reserve. Whether any of them will actually work, though, is a completely different thing, isn't it?'

'Our gardener, Jill, is very good at fundraising. She's on the community hub for the village and gets involved in all sorts. I'm sure she'd be more than happy to help if you've any questions.' Nicola tilted her head as she tapped on her mobile and scrolled through to the calendar. 'In fact, it's Meadowfield's village meeting tomorrow evening. Why don't you come along? You'll get a sense of the community and will probably get some ideas. Besides, you're practically a resident now, being as you're staying here for so long.'

'Umm, maybe.' Polly nodded thoughtfully. 'Yes, okay. I'll come if you don't think it'll be weird as I haven't actually moved here permanently yet.'

'Not at all.' Nicola nodded before looking across at the kitchen door. 'Evening, Zac. Can I get you anything?'

Twisting in her chair, Polly watched as Nicola stood up and walked across to Zac. Great, this was all she needed, him to come and sit down just as her creativity was finally flowing.

'Just a coffee. I'm happy getting it myself.' Zac smiled one of his signature grins reserved for anyone but Polly as he placed his briefcase carefully on the closest table.

'Don't be daft. Go take a seat and I'll get you one.' Nicola smiled as she reached for a clean mug.

'Thanks.' Zac looked pointedly at Polly as though weighing up his options before picking up his briefcase again and waiting as Nicola poured him a coffee.

Turning back, Polly looked out of the window into the garden. She could just see Zac's faint reflection in the glass as he chatted with Nicola. She shook her head. Stacey didn't know what she was talking about. If Polly brought up the kiss, it'd only make things even more awkward between them.

Returning to the table with a mug for herself, Nicola slid back into the chair she'd previously vacated. 'Am I disturbing you?'

'No, not at all. I need a bit of a break.' Polly grinned. If she were honest, after spending the entire afternoon holed up in the office with the King of Cold Shoulders, she was glad of the company and the chance to talk normally with another human being.

Taking a small sip of her coffee, Nicola then lowered her mug and nodded towards the door. 'What's going on with you two? He couldn't get out of here quick enough and the room temperature dropped at least fifty degrees when he walked in.'

Polly shifted in her chair as she wrapped her hands around her mug. 'It's that obvious?'

'Just a little.' Nicola grimaced. 'Don't share if you don't want to, though. I'm being nosey.'

Polly took a gulp of coffee. It might be good to talk, to get a different perspective on the situation besides Stacey's. Stacey was loyal to the bone, so maybe a neutral opinion on it all might be beneficial. 'I don't mind. It'll probably be good to get someone else's take on it, anyway.'

Nicola nodded.

Moving her coffee mug to the side, Polly placed her hands palm down on the surface of the table in front of her. 'Right, so, I... umm used to teach part-time, while volunteering at the Cotswold Wildlife and Wilderness Trust headquarters where Zac worked.'

'And you never got on?' Nicola frowned.

'No, we did. We used to get on really well and then my friend, Stacey, threw me a leaving party when I finally quit my teaching job and invited people from the trust too.'

'Oh.' Nicola raised her eyebrows.

'Exactly. Zac and I both had a bit too much to drink, and we ended up kissing. I'd always had a bit of a crush on him so thought great, but he obviously felt the complete opposite because from then, things have never been the same and he now hates me.' She turned her hands upwards. 'And I don't know why. I mean, mistakes happen at parties, don't they? Especially where drink is involved. He didn't feel the same way about me as I did about him, and that's fine. Whatever. But it didn't mean he had to be frosty with me.'

'And this is how things have been between you since then?'

Polly nodded. 'Yep. For over four months now. It's ridiculous. You'd have thought he'd have forgotten about it by now, wouldn't you?'

'Maybe you should talk to him and clear the air? If things were fine between you before, then hopefully by addressing it, things should go back to how they were.'

Polly scrunched up her nose as she slid her mug back in front of her. 'There's an added complication now, though. We're both pitted against each other for a promotion. One that it turns out that we'd both been promised by our old boss.'

Nicola whistled through her teeth. 'Ah, now I can understand how that might be awkward.'

'Exactly.' Polly nodded as she picked up her mug again. Taking a sip, she let the sugary coffee pool in her mouth. The word awkward didn't even describe how she felt. Heck, she didn't think she had the vocabulary to describe how she felt.

'Still, talking about things, the kiss and the promotion, might help matters?'

Polly swallowed. 'Maybe.'

Nicola tapped the screen of her phone. 'Yikes, I'd better get going. I didn't realise that was the time. Have a think about it and I'll see you in the morning.'

'Will do, and thank you for listening.' Polly leaned back in her chair as Nicola headed out into the hallway. That was two people who had advised her to talk to Zac and clear the air. And that was just today. Yes, Stacey couldn't be trusted – if she had her way she'd have Polly declaring her undying love to Zac just to see her best friend in a relationship, but Nicola... Nicola was impartial. She was a stranger looking in.

Yes, maybe she would speak to Zac, clear the air. Maybe she should even offer up a truce about this promotion. Just because they were going after the same job, it didn't mean they had to be hostile towards each other. It wasn't as though either of them had known what was going to happen. They couldn't have predicted finding themselves in this situation. Yes, clear the air, get the awkwardness of the kiss gone and also agree to be friendly towards each other. It would be worth her humiliation in bringing up the party incident just to achieve a frost-free work environment.

Taking another sip of her coffee, Polly smiled to herself. The next three months might just be bearable. Placing her mug towards the edge of the table, Polly riffled through the pile of papers before deciding on one idea to expand – rejuvenating the visitor centre's hallway. The first step into making any of their visitors care more for the reserve would be to show it in its best light. And an exhibition displaying the improvements previous funds allowed might just encourage people to dig into their own pockets.

With the pen poised to write, Polly glanced at her mobile as a notification flashed across the screen. It needed charging. Picking up her bag from the floor, she delved through the collection of notebooks, pens and half-used tissues searching for the charger. Drat. Where had she left it? She'd definitely brought it down with her this morning and she could have sworn she'd popped it in her bag to take to work.

Ah no, it was in the sitting room. She'd charged her phone there for a few minutes before breakfast whilst she'd enjoyed her first coffee of the morning, thanks to Laura.

Right, she'd fetch her charger and then get back to the mind mapping. Standing up, she hurried through the kitchen door and crossed the hallway. The sooner she could get back to her work, the better. She'd spent all her time dithering at the office, trying to think of ideas so now they were flowing she didn't want anything to get in the way.

Zac's voice rose from inside the sitting room, and she halted in her tracks. Did she go in? Run in, retrieve her charger before racing back out? It would hardly disturb him, would it? Besides, if he was on a particularly private call, he would have taken it in his room. She'd be quick. Placing her hand on the door handle, Polly readied herself to dart in and out, but before she had the chance to push the door open further, Zac's tone changed as his voice dipped.

'Yes, Dad, that's what I'm asking. And, personally, I don't think it's much to ask, considering.'

He was talking to his father. He wasn't asking him to sponsor the reserve, was he? Polly pursed her lips as she felt a rush of anger shudder through her. Why hadn't she seen this coming? She'd known his parents had been huge benefactors in the past, but that had been just over a year ago now. She should have known Zac would turn to his wealthy family to basically buy him the promotion. And that's what he was doing – by getting them to pledge money to the reserve, he was still technically fundraising, doing his job, just in the most unjust way.

'That's right.'

Polly jumped back as his voice grew louder and she realised he was walking towards the door. Turning on her heels, she ran back through to the kitchen at such a speed she almost skidded on the newly polished oak floorboards. Once in the sanctuary of the kitchen, she quietly closed the door before heading back to her table by the window.

He was cheating! That's what this was – cheating! Plain and simple. She'd assumed he'd planned to ask some business contacts from his old job in marketing to sponsor the reserve, and that would have been close to cheating, but this! He was raising the money by asking for handouts from his parents!

Sinking into her chair, she rubbed at her eyes. Despite the coffee, she suddenly felt exhausted and the ideas she'd been feeling so excited about only moments earlier felt ridiculous. Childish even. She couldn't win.

13

Shrugging her tote bag off her shoulder, Polly dropped it to the floor before kicking it beneath her desk. The office was empty, but then she'd caught the earlier bus, so what had she expected?

After a night spent tossing and turning after almost walking in on Zac taking that call, she'd given up even attempting to sleep at 4 a.m. and had spent the next couple of hours doom-scrolling social media in a lame attempt to take her mind off her dire situation before deciding to just get up. At least she could take a walk around the reserve before deciding whether to hand her notice in right away or wait until the dreaded day of doom when Zac could gloat to her face, knowing for sure he'd bagged the promotion.

Gazing out of the window, she watched as a lone dog walker unclipped his dog's lead and let it run ahead along the winding path, pausing every few feet to sniff the undergrowth. Polly swallowed. She'd expected it to be a little busier at this time of the morning. An early-morning stroll through the reserve would be the perfect way to start a workday, surely? In fact, now she thought about it, besides the group of runners she'd spotted twice now over the last few days and the odd parent walking with children clasping bags of food to feed the ducks, it hadn't been that busy. The reserve attached to the head office where she'd volunteered had always had a constant footfall, people enjoying the area at times to suit them even in the dead of winter.

Besides, the weather was nice today. Uncharacteristically warm for late October. The sky was a beautiful clear blue and there was the crispness in the air which Polly craved during the warmer months. The trees lining the pathway had already turned an assortment of colours, from rustic reds to fiery oranges and yellows, their leaves carried on the slight breeze, clustering beneath their trunks, tempting piles for visitors young and old to crunch through. She'd miss this place.

Shaking her head, she knelt down and pulled her metal water bottle from her bag before tugging her striped scarf off and re-wrapping it properly in place. Fastening the top button on her coat, she turned, ready to leave for her walk, pausing as she felt her arm knock her bottle and heard it drop to the floor with a clang.

Drat. She watched as it rolled across the floor before knocking into the small wastepaper bin between her and Zac's desk, the contents duly spilling across the thin threadbare carpet.

Sighing, she sank to her knees and began to gingerly pick up the banana skin she'd thrown in there yesterday, the once waxy yellow already turning a mushy brown. Yuck. As she began picking up the rest of the rubbish – fortunately a combination of crisp packets and discarded notebook pages – she paused as the words 'Matthews Marketing Ltd' caught her eye. Isn't that where Zac had worked before making his career change into conservation?

Taking the discarded paper, she stood up and unfolded it. Laying it on her desk, she smoothed out the creases and frowned. It was a list of companies, all wealthy-sounding corporate ones by the looks of it. Some had ticks next to them whilst others had been scored out with a heavy line through the middle. She'd known Zac would be taking the route of corporate sponsorship in order to raise the funds. Plus, he now had his dad on board, if last night's conversation was anything to go by.

Picking the paper up, she turned it over and frowned as she spotted an array of numbers scribbled in a list. Great, she literally had no chance if that was how much he'd secured already. Scrunching it back up, she threw it into the bin before retrieving her bottle, placing it on her desk and heading to the door.

As soon as the cold autumn air hit her cheeks, Polly let the tears begin to fall. This was it. It was over. Her new life in Meadowfield was over. Heck, her new career was over, too. Maybe she should message Stacey and ask if there were any jobs going back at Daisy Chain Primary. She'd suggested there was, and if not, she'd know of at least one teaching vacancy. That was one positive of there being a teacher shortage, Polly supposed.

Swiping at her eyes with the back of her hand, she crossed the narrow bridge over the stream and just kept walking. As she ambled alongside the lake, not even the early-morning sun reflecting on the dark waters could raise a smile. She just felt... bereft. She'd worked so hard to get here. So hard, and now all she could do was to focus on the truth lying in front of her. She had to leave.

At least her grandparents' flat hadn't sold. Silver linings and all that. If it had, she'd be homeless as well as jobless.

She laughed, the sound hollow even to her own ears.

'Excuse me, please?' a voice called from behind.

Taking a deep breath, Polly quickly wiped her cheeks dry with the end of her scarf before plastering a smile on her face and turning around. A young couple with a toddler happily gripping a yellow teddy in her pushchair walked over to her. 'Hi, can I help?'

'Sorry to bother you, but little Maddie here is desperate to feed the ducks. It's our first time here and we're not sure where to go.' The woman smiled kindly.

'Oh... umm... there's a little jetty on the other side of the lake by the swing park, which is a great place to feed them.' Polly pointed ahead to where the path curved around the lake.

'There's a park here too?' The woman looked down at her daughter. 'Did you hear that, Maddie? A swing park! Shall we have a play in the park after feeding the ducks?'

The small girl kicked her yellow wellie boots against the footrest of the pushchair whilst holding her teddy in the air and nodding.

'Thank you.' The man nodded and began walking in the direction Polly had indicated.

As she watched them amble past her, Polly frowned. 'Sorry, can I just ask you something?'

'Yes, of course.' The woman paused and turned back to face her.

'Are you new to Meadowfield?'

The woman shook her head. 'No.'

'But this is the first time you've been to the reserve?' Realising the questions she was asking might sound a little odd coming from a total stranger, Polly pulled her lanyard from beneath her buttoned coat and brandished it in the air. 'Sorry for the questions. I work here and we're looking at ways to improve the reserve, how to make it more visitor-friendly and the like.'

'Oh, right.' The woman smiled. 'No, we've lived in Meadowfield for about a year and a half now.' She glanced at her partner, who nodded. 'But, to be honest, we've never really ventured up here to the reserve. If we'd known there was a swing park here, we probably would have done.'

'Okay, thank you.' Polly waved at Maddie as the woman turned the pushchair back around and they continued on their way. Huh. How hadn't they realised there was a park here? If they'd been living in Meadowfield for over a year, they must have spoken to people who frequented the reserve, mustn't they?

Polly turned towards the lake and watched as two gulls dipped and dived across the water, no doubt chasing an early-morning snack. It really was beautiful here. Peaceful, tranquil. And it had so much to offer the local residents and people travelling from further afield, too. From what she knew about the local area, Meadowfield Reserve was the biggest one in at least a twenty-mile radius. It should be attracting families, dog walkers, runners, wildlife enthusiasts, everyone.

There was everything here – a park, birdwatching hideaways, the lake, a meadow, a café, everything anyone could want from a reserve, so what was the problem? What was stopping people from visiting? Yes, it was a little way out of the village centre, but there was a good car park, which was free, and it was only a short walk from the outskirts of the village. Yes, she'd taken the bus the last couple of days, but she could definitely walk here in the future.

So location wasn't a problem. She drew her thumb to her mouth and bit down on the nail. She needed to figure this out. Even if she wasn't going to get the promotion, maybe she should hang around for the three months before quitting. She had her accommodation paid for and, yes, the wage for this role wouldn't allow her to get her own place but she should at least see these three months out. After all, working full time for the trust had been her dream. If she could have it for even a short while before going back home and facing reality, then maybe she should.

Plus, there was the chance she could actually make a difference here.

Meadowfield Reserve was stunning and if she could at least draw a few more daily visitors to the reserve, then she'd have felt she'd contributed a little something to the future of the trust before turning her back on her dreams and heading back to her old life.

Yes, that's what she'd do. She couldn't compete with Zac, but that was okay. Well, not okay, but she could still do something.

14

'Meeting in five minutes, folks.' Declan's voice rose above the general chitchat in the office.

Barely looking up from her desk, Polly nodded before scribbling more ideas down into her notebook. With her head bent and her elbow lounging across the desk in front of her, she had filled five sheets of paper with details of events they could put on and improvements they could make to the reserve to entice people in. Plus, she had the fundraising ideas she'd worked on all evening before she'd overheard Zac's phone conversation. On her way back from her walk, she'd passed the small café whose staff had been sitting outside, their hands wrapped around hot mugs of coffee as they waited for a passing customer, and after speaking to them she now knew today wasn't an overly quiet day, this was the norm. It was normal to have very few customers, very few passers-by.

Stabbing the page with her pen, Polly finished her sentence with a full stop and leaned back in her chair. After feeling as though she'd likely be telling her colleagues she'd be leaving during today's meeting, she was now going to be sharing her vision of the future of Meadowfield Reserve. And she couldn't wait.

She glanced across at Zac, who, in that instant, looked up from his laptop and met her eye. Quickly looking away, Polly slipped the papers into her notebook and stood up, ready to head towards the meeting room.

'You were here early today.' Standing up, Zac pushed his chair under his desk before tucking his laptop beneath his arm.

'Yes.' Polly nodded. How had he noticed? He'd have been leaving Pennycress after her as the car journey to the reserve took minutes compared to the half-hour it took on the bus as it weaved along an abundance of streets, stopping off and collecting travellers as it made its lazy way along the road. She hadn't been in the kitchen when he'd come down for breakfast. That must have been it.

'Okay, people. Grab a cuppa and join me around the table please.' Declan poked his head out of the door leading to the meeting room before disappearing again.

Polly followed Zac into the meeting room before slipping into a chair next to Vicki. 'No Rolo today?'

Shaking her head, Vicki smiled. 'Not today. My flatmate Pearl is off work, so she's kindly agreed to be on Rolo duty today.'

'He's doing okay, though?' Polly tucked her pen inside her notebook, keeping the loose pages with her notes on easily accessible.

'He is.' Vicki grinned. 'It's impossible not to develop a soft spot for him, isn't it?'

'He is rather cute.' She could understand why Vicki chose to spend her free time rescuing and caring for wildlife. 'It must be really rewarding volunteering to help at the wildlife sanctuary like you do.'

'It is.' Vicki stretched her arms out above her head and yawned. 'It's tiring too, though. I was there until gone midnight last night as we had a couple of emergencies brought in and then—'

'Thank you, folks.' Sitting down heavily in his chair at the head of the table, Declan cheerfully cut across the chatter. 'Okay, on today's agenda is a general catch-up. I'd like to hear about your visit to the school yesterday, Art and Vicki, and your visit to Stratford-upon-Avon Reserve, Dennis. Then we'll have a catch-up with Zac and Polly, if that's okay? No pressure though, we know you're new here and have been thrown into the deep end, so to speak.'

Polly nodded. For the first time since starting her job, she didn't feel the pressure. She'd accepted she wasn't going to get the promotion and, instead, she was ready for the challenge of ensuring her time at Meadowfield Reserve wouldn't be for nothing. She was ready to talk about her ideas and, fingers crossed, get the go-ahead she needed from Declan in order to proceed with them.

As she listened to Art, Declan and Vicki recount their week's work, she fiddled with her pen. It felt strange listening to Art speak about the school assemblies he'd been giving as outreach and education officer, to raise awareness of their conservation work. That should have been her.

'...And I think every pupil and teacher alike now knows to check any bonfires for hedgehogs before lighting them,' Art finished with a grin.

'That's fantastic, thank you. It sounds as though you've had a very productive week.' Declan nodded to Art before fixing his eyes on Zac and Polly. 'And now to our two new recruits, our fundraising and development officers, Zac and Polly. Who'd like to go first?'

Feeling herself put on the spot, Polly felt a flutter of nerves as she waved her hand in Zac's direction. 'I'm happy with you going first, Zac, if you like?'

Nodding, Zac cleared his throat and gave her a cursory nod. 'Thank you. Right, I've spent the week focusing on developing sponsorship deals with some corporate companies.'

'Ooh, corporate companies! I don't think we've ever had any sponsorship deals before.' Leaning forward, Declan laced his fingers together. 'Tell me more.'

'Of course.' Zac clicked on his keyboard before continuing. 'It's early days and I'm building up trust between myself and the companies so far. At the moment, I'm working on formal proposals and will begin visiting them over the next few weeks, but if I secure even half of the sponsorships, we'll reach our funding target for this year.'

As a chorus of oohs and ahhs filled the small room, Polly zoned out of the conversation, while Declan, Art, Vicki and Dennis fired questions at Zac and marvelled over his answers. The truth of the matter was that Zac already had the contacts. He'd come into the job with an advantage. She gripped hold of her pen and reminded herself that it didn't matter. She was no longer here to compete; she was here to make her time at the reserve worthwhile. She was here to make a difference. Or to try to. Now everyone had been wowed by Zac's development with the funding situation, her plans would look like nothing in comparison. The work she'd been focusing on would only lead to money coming in dribs and drabs, not anything close to how grand Zac's proposals were. Still...

'Polly?'

Declan's voice cut into her thoughts and she snapped her head in his direction, immediately realising the room had gone quiet as people waited for her contribution. 'Oh, umm... sorry. Er, Zac, your funding forecast sounds amazing.'

'Thank you.' Zac's voice was clipped as he slowly closed his laptop.

'And yourself? Are you in a position to give us an update on what you've been working on?' Declan smiled warmly. 'It doesn't matter if you want to skip an update this week. We know you're both new and wouldn't really expect such progress within your first week.'

Mentally shaking herself, Polly tried her best to fill her voice with a confidence she suddenly found lacking. 'No, I'm happy to give you an update. I've been working on a few ideas. Although I'm afraid they won't be able to compete with Zac's in terms of money raised, I'm still hopeful they can make a little impact to the reserve in the long run at least.'

'Great.' Declan rubbed his hands together. 'I look forward to hearing all about them.'

'Okay.' Taking a deep breath, Polly pulled the loose pages from her notebook and gripped them in her hands. 'It's occurred to me that the reserve might not be reaching the number of visitors it potentially could. Does that sound fair?'

'Quite fair, yes.' Declan nodded as he stroked his beard thoughtfully. 'I think it's always been a bit of a problem with the reserve being a little out of the village.'

'Yes, yes, I understand that, but we have a lot on our side in that respect: we have a regular and reliable bus service, a large free car park and its position isn't too far from the village to entice dog walkers and people wanting to stretch their legs before reaching us.'

'True.' Declan held his hand out, allowing her to continue.

Laying her papers in front of her, she gripped the arms of her chair and pulled herself in an inch. 'I think there're improvements we can make to encourage more visitors. Both by raising awareness of all the reserve has to offer to the local community, as well as things we can do here at the reserve to make people's visits as enjoyable and informative as possible so they're more likely to not only return, but also to talk about their experience with their family, friends and neighbours, which will then grow our visitor numbers too.'

'What sorts of things are you thinking of?' Vicki looked towards the small pile of papers in front of Polly.

Was she going to do this? Could she get across her ideas without coming across as dismissive of past attempts at raising interest in the reserve? Polly bit down on her bottom lip. This was why she was here, a fresh set of eyes. That's what was expected of her. It was quite literally her job. 'Right, I've brought a few initial ideas to share to begin with. I must warn you, they're just notes at this time. I'll work on getting some more details down, though. If you all think they're worth it, of course.'

'Great, great. Let's hear them.' Declan nodded.

This was it. Polly took a deep breath and tried to focus on slowing the pace of her voice, one thing she'd always struggled with when giving assemblies at school. 'Right, well, to begin with, I've focused on ideas to make the reserve more accessible to people once they get here. So, with that in mind, my first proposal would be to update the reserve map. I know we already have one, but it's not in a very prominent position.' Now that was an understatement. She'd had to fight her way through a ton of spindly branches which had encroached onto the map's board. 'I was thinking it should be by the car park, on the main path leading into the reserve. That way, people new to the reserve will be able to take a look and familiarise themselves.'

'We've been meaning to update that map for a few years now. I'm pretty sure the new birdwatching hideaways aren't even on there.' Declan scribbled in his notebook.

'And once people are in the reserve, because it's so big, I thought we could perhaps put up a few signs. Just pointing people in the direction of the main attractions to begin with, before working on a few distinct routes visitors could take depending on whether they were wheelchair and pushchair accessible, shorter, longer, that type of thing. A woodland walk, perhaps?' Keeping her eyes fixed on her scribbles, Polly shuffled through her papers until she found the next one. 'And then there is this place, the visitor centre. I feel the foyer leading through to the toilets is a great space to encourage people to care for the reserve. We could update the displays, make them fresher, with maybe some before and after photos of parts of the reserve, to show visitors where their donations go.'

'And move the donation box from the car park to the visitor centre? To be close whilst people are thinking about donating?' Vicki tapped her pen against the table excitedly.

'Or have both. There's no reason we can't keep the one in the car park to catch people as they leave and have a new one by the displays.' Art pointed his finger towards Declan's notebook.

'Yes, yes. Good, very good.' Dipping his head, Declan added to his notes.

'I know we're not going to raise anything anywhere close to the amount Zac has proposed to raise from corporate companies but...' Polly shrugged.

'No, I get it.' Declan stabbed his pen in her direction. 'We need to make people care. If they care about the reserve, they're more likely to donate. Plus, once we've got them here, there's nothing stopping us from putting on special fundraising events.'

'Exactly. If we can increase the footfall to the reserve, there's so much more we can do. We could set up little Santa trails at Christmas, where children have to spot a certain number of pictures of reindeer or something around the reserve. If we charge them, just a bit, we can give them a prize at the end and raise money that way. We can do the same at Easter and Halloween. We could host fun days and charge stallholders to set up stalls.' Polly pushed her papers into the middle of the table, spreading them out, her ideas in full view.

'And the café. With more people visiting the reserve, the café is bound to make more and some of the profits go back into the reserve, don't they?' Dennis glanced at Declan for clarification.

'That's right.' Picking up one of the papers, Declan raised his eyebrows. 'You've worked hard on this, Polly. I'm impressed. With the tweaks and improvements you're suggesting, how much do you expect we can increase our footfall?'

'Oh, I'm not sure. Sorry.' Polly picked up her pen again, twisting it in her hands. 'I've not got that far with these ideas, but I have thought I'd quite like to visit some other reserves in the vicinity to gauge an idea of how well they're doing with regard to visitor numbers.'

'Good idea.' Declan nodded. 'I look forward to seeing how this goes.'

'Thank you.' Polly grinned as relief flooded through her body. 'I know it's not rocket science but...'

'Nope, it's great. As I think I mentioned when you and Zac first arrived, we've had a few too many changes on the staffing front and after being understaffed for so long, we've let things slip. Things like this.' Declan waved his hand across the table, indicating Polly's papers.

Polly nodded as she felt the fierce rush of self-consciousness warm her cheeks. She was pleased everyone had taken so well to her plans and she was relieved to hear Declan didn't feel she was undermining anything which had been attempted in the past.

'Thank you all. We'll regroup next week and see how everyone's getting along.' Declan turned back to the page of Polly's notes he was holding.

With the meeting declared over, Polly watched as Art, Dennis, Vicki and Zac filtered outside before standing and collecting her papers. She shuffled them into a neat pile as she waited for Declan to finish perusing the last one.

'Here you go.' Standing up, Declan passed her the paper before lowering his voice. 'I'm very impressed. You've come in here and spotted the root of the problem with the reserve: the lack of regular visitors. Not only that, but you've suggested solutions too.'

'I've tried to.' Polly looked down as she slipped the paper Declan had given her into the pile with the others.

'Marvellous job. You continue like this and I'm going to have a really tough time choosing who takes over my role.' Declan turned to the door, patting her on the shoulder as he left.

'Oh, umm, thanks.'

Had he really just said that? Was she still in the running to get the promotion? Even though there was no chance of her raising as much as Zac could?

As she heard the click of the door shut behind her, Polly sank back into her chair in the now empty meeting room. All was not lost. She still had a chance at this, a chance at her new start. And if that was the case, then she knew one thing: she would work her butt off to succeed, or failing that, just so she knew in her heart she'd given it her best shot.

15

Polly yawned as she walked up the garden path towards Pennycress Inn. After staying late at the office surveying the few visitors they did have to the reserve and working on more proposals, she was ready for her bed. There was nothing more she wanted than to throw herself onto the ridiculously comfy mattress and pull the squishy duvet over her head. Only then would she be able to turn her brain off and quiet the whirring of ideas.

Now she knew she was still in the running for the promotion regardless of bringing in less funding than Zac, her mind was brimming with thoughts and she was excited to get them down on paper, but she did need to give in to her body as it screamed at her to rest.

As she climbed the steps up to the decking which wrapped itself around half of the inn, the door opened in front of her and Laura, Jackson, Nicola and Zac spilled out. 'Hi.'

'There you are. Aren't we glad you're back now. I was worried we'd miss you.' Laura tucked her arm through hers as she spun Polly around back to face the gate again.

'Huh? Sorry, where are you going?' Polly glanced over her shoulder, catching a glimpse of Zac deep in conversation with Jackson and Nicola.

'To the community hub meeting.' Laura grinned at her as they made their way through the garden. 'You hadn't forgotten, had you?'

'The community hub meeting? Of course.' She had forgotten. The conversation with Nicola yesterday evening where she'd agreed to go along had completely escaped her mind.

'It's a village meeting. Nicola said she'd mentioned it? Everyone living in Meadowfield goes along and the mayoress, Miss Cooke, runs it. We discuss different events coming up in the village, or any problems people have.' Laura lowered her voice and leaned in closer. 'And I say "discuss", but what I really mean is Miss Cooke talks at us.'

'Oh right. Yes, Nicola did say. Sorry, it must have slipped my mind.' Polly pulled her bag higher up onto her shoulder.

'No worries. Obviously you don't have to come, but we thought it might be nice for you and Zac, seeing as you're both staying with us for a while.' Laura glanced across at Polly. 'You absolutely don't have to, though? I've just forced this on you, haven't I?'

Polly laughed. 'No, it'll be good. I'm glad Nicola mentioned it and I'm happy to come.'

'Are you sure?' Laura slowed down.

'I'm sure. In fact, it could be super helpful to my work at the reserve.' The meeting would be the perfect place to gauge people's interests and might give her some more ideas as to how to entice people to venture there.

'Really?' Grinning, Laura picked up speed again.

'Yes, really. I'm focusing my efforts on trying to get more people to come across to the reserve and explore. There's so much it has to offer, but I just don't think we're getting people there in the first place.'

'I must admit I've never been.' Laura frowned.

'Can I ask why?'

'I'm not sure, really. I guess I've just assumed it's a place for people to walk their dogs around, or for parents to take their kids to feed the ducks.'

As they rounded the corner, they were met with a crowd standing around in front of what looked like an old community hall and Polly realised that Laura hadn't been exaggerating when she'd said most of the villagers turned up to the meetings.

'I'll have to drag Jackson up there for a wander when we've got a spare minute.' Laura waved towards a couple surrounded by four children, one in a buggy and three of varying ages up to a young teen. 'Jill! Gerald!'

Turning, Jill grinned as she pushed the buggy towards them. 'Hi, Laura. Hi, you're Polly, right? I remember you arrived during Willow's party at the inn? I'm glad to see we didn't scare you away.'

'Haha, definitely not.' Polly grinned.

'Good.' Jill leaned over the buggy and passed two little wooden figures to the toddler. 'Here you go, Kasey. Play with these.'

Polly waved at the toddler. 'Hello.'

'Polly is working at the nature reserve, alongside our other long-term resident, Zac.' Laura waved her arm behind her.

Jill raised her eyebrows. 'The nature reserve, you say? Wow, that must be an utterly incredible job! Getting to work in nature all day every day and for such a good cause, too.'

'Oh, I'm based in the office, mostly.' Polly fiddled with the straps of her tote bag as it dug into her shoulder.

'That's a shame, although I bet you've got an amazing view. And to have all that space and wildlife just outside your office...' Jill glanced behind her and waved her husband over. 'We love it up there, don't we, Gerald?'

'Where?' Gerald questioned before holding out his hand towards Polly. 'Nice to meet you. I'm Jill's other half, Gerald.'

'Good to meet you too.' Polly smiled.

'The nature reserve,' Jill continued. 'There's so much to do there. Of course, not as much as some other reserves around here, but it's definitely the biggest.'

'Well, that's what we're hoping to change. There's so much potential to do great things there, to make the experience so much more interactive for visitors.' Jill was the first person Polly had spoken to outside of work who seemed to be on the same page as her, who could see what the reserve could be with a little thought.

Laura placed her hand on Polly's forearm and laughed. 'I knew you two would get along, but we'd best get a move on and get inside before we're told off.'

Polly looked towards the door into the village hall. An older woman wearing a sage green coat and sporting large matching earrings, which almost brushed against her collar, was standing there, propping the door open whilst ushering people inside. She glanced back in the direction they'd come, searching for Zac's dark hair in the gathering of people, but he wasn't there.

'Ah, we'd best get a wriggle on. See you inside.' Jill turned, pushing the buggy with one hand as she herded her children towards the door with the other. 'Come on, kids. Now remember, best behaviour in front of Miss Cooke. You promised.'

'That's our cue too.' Laura led them towards the entrance.

Taking a final look around to see if she could spot Zac, Nicola or Jackson, Polly nodded and smiled as Laura introduced her to a number of people she'd never remember the names of. Once they reached the front of the entrance and the woman in green, Polly paused as the woman shot her hand out and clasped hers.

'Welcome, welcome. It's nice to see another new face. Who might we have here?'

'Hi, I'm Polly. I'm staying at Pennycress Inn.' Polly gritted her teeth as the woman shook her hand with more gusto than necessary.

'Polly, this is Miss Cooke, Meadowfield's esteemed mayoress.' Laura waved her hand between Polly and Miss Cooke. 'Polly is staying with us for a few months and hoping to settle here, so I thought it would be nice for her to get to know the village a little better.'

'Ah, I take it you're also working at the reserve? Lovely. The more the merrier. Come on through.' Miss Cooke dropped her hand and waved her into the hall.

That answered that question then. Zac must already be inside. How else would Miss Cooke have known Polly was working at the reserve?

Pausing just past the doors, Laura stood on her tiptoes and scanned the large hall. 'There they are. Over there.'

Following Laura, Polly weaved her way through the throng of people heading down the large aisle between chairs towards the back of the vast stone building. It seemed like a sweet tradition, having a village meeting. There had been nothing like that where she'd grown up. Yes, her grandparents had known almost everyone in their block of flats and in the street and her grandma had taken Polly along to her WI meetings a few times, but apart from chatting in the street or popping round friends' homes for a natter over a cuppa there hadn't been any organised events within the community such as this. And people were turning in their seats, smiling at each other, chatting in groups. It was nice.

'Hold on. I'm just waiting for Charlie.' Nicola stood up from her chair at the end of the aisle and ushered Polly through. 'You go first.'

'Where's Jackson?' Laura glanced around.

'Ha, Miss Cooke has roped him into helping with the microphone or something.' Nicola shrugged. 'There was some drama as we came in and she kidnapped him. Wrong place and wrong time for him, I'm afraid.'

'Oh.' Laura twisted to look behind her and waved towards the stage as Jackson struggled with a large box. 'Oops, that'll be him tied up all meeting then. Go on, Polly, you go first.'

16

Polly squeezed along the row of chairs, her heart sinking as she realised she was going to be sitting next to Zac. She'd spent enough time beside him at work and now it looked as though she'd be right beside him for the next hour or however long these village meetings usually took. At least at work she had the wastepaper bin to separate their desks, here the chairs were so close together that physical contact was likely to be unavoidable. Slipping her tote bag from her shoulder, she perched on the chair, her bag on her lap. 'Hello again.'

'Evening.' Zac nodded before turning back to the front, his eyes following Jackson as he continued to shift boxes around the stage.

'You could always go and offer to help him.' Biting her tongue, she refrained from adding 'because you look as though you want to be anywhere besides sitting next to me' and instead plonked her bag on the floor and kicked it under the seat. Inching it further back, she cursed under her breath at the familiar tinkly sound of her metal water bottle as it once again escaped the confines of her bag. And yep, there was the rolling sound. Great. Leaning forward, she looked between her legs and, sure enough, there it was sitting smack bang in the middle of the floor beneath her chair. There was no way she'd be able to reach it like this. Scooting off the edge of the chair, she dropped to her knees at precisely the same time as Zac knelt down, coming forehead to forehead with him. 'Ouch!'

'Sorry. Let me.' Waiting until she'd stood up and to the side, Zac reached beneath her chair and retrieved her bottle, holding it aloft in much the same way as she had always envisaged him receiving trophies as the college football hero or some such.

'Great. Thanks.' Taking the bottle, her fingers swept across his, causing him to snatch his hand back so quickly that if it wasn't for the fact Polly shot her other hand out, the bottle would have ended up crashing to the floor once again. As soon as he'd sat back in his seat, she sank back on hers, inching her chair across the hardwood floor as far away from him as she could. Why had he reacted so dramatically to their fingers touching? Was she that repulsive that he thought he'd catch something from merely brushing her skin? Huh, he hadn't been so worried about that at her leaving party.

'Finally, he's dismissed.' Laura laughed as she shimmied her way down the row of chairs, Jackson following closely behind, a frazzled expression fixed to his face. 'Quick, sit down and hide before she realises she needs you for something else.' Placing her hand on his shoulder, Laura gently guided him into his chair.

'Haha, I don't need to be told twice.' Sitting down, Jackson slumped against the back of his chair and slid his legs forward, ducking his head down out of view behind the people in front.

Polly watched as people stopped talking, and a hushed silence filled the hall. She glanced across at Zac, whose gaze was fixed on Miss Cooke as she took to the stage. She understood it now. After all these months wondering what she'd done to wrong him, she understood. He just didn't like her. Not like that. Or in any way, it seemed. The kiss had been a mistake, which, yes; it had been, she agreed. Everyone knew that relationships at work weren't such a good idea. Fair enough. But it wasn't just that. He'd changed the way he acted around her and just now she could have sworn he'd have rather had the floor swallow him whole than have to endure a moment's touch from her. No, it all made sense. He'd done all of this to make sure she hadn't got the wrong impression from that kiss.

'Where's Charlie? He promised he'd come.' Leaning forward in her chair, Nicola whispered along the line. 'I don't want to endure this by myself.'

'There he is,' Laura stage-whispered back as she pointed towards the door of the village hall.

'Fingers crossed he isn't noticed.' Nicola grimaced.

'Our lovely mayoress loves Charlie. If anyone can get away with being late, it's him.' Jackson chuckled quietly as everyone's eyes moved to the creaking door as Charlie tried and failed to slip inside without being spotted.

'Ah, Charlie, you're here. Come on in and pop yourself in a chair.' Miss Cooke smiled brightly as Charlie muttered an apology and half walked, half ran down the aisle towards them.

'Told you.' Jackson spoke a little too loudly and tried to cover his words with a cough.

Polly smiled despite herself. She could picture herself living here, finding a place of her own, feeling at home. The people she'd met in such a short space of time were already beginning to feel like friends and the community feel of Meadowfield was obvious.

If only she didn't have to endure Zac's awkwardness at work. She crossed her arms, her bottle still clasped tightly in one hand. Still, she wasn't going to allow herself to focus on him and his weird ways. No, instead she was going to focus on the fact Declan had promised her she still stood a chance at winning the promotion. That was why she was here, and that's what she needed to remember. She wasn't here to try to decipher Zac Sinclair's thought patterns. She was here for her and for her chance at a fresh start. Everything else she needed to put out of her mind. To push it out of her mind, the house (or building) and the universe, as her grandma had always told her to do when she awoke from a particularly awful nightmare.

'...So please welcome our newcomers, Zac and Polly.' Miss Cooke clapped her hands once as she located them both in her audience.

'Oh, umm...' She should have been listening. Was she expected to say something? Had she asked them a question?

'Many thanks. Very happy to be here.' Zac straightened his back and looked around the packed hall, smiling.

Drat. That was everyone tuned into Zac's charms then. She should have been on the ball, she should have thanked Miss Cooke first instead of floundering. Once again, Zac had got the upper hand and, once again, everyone would think he was the friendly one and she the stand-offish one.

Polly opened her mouth to speak before clamping her lips together again as Miss Cooke continued. It was too late now. She'd missed her chance.

'And now I'll hand over to Jill, who would like to speak to you all about

Meadowfield's upcoming village bonfire.' Miss Cooke stepped back as Jill and her children clambered onto the stage.

'Thank you, Miss Cooke. And to begin my chat with you all about Bonfire Night I have four very excited children who have worked very hard to practise this dance for you. I'm told it's called "Pop, Fizzle and Bang".' Jill leaned down as her young daughter, Willow, ran across the stage to her, tugged the hem of her mum's jumper and whispered in her ear. Straightening her back again, Jill grimaced. 'I'm sorry, it's called "Bang, Fizzle and Pop".'

The group of children took their places in the centre of the stage as the youngest, Kasey, still strapped securely in his buggy, began banging a wooden spoon against an upturned saucepan. His siblings pranced and danced their way across the small stage, jumping up and down to the beat. The teenager, clearly coerced into participating by his younger brothers and sister, spent the time half-heartedly joining in whilst trying his hardest to avoid eye contact with his audience.

As the group finished and the children took a bow, a round of applause erupted and filled the cavernous hall.

'What a wonderful surprise. Thank you, children.' Miss Cooke rose her voice as the applause subsided. 'What a lovely way to begin your mum's talk.'

As the children filed off, the eldest rolling Kasey's buggy to the edge of the stage where Gerald lifted him, buggy and saucepan included, down with ease, Jill beamed, her face full of pride. 'Thank you. Right, so now you have an idea of what to expect, I'll continue and would like to share that we're once again having the bonfire and fireworks on Guy Fawkes Night on the primary school playing field.'

A cheer sounded from the front of the hall and Jill paused before continuing.

'We'll be having food trucks and stalls around the perimeter of the play-ground, weather permitting of course, so there's no reason for any of you to be slaving away over a hot stove before coming to enjoy the fireworks. We'll have stalls inside the school hall too for you to peruse at your leisure before the fire-works.' Jill looked around the hall before indicating towards where Laura, Jackson and Nicola were sitting. 'Plus, this year we're very lucky as the lovely Laura, Jackson and Nicola from Pennycress Inn will be handing out free sparklers to all attendees and will also be serving mulled cider and toffee apples, so be sure to pop by Pennycress on your way to the school.'

'Thank you, Jill. It sounds as though it will be a wonderful night, as always.' Miss Cooke began walking back towards the lectern where Jill was standing. 'And I for one shall look forward to treating myself to a nice warm mulled cider.'

'Thank you, Miss Cooke.' Jill turned back towards the hall. 'Oh, one last thing, we do have a little more room for a few more stalls, so if you'd like to join us and haven't spoken to me, please do catch me sometime this week.'

'Fabulous.' Miss Cooke took over, Jill now dismissed.

Polly felt Zac shift in his chair next to her and looked across at him. He was leaning forward, his elbows on his knees, his head dipped and his mobile in his hand. She opened her mouth to say something to him before thinking better of it and turning back to the stage again. If he got caught, then let him take the punishment, whatever that might be, but the way Laura and Jackson had been talking about the infamous mayoress, she wouldn't like to be in his position if he was caught not paying attention.

She picked at the cuticle on her thumbnail. Although, this was Zac, the golden boy, the man who had everyone fooled by his charms. He wouldn't get caught. And if he did? Well, he'd only go and talk himself right back out of it again. Pulling on her skin a little too forcefully, she winced as it began to bleed. Drat.

'Take this,' Zac whispered as he held out a pale blue handkerchief, folded precisely into a small square, his eyes still fixed on his phone as the screen lit up with a new message.

Looking at the handkerchief in his hand, Polly widened her eyes. Of all the people she'd expect to step in and offer her help, Zac was the last on the list. No, in fact, he wasn't on the list at all.

'Thanks.' She grunted back at him as she took it. Looking down at the pristinely clean handkerchief in her hand, she glanced back across at him. What if she stained it? That would only give him something else to hold against her, wouldn't it?

Zac glanced up and nodded at the hankie as if indicating she should use it, before turning his attention quickly back to his phone.

Shrugging, Polly wrapped the soft fabric around her thumb. She needed to put him out of her mind. Not that it was easy being as he physically filled every space she went, the office, the inn, even here in a random village meeting.

She unwrapped the handkerchief from around her thumb and peeked at the damage she'd caused. She knew one thing, and that was that she'd be omitting a few details from tonight's tale when she recounted it to Stacey. Her friend would only read something completely ridiculous into the fact Zac had retrieved Polly's bottle for her and passed her a hankie. Knowing Stacey, she'd embellish it to the point that Sir Zachary was riding into the hall on his white horse to rescue her from a pit of snakes or something equally deadly.

Besides, she wasn't thinking about Zac. Not from now on, so she wouldn't be talking to Stacey about him anyway.

17

Pausing in front of the office door, Polly pushed the hood of her coat down and watched the rainwater drip onto the tiled floor of the large foyer. She was late. She'd decided to take the bus again this morning because of the downpour, but the bus had broken down at the stop before the reserve and so faced with the prospect of waiting ages for a replacement, she'd braved the rain and walked the rest of the way. But at least it had given her time to think a little and she might just have thought of a way to speed up raising awareness of the reserve.

With her hand on the door handle, she jumped back as Declan's cheery voice boomed through the door before it opened.

'Ah, Polly! There you are. We'd begun to think you'd run out on us.' Declan chuckled as he held the door open for her.

'Sorry, bus trouble,' she muttered as she began to walk through into the office. Thinking better of it, she turned to him. 'Actually, I was wondering if I could have a quick word at some point today, please?'

Pausing with his back against the open door, Declan hitched the sleeve of his coat up and glanced at his watch. 'Ah, any other day I'd be all yours, but I've got a meeting at HQ to go to this morning and will be out all day. Can it wait?'

She hopped from foot to foot. With the idea fresh in her mind and with the limited timeline, she really wanted to get back to Jill today if there was an any possible way she could pull this off.

Watching as she dithered on the spot, Declan shook his head slightly. 'Walk and talk with me. That's the best I can do if it's urgent.'

'Great. I'm happy to walk and talk.' Turning, she followed him back the way she'd just come and pulled her hood up just before they stepped outside.

After holding the door open for her, Declan followed and lifted his face to the sky before raising his own coat hood. 'There's something refreshing about this weather, isn't there? Something revitalising.'

Polly swiped at her face as a fat raindrop landed squarely on her forehead. Refreshing? That's not the way she'd have described it after walking half a mile through it and getting drenched. She could feel her wet jeans sticking to her legs and that definitely didn't feel particularly revitalising, either. 'Yep, it sure is.'

'What can I help you with?' Turning to her, he held the edge of his hood back so he could see her.

'Zac and I went to a village meeting last night and I just have a couple of ideas to run past you. They're to do with the upcoming Bonfire Night, which is why I wanted to get your opinion on them today.' Polly batted a raindrop dribbling off the end of her nose.

'In Meadowfield?'

'Yes, that's right. The community hub have organised a bonfire and fireworks display at the local primary school and will be having food trucks and some stalls inside the hall too.'

'And what were you thinking?' Turning, Declan began walking slowly in the direction of the car park.

Walking beside him, Polly took a deep breath before blurting out her ideas. 'Well, I was thinking we could hire a food truck on behalf of the reserve café and offer hot drinks and some of the food which is served there. And we could also set up a stall inside, print some leaflets and maybe run a competition to win a stuffed toy or something. Anything really just to let people know the reserve is still here, still open and has a lot to offer the people of Meadowfield.'

Declan paused and turned towards her. Tilting his head, he nodded slowly. 'I can see how this could work.'

'Yes, I really think it might. Of course it'll cost us, but I reckon we'd get our money back and make some besides. Plus, it'll be worth the outlay to get the word out. I know we've spoken about how we can improve visitors' experience of the reserve and I know we won't be able to implement everything in time, but I do think a lot of villagers just don't see it as a place to come.' She shook her head. She wasn't making any sense. 'We need to raise awareness if we're going to attract more visitors.'

'Okay, okay.' Rummaging in his pocket, Declan pulled out a bunch of keys. 'Make the necessary enquiries. See if it would be possible. Check there are still stalls available, speak to Helena and Jarvis at the café and ask their opinions and if they'd be willing to help and we'll go from there. How does that sound?'

'Great. Absolutely great. Thank you.'

'No worries. I like it.' Smiling, he held his keys out and clicked the fob, the hazard lights flickering to life on an old Ford Escort.

'Okay.' Polly nodded, a slow grin spreading across her face. She'd got his approval. He thought the idea was a good one.

'Now go inside and get yourself dried off before you catch your death or nothing will get done.' Nodding towards the visitor centre, Declan chuckled before turning and making his way to his car.

Laughing, Polly spun on the spot, suddenly forgetting how cold and wet she was. If she could organise this in time, it could make a difference. It could be a relatively easy and quick way to remind the villagers of the reserve's existence and bring in some money.

18

Settling back into the chair at her desk, Polly rubbed her hands together, willing the cold red skin to warm up. After calling Pennycress Inn hoping that Jill might be there, she'd got the go-ahead that there were still stalls available and space for another food truck. She'd also spoken to Helena and Jarvis who ran the reserve café, and they were suitably excited at the prospect of pulling more customers in.

'How did it go? Are Helena and Jarvis keen?' Wheeling her chair towards Polly, Vicki stopped in front of Polly's desk before readjusting the cotton scarf draped around her shoulders as a bushy browny-red tail flopped out.

'Who have you brought to work today?' Leaning forward, Polly smiled as Vicki folded the fabric down a little to reveal a small sleeping squirrel.

'Nutkin. He's been hand-reared since a member of the public found him trapped inside a skip on someone's driveway.' Vicki grinned as she gently let the fabric cover him again. 'Don't let this fool you, though. When he's awake, he's an utter pest, which is why I've had to bring him to work today. I'm looking after him for a few days while, Betty, who he's staying with, goes on holiday and it's got to the point that I have to separate him and my flatmate's cat as Nutkin here just terrorises her.'

'Oh.' Polly couldn't help but laugh. 'Appearances can be deceptive.'

'They definitely can.' Vicki picked up a pen from Polly's desk and began winding it around her fingers.

Polly looked towards the door as Zac strode through. Yep, he was another example of appearances being deceptive.

'So, go on, don't keep me in suspense. Are we having a food truck and stall at the bonfire and fireworks display?' Vicki tapped the pen gently against the edge of the desk.

'Sorry, yes. Helena and Jarvis are more than happy to organise and run the truck. They were pretty excited about the potential to drum up business.' Polly opened her notebook and crossed off the task of finding a food truck from her list. It made sense Helena and Jarvis making the arrangements. They knew what they'd need for a start, and she was grateful they'd been happy to organise it all.

'So, it's going ahead, then?' Vicki grinned. 'I don't think we've ever been part of such a big event since I started here three years ago.'

'I just hope it works.' Polly lowered her voice as Zac took his seat at the desk next to her, the aromatic fumes of fresh coffee enveloping her. She'd hardly sat down all morning, let alone had time to grab a coffee. She'd just have to breathe a little deeper and hope the aroma supplied her with the caffeine too.

'It will do. I have great faith in you.'

'Umm, thanks.' As excited as she was, she just couldn't shake the feeling that if this event fell flat for them, then she'd not only be letting herself down but the reserve too.

'Is that your phone?' Vicki pointed to Polly's bag stashed beneath the desk as her cheerful ringtone filled the office.

'Oh, yes.' Shaking herself from her thoughts, Polly leaned down and picked up her bag before rummaging through and pulling out her phone. It was David from the estate agents. 'Sorry, I'd best take this.'

'Yep, catch you later.'

Polly watched Vicki wheel her chair back to her desk as she jabbed the Accept Call button and held the mobile to her ear. 'Hi, David. All okay?'

'Hi, Polly. And yes, all is okay. Thank you for asking. In fact, it's more than okay...' He took a dramatic pause.

Polly tried to quiet the flicker of excitement in the pit of her stomach. Had the flat been sold? Even a few days ago, she would have been torn as to whether to accept an offer or not, but now, with things looking up and finding out she still had a chance at the promotion, it would be a weight off her mind. 'It's sold!'

David's voice grew hesitant. 'No, no. We're not quite there yet, but I do have a viewing booked in for Monday morning.'

'Oh, right.' She ran the pad of her finger along the edge of her notebook, tracing its outline. Another viewing, another disappointment to follow. They'd been here before. Numerous times.

'Don't sound too disheartened. I have a good feeling about this one. The couple viewing are new developers building a portfolio who have recently bought up several other properties locally.'

'And you really think they might take on my grandparents' flat?' She glanced across at Zac, who was seemingly busy tapping away on his laptop.

'I think if we go about this the right way, there might just be a good chance.'

Go about it the right way? 'What do you mean?'

'I mean, I think we should take the necessary steps I suggested to increase our chances of success.'

Ahh. 'So, to declutter a little?'

'Nope. To declutter a lot and to redecorate.' David took a sharp breath in. 'I'm not talking about putting up wallpaper or painting woodwork or anything. I'm just suggesting we paint a few walls white or magnolia, that's all. Focus on the living room and the master bedroom, give our buyers a chance to see the flat's potential.'

Declutter a lot? Paint? And what did he mean by 'we'? The royal we, that's what he meant. 'I don't know...'

'I know it's a family home, the one you grew up in, but sometimes that level of someone else's stuff puts off buyers. They don't have the ability to be able to see what could be.'

'I thought you said they were investors? They wouldn't be living in it, so why would anything put them off?' As great as it would be for the flat to be sold, she really needed to get organised for the upcoming event at Meadowfield's Bonfire Night. A week, that's all they had. A week to organise the stall, leaflets, competition prizes. Leaning forward, she pinched the bridge of her nose.

'They're new to this. Inexperienced. We don't want to give them any reason to walk away, do we?'

'No, I guess not.' Polly drew a small circle in the corner of her page. The phrase chicken and egg sprang to mind – if the flat didn't sell, she wouldn't be able to relocate, but if she spent the weekend prepping for the viewing at the expense of organising her first fundraising event, she might not even get the promotion, anyway.

'Good, good. I'll leave it all in your capable hands, then.'

And then he was gone.

Polly pulled the mobile from her ear and stared at the blank screen. She knew he was right; she knew she needed to do the work he suggested, but how was she supposed to fit it all in? How was she supposed to declutter, paint and source prizes, design and organise leaflets, all in one weekend? Two days, that's all she had. Two days to complete two tasks which had the potential to shape her future. Yes, she had next week to work on the Bonfire Night fundraising stall, but if she was going to have time to source prizes, print leaflets and everything else that needed doing, she had to make a good dent in the preparations as soon as she physically could. She needed to know what she had to source, what was being included in the leaflets...

'Polly? Can I have a quick word?'

Twisting in her chair, she watched as Declan entered the office and pointed towards the meeting room. Wasn't he supposed to have had meetings all day? He wasn't even going to be in the office, he'd said. 'Coming.'

'Vicki, can you join us too, please?' Declan called across the room towards the other woman, who stood up slowly, her hands scooped beneath the fabric scarf.

Standing up, Polly picked up her notebook and pen before looking longingly at Zac's coffee mug, still steaming with the hot, delicious liquid. Making her way into the meeting room, she crossed her fingers beneath her notebook. *Please don't say the whole thing is off.* She'd worked so hard today to get things in place for the Bonfire Night event. She didn't know what she'd say if he backed out now.

19

'Sit down, sit down.' Walking behind the table, Declan hefted his bag onto it before pulling out books and papers. After riffling through the papers, he pulled one out triumphantly. 'Here we go!'

Slipping into the chair opposite, with Vicki at her side, Polly shifted her seat under the table, still unsure whether this impromptu meeting was a good thing or not. 'Is everything okay? How was your meeting at HQ?'

'My meeting was great, thank you, Polly. Very good indeed and very insightful.' Declan nodded as he shoved the rest of his belongings back into his bag, leaving out the one sheet of paper he'd found earlier. 'In fact, everyone was very excited about your proposal for Meadowfield's Bonfire Night and producing information leaflets about the reserve too.'

'They were?' Polly widened her eyes, the nervous butterflies in the pit of her stomach somewhat abating.

'Absolutely. Which is why I've called you in here now.' Declan sat down and shifted his chair closer to the table too. 'I didn't want to waste another minute.'

'Oh, right.' Polly grinned as she turned to a fresh page in her notebook. Who was he referring to who had liked her idea? The other project managers of various nature reserves? It must be. And Mr Bob must have been there too. She'd love to know what he'd thought of it.

'A couple of other reserves have also taken it upon themselves to get some leaflets printed and so I have...' He picked up the sheet of paper and held it aloft. 'A list of things you may wish to think about including.'

'Oh, that's great.' Polly nodded as she picked up her pen. She'd had a few ideas on what to include and had begun to draw a quick mock-up, but she could certainly use anything the other reserves had found to be successful.

'Don't worry about taking notes. I have the list here. You can have it.' Shaking his head, he waited until his reading glasses had dislodged themselves from the midst of his flock of white hair and settled on the end of his nose before continuing. 'I'm sure you have already thought of at least a few of these, but such things as a map, how to get here, things to do once here... that sort of thing.'

'Thank you.' Leaning over, Polly took his list in her hand before settling back in her seat and skimming over it. 'Oh, the options on what visitors could bring to feed the ducks is a great idea.'

'Yes, yes. I thought so too. Particularly being as a lot of people know old bread isn't a good idea and worry about what else to bring.'

'That's right.' Vicki placed her palms on the table. 'I've got an idea. Why don't we suggest to Jarvis and Helena that they could sell duck feed at the café? Little bags for fifty pence or so. We'd make a profit and the ducks will love it too.'

'I love that idea.' Polly smiled.

'Thanks.' Vicki grinned as she gently rearranged the scarf hammock around her neck, securing Nutkin.

'This is great, all of these ideas about how we can improve the reserve.' Declan pushed his reading glasses back onto the top of his head before lacing his fingers together. 'I can feel it now. The reserve is going to be in the best shape it's ever been before I retire. What more could I ask for?'

'Well, you asked for fresh eyes and that's what you got.' Vicki pointed her forefingers towards Polly. 'You're making us consider the reserve from a different perspective and seeing it for the first time again.'

'That you are, Polly. Great work.'

'Thanks.' Looking down at the blank page in her notebook, Polly tucked a loose curl behind her ear, a fierce blush creeping across her face. This was what she'd wanted. She'd wanted to make a difference, and Declan, Vicki and now project managers from other reserves in the trust seemed to be believing in her.

'Right, well, I'll leave this in your capable hands whilst I get off. Have a lovely weekend, both of you.' Standing up, Declan pulled his heavy bag from the floor before leaning it against the table and pulling out another piece of paper. 'Oh, Vicki, here have this. It's a list of printers the other reserves have used and recommended for their leaflets. Might you want to take a look and see if they have any availability at short notice?'

'I certainly can, boss.' Cradling Nutkin through the cotton scarf with one hand, she stood and reached across the table, taking the paper. 'I'll give them a ring round before I leave today.'

'Good, thanks, Vicki. Don't stay too long, mind. It's almost time to go.'

'I won't. I don't need to be told that twice.' Laughing quietly, Vicki headed to the door, Declan behind her.

As the door to the meeting room closed softly behind them, Polly looked down at the list in her hand once more. How was she ever going to get everything done? With just a week until the Bonfire Night celebrations, how was she supposed to design the leaflets by Monday, declutter her grandparents' flat and paint two rooms? It was impossible. Completely impossible.

Standing up, she walked across to the small refreshment area and jabbed the kettle on. She had half an hour left at work and then she'd just have to hurry back to Pennycress Inn, pack a weekend bag and grab the first bus to the train station. Maybe if she could get back to the flat by eight, then at least she'd have a few hours to start decluttering.

She poured herself the long-awaited coffee, spooning not one but two sugars into the dark liquid before adding a splash of milk. She had a feeling she might need those two sugars if she was going to stay awake. Sitting back in the chair she'd shortly vacated, she turned her notebook upside down and opened it up to the last page. Scribbling the title 'To-Do List' at the top, she downed half her coffee, barely registering how hot her drink was.

Holding the mug in one hand, she began writing down the tasks she'd have to complete this weekend, both for the reserve and back at the flat. It was just typical that both work and life stuff had the deadline of Monday morning. She needed to get the leaflets off to the printers if there was any hope for them to be ready for Bonfire Night and David was showing the investors around on Monday, too. Work and home. Both needed completing if she were to have a chance of staying on in Meadowfield, so both were equally important. And possibly both equally time-consuming too.

Lowering her mug to the table, she leaned back in her chair; the backrest creaking slightly in disgust that she wasn't hunched over the table working. Covering her eyes with the palms of her hands, she tried to clear her head. Not that it was any use. She had too much to do. Too many commitments this weekend. How was she going to get them done? Even if she focused on one or the other, it would take a minor miracle to get either of them completed in time, and to a standard she was happy with, too.

'Polly! You frightened the life out of me. I thought the office was empty. I was only popping my head around the door here to check the kettle had been switched off at the wall.' Standing in the doorway, Harold waved his bunch of keys in the air, the metal clinking together. 'Time to go home and enjoy the weekend.'

Pushing her chair back into a sitting position, Polly glanced at the clock. It was ten to six. She must have been in here writing her to-do list for over an hour. How did that even happen? Standing up, she grabbed her notebook, pen and the empty coffee mug and turned to Harold. 'Sorry, I didn't realise what the time was.'

'No worries. Just don't want you getting locked up in here for the weekend, now do we?' Harold held the door open for her as she hurried back into the office.

At her desk, she placed the mug down. It would have to wait until Monday to be washed; if she missed the six o'clock bus, she'd be stuck there for at least another hour. 'Sorry, I'd best get going. My bus is at six.'

Whistling through his teeth, Harold locked up the meeting room. 'You should get a wriggle on then. You've only got a few minutes.'

Grabbing her tote bag, she shoved her notebook and pen inside before glancing back at the mug. She couldn't leave it until Monday. It would become the classic office science experiment. Besides, no one else had left any dirty mugs on their desks. Picking it up, she glanced at the clock again before dithering on the spot.

'I'll sort that for you. I've got two of my own to wash up, as I missed the last dishwasher call.' Harold nodded towards the mug in her hand.

'Are you sure? I feel bad leaving it for you.' Polly bit down on her bottom lip.

'No worries. It's only a mug. Off you go, love, before you miss your bus.'

Walking towards the door out to the foyer, Harold pulled it open, his back against it, as he held his hand out.

'Thank you. I owe you.' Walking over to him, she gave him the mug before slipping through the door. Two minutes. She had two minutes to get to the bus stop.

'Enjoy your weekend,' Harold called after her before the office door clicked closed again.

'You too,' she called feebly as she made her way through the foyer. If she knew one thing, it would be that she wouldn't be enjoying this weekend. In fact, this weekend was set to be one of the hardest she'd had since losing her grandma.

20

Letting the front door to Pennycress Inn close softly behind her, Polly ran towards the stairs, pausing on the first step up as Laura emerged from the kitchen.

'Hi, Polly. How was work? Are you joining us for dinner tonight?'

'Umm, sorry, not tonight. Thank you though. I've got to go back home this weekend.' She pulled her tote bag higher up on her shoulder, her metal water bottle digging into her side.

'Ooh, I bet that will be nice then. Catching up with friends, are you?' Walking across to the bottom of the stairs, Laura folded the tea towel in her hands.

Polly gripped her fingers around the straps of her bag. If only that was what she was doing, a catch-up in person with Stacey was just what she needed, but there was no chance she'd have any time for that. Although, thinking about it, she might just be able to rope her into helping. 'I'm not sure I'll have time, to be honest. I've got some bits to do for work and also have to get my grandparents' flat ready for a viewing on Monday.'

'Oh, it sounds like you have a busy time ahead of yourself, then.' Laura glanced towards the kitchen door as the oven timer beeped. 'Oops, I'd best go and get that out of the oven.'

'It smells delicious.' Polly smiled as Laura hurried back through the hall-way. It was strange how, in such a short amount of time, she'd begun to think of Pennycress Inn as her home. Which was odd because it was an inn, and also because she hardly knew Laura, Nicola and Jackson. But after spending time with them during breakfasts, dinners and coffee breaks, she felt as though she'd known them a whole lot longer than she actually had.

Shaking her head, she headed up the stairs. If she'd read the bus timetable correctly, then she had about fifteen minutes to pack and get to the bus stop. Not long, but definitely doable.

In her room, she pulled her battered old suitcase from where she'd stashed it beneath the bed before tilting her head and looking at it. She wouldn't need all that much stuff for just a weekend and the thought of hefting that big thing onto various buses and trains filled her with a dread she didn't need, not today. Nope, she could fit a change of clothes and her toothbrush in her tote bag. Besides, she'd left what she hadn't been able to fit into her suitcase back in the flat, so she'd be able to find old clothes to wear for painting.

Pushing the suitcase back under her bed, Polly pulled a few things from the drawers before shoving them in her tote bag. Yep, it was bulging at the seams, but it would be a whole lot more convenient than carrying her battered suitcase around. Pulling it onto her shoulder, she grabbed her coat and headed out onto the landing.

As she opened the door to her room, she paused, her hand on the door handle. She could hear voices in the hallway. Nicola's, Laura's and Zac's. Great. She glanced at her mobile to check the time. She literally had ten minutes before the bus arrived. She didn't have time to wait until Zac had disappeared and the coast was clear.

Sighing, she took a final look around her room, the soft bed tempting her to enjoy a lazy weekend, and closed the door softly. Hopefully, she'd be able to slip out without being noticed. The last thing she wanted to do was to high-light how awkward things were between her and Zac, and only more so since the conversation they'd had on the phone with Mr Bob. Not in front of Laura and Nicola, who had been nothing but welcoming and friendly. Yes, after their conversation Nicola was aware of the history between them both, but she didn't want it to affect things here. She didn't want them to feel any awkward vibes in their bed and breakfast.

Walking down the stairs, Polly was careful to keep to the edge nearest the wall, away from any of the squeaky floorboards she'd noticed, and with her head down, she crept across the hallway, holding her breath and hoping she wasn't spotted as she made her way to the front door. Laura and Nicola had their backs towards her, and she was certain Zac wouldn't want to engage in conversation even if he did see her.

At the front door, she turned around and called over her shoulder so as not to appear rude, before hurrying outside. 'Bye. Have a lovely weekend.'

'See you Sunday, Polly.'

Polly heard Laura's reply as she closed the front door and breathed a sigh of relief. There was only so much Zac time she could handle, and she'd definitely had enough for the week. In fact, in a weird way, she was pleased to be going back home. She made her way down the path through the front garden and opened the wrought-iron gate.

Huh, no, that wasn't true. She'd have given anything to hole up in Pennycress for the weekend, work on designing the leaflet for the reserve at her leisure and take a wander into the village centre for lunch, but instead she had to face the one thing she'd been putting off since her grandma had passed away.

Checking the time again, she closed the gate and picked up her pace. She had two minutes. That was fine. The bus stop was only at the end of the road and by the looks of it, someone else was waiting for it too, which meant that it hadn't got there early. That was always a good thing.

'Hi.' Coming to a halt next to the small wooden bus shelter, she smiled at the woman standing there, her short white hair set into perfect curls.

'Evening.' The woman turned to face her, the large bag sitting by her feet shifting slightly as she did. 'You were at the village meeting, weren't you? One of the newbies staying at Pennycress? That's right, isn't it, love?'

Polly nodded as she lowered her own bulging tote bag to the floor, resting it against her ankles. 'Yes, that's right.'

'Ah, I thought I recognised your face. Lovely to meet you properly.' The woman held her palm against her chest. 'I'm Mrs Pierce, or Enid, should I say. I run the bakery in the centre of the village. I don't think you've been in yet, have you?'

'It's nice to meet you too.' Polly smiled. 'I haven't had a chance yet, no. I was rather hoping I'd have the time to pop in for lunch this weekend, but I've been called away back to my hometown.'

'That's a shame. Saying that, I'm away this weekend too, although, of course, the bakery will still be open.'

'Are you off anywhere nice?' Polly stuffed her hands in her coat pockets. Why had she asked? Now she had, Mrs Pierce would likely ask her too, and she wasn't sure she wanted to have that conversation with a near stranger, however pleasant she seemed.

'I'm going to my granddaughter's for the weekend. Her and her husband have just had their first baby – my first great-granddaughter, can you believe it! So, I'm going round to meet the little angel.' Mrs Pierce glowed with pride.

'Oh, wow. Congratulations! That's amazing. I bet you can't wait to meet her?' Polly forced a smile, thinking of how much her own grandparents would have wanted to meet their own great-grandchildren. She took a breath in, the near freezing evening air filling her lungs.

'I can't. And it's great-grandma duty to spoil the little mite rotten, so I've been buying clothes and toys ever since I found out my granddaughter was pregnant.' Mrs Pierce lifted a large carrier bag in the air, one Polly hadn't even noticed she was holding.

'Haha, that's fair enough. I'm sure they'll all be thrilled with your gifts.' Polly laughed.

'I hope so. There'll only be more to come.' Mrs Pierce chuckled before hitching up the sleeve of her thick coat and checking her watch. 'That's odd. The bus is over five minutes late now and that's one thing the local council usually pride themselves on, the regular bus service through the villages.'

'That is strange.' Polly glanced one way and then the other. Since arriving at Meadowfield, the buses had run like clockwork, which she'd been grateful for being as she'd relied on them to get to work. That was apart from this morning's incident with the breakdown, but that had been out of anyone's control.

'Oh look, that's Miss Cooke's little Smart car, isn't it? If anyone knows what's going on, it'll be her.' Mrs Pierce stepped forward towards the edge of the kerb and waved her hand in the air as a red Smart car made its slow way along the road towards them.

'Careful...' Before Polly could even get the word out, Mrs Pierce lowered her arm as the car slowed to a stop beside her and, sure enough, the window was wound down to reveal Miss Cooke sitting behind the wheel.

'Evening, Enid. Evening, Polly.' Miss Cooke frowned. 'You do know the bus service has been cancelled this evening, don't you? I did add a post to the local social media page.'

'Oh, I'm not on any social media.' Mrs Pierce waved away such a ludicrous idea with her hand. 'The bus service is cancelled? I was just saying to Polly how well run the public transport is around here. How well organised it is.'

'Well, unfortunately, not this evening. After the early-morning bus ran into some engine trouble, it was decided that the service would only run until half past six and then they'd redirect things to busier routes to make up for being a bus down.' Miss Cooke shook her head slightly.

'Oh dear, oh dear. I'm meant to be going to Charlotte's this evening. Gary offered me a lift, but I didn't want to be an inconvenience, so I promised them both I was perfectly capable of getting there on the bus. They've just had their little baby, you see.'

'Congratulations, that's marvellous news! Do they still have that little place in Nettleford?'

'Yes, that's right. It's not far, but now I'm going to have to wait until morning.' Mrs Pierce looked down at the ground, crestfallen.

'I'm off that way, anyway. There's a book club I want to check out, so I'll drive right past Charlotte's house.' Leaning over, Miss Cooke popped open the passenger door and pushed it open. 'Hop in.'

'Are you sure?' Leaning down, Mrs Pierce picked up the bag by her feet before glancing back at Polly. 'What about you, love? This is going to be a great inconvenience for you, isn't it?'

Polly shrugged, trying hard not to let the panic bubbling in the pit of her stomach show. How was she going to get back home? She'd have to get a taxi to the train station, which would cost a lot whilst she was supposed to be saving every penny she could in order to build her new life here. 'I'll be okay. I'll grab a taxi.'

'Good luck with that. They'll be busy this evening, what with the absence of the bus. Make sure you get on the phone to them as soon as you can.' Miss Cooke raised her voice as Mrs Pierce bundled her bags into the back seat before sitting down.

'Good point. I will. Thanks for the heads-up and have a lovely weekend at your granddaughter's, Mrs Pierce.'

'Thank you, love. You have a good weekend too.' Mrs Pierce closed the door seconds before the car pulled away again.

If Polly hadn't had that coffee and wasted time writing her to-do list before leaving the office late, she'd have not missed the last running bus and she'd be on a train on the way home right now. She bit down on her lip as she picked up her tote bag. Holding it up, she glanced at the bottom. The fabric was discoloured from the damp path. Brushing it off with her hand, she then hooked it over her shoulder and turned back to the inn.

It wasn't so bad. Sure, she'd have wasted an hour, two at the most by the time a taxi came and she finally got on her way home, but she still had this evening and Saturday and Sunday – two whole days – to get things straightened at the flat. Besides, she could only do as much as she could.

Maybe Miss Cooke was right, she should join the village social media group. That way she'd be alerted to things such as the buses not running and the like. Pulling her mobile from her pocket, she sighed as the heavens opened and a torrent of rain fell.

Perfect. Shoving her phone back into the relative safety of her pocket, Polly pulled her hood up, put her head down and retraced her steps back towards the inn.

21

In the short time it took Polly to hurry back down the road and up the garden path to the front door of Pennycress again, she was soaked, the fat raindrops incessantly beating against her coat and working their way through the fabric to her clothes beneath. Huh, maybe it wouldn't be so bad if the taxi did take a little longer. At least she'd have a few minutes to change into something dry.

Running up the few steps to the front door, she lowered her hood, rung out her hair and shook herself, hoping to limit the amount of water she'd be bringing into Laura's nice clean hallway. Taking a tissue from her pocket, she began to dab at her face just as the front door swung open and she came face to face with Zac. She lowered her hand, the tissue still crumpled in her palm, and frowned. What were the chances?

'Polly, you're drenched.' Zac's clipped tone broke the silence.

'I know.' Pausing, she waited until he'd stepped aside until walking into the hallway and the welcome warmth from the central heating.

'I thought you were getting the bus?' Zac closed the door behind him.

'And I assumed you were heading out, being as two seconds ago you opened the door.' She shook her head. 'Sorry, I didn't mean—'

'It's fine. I was. I am.' Zac frowned.

'Polly! You're back!' Nicola appeared from the kitchen door, a tray with three mugs on it in her hands. 'Changed your mind and decided to spend the weekend in Meadowfield?'

'No, I... The bus has been cancelled.' Polly stuffed the wet tissue back in her pocket.

'Oh really? That's rubbish. Where did you say you were going? Zac's on his way out. Maybe he can drop you at the train station? Or, if not, if you give me a few minutes to grab my car, I can take you?' Nicola slid the tray onto the reception desk before joining them at the door.

'Oh no, don't worry. I'll call a taxi. Thank you though. It won't take long and once I'm on the train back to Featherford, it's an easy enough journey.' If you didn't count the changes, that was. But she wasn't about to add that.

'Featherford. Of course, you're both from that way.' Nicola slapped her forehead. 'I'm sure Zac won't mind giving you a lift.'

'No, it's fine, thanks. I'll grab a taxi to the station. I don't want to put anyone out.' Polly glanced quickly at Zac, hoping for backup. Neither one of them wanted to be cooped up together in the confines of a car, even if the train station was only a twenty-minute drive away. And what was Nicola trying to do anyway? Force a truce on them?

'I didn't mean the train station. I meant Featherford.' Nicola placed her hand on Zac's forearm. 'That's where you're headed, isn't it?'

'Er... yes.' Zac pulled at the collar of his coat.

He was clearly uncomfortable at the mere thought of Polly sharing a car with him, and she didn't blame him, either. The prospect of walking a million miles in this rain in a pair of four-inch stilettos suddenly seemed preferable to car sharing. 'Honestly, I couldn't. Zac's in a rush.'

'That's fine. So are you.' Nicola turned her attention back to Polly.

'Yes, but we don't live anywhere close to each other. Our homes are on the opposite sides of town.' Now that wasn't a lie. After attending a Cotswold Wildlife and Wilderness Trust gathering Zac's parents had hosted a couple of years back, she knew Zac lived in the posh end of town and her flat was at the... other end.

Either seeing right through Polly's excuses or else hell-bent on turning her plan into a reality whatever the obstacles, Nicola continued. 'Not far then. Zac?'

Zac cleared his throat as Polly noticed his knuckles turning white from their grip on the handle of his small, wheeled suitcase. 'It would be my pleasure.'

Polly coughed, a lump suddenly forming in her throat. His pleasure? Is that why he looked as though he was sucking on the sourest sweet in the world then? It was clear he was about as happy with this situation as she was, but what else could she say? The easiest thing would be to agree to the lift and then once outside and out of sight from Nicola she could say thanks but no thanks and let both of them off the hook. 'Perfect. Thank you.'

'See you on Sunday, Nicola. Have a great weekend.' Zac held his hand up in a wave before pulling the front door open once again and nodding for Polly to go through first.

'Hold on, Polly. I'll grab you both a slice of Laura's fruit cake for the journey.' Cupping Polly's elbow, Nicola ushered her through to the kitchen, the door closing behind them as she hurriedly cut two chunks of cake and placed them in a Tupperware box.

'Thanks.' Taking the small plastic box, Polly turned to leave before Nicola held her hand against the door. Turning back around, she saw it now, that glint in Nicola's eyes. What was she up to?

'This will be the perfect opportunity for you to talk about the kiss and to clear the air. With the two of you being alone together.' Nicola grinned.

Polly opened her mouth before closing it again, her mind clear of how to respond.

'Genius idea, right?'

Finally finding the words, Polly stage-whispered, 'No, it'll be too awkward. I can't bring that up.'

'Sure you can.' Pulling the kitchen door open again, Nicola ushered Polly back out into the hallway, a large smile spreading across her face. 'I've just packed a little slice of cake for you both for the car journey. There's nothing better than a good old natter and a slice of fruit cake, as my mum always says.'

Frowning slightly, Zac nodded. 'Thank you.'

'Right off you both go, then. Have fun.' Taking the door handle, Nicola waited for them to go through before waving at them. 'Bye.'

'Bye.' Holding her hand up in a wave, Polly reluctantly followed Zac around the back of the house to the inn's small car park. As they rounded the corner of the inn, Polly glanced behind her, half expecting Nicola to be tailing them to make sure she got in the car. After seeing the coast was clear, she stopped. 'Zac, thanks for the offer, but I'll call a taxi.'

'I can take you.' Setting his suitcase by his feet, he pulled a single car key from his pocket.

'No, it's fine.' Polly shook her head quickly and turned away, ready to sneak past the front door and down the garden path.

'Honestly, Polly. Nicola is right. We're both heading to the same place. It makes sense I give you a lift.' He glanced at the Tupperware container in her hand. 'Although, I'd appreciate you not eating that in the car.'

Blinking, Polly frowned. That's what he was worried about? A few loose cake crumbs being dropped into the footwell of his car? Surely the fact he'd just agreed to spend the next two hours alone with her trumped the small inconvenience of a cake crumb or two?

Clicking his car key, Zac stood patiently as Polly dithered on the spot. What was she supposed to do? She could hardly decline his invitation of a lift now, could she? After all, Nicola was inside, and he wasn't being forced into anything right now. She'd fully expected him to agree to her getting a taxi. She wasn't prepared for this. She wiped a loose strand of hair from her nose, the unrelenting rain streaming down the inside of her coat sleeve as she did so.

'I'd rather get out of the rain sooner than later.' Zac pierced her thoughts.

'Right, of course.' She closed her eyes momentarily. She supposed the prospect of either making small talk or sitting in awkward silence for the next couple of hours was a small trade-off for getting in the warm and dry. And sitting in relative comfort rather than swapping trains in the dark. 'Okay. A lift would be great. Thank you.'

Holding his arm out, he indicated his car, a sleek dark blue Audi. Older than she remembered.

'Thanks.' Walking past him towards the car, she mumbled quietly as he slipped in front of her and lifted the lid to the boot. Placing her tote bag carefully in the corner of his empty boot, she realised the fabric was decidedly wet and that any clothes she'd brought with her would need drying out as soon as she got back to the flat.

As Zac lifted his small suitcase next to her bag with ease, Polly began making her way around to the passenger side, surprised that Zac managed to reach the door first and hold it open for her. 'Umm, thanks.'

Without uttering a word, he waited for her to bundle herself in before closing the door softly and hurrying round to the driver's side.

Polly balanced the Tupperware box on her knees as she clipped her seatbelt in. She should have put it in the boot with her bag. He'd no doubt be super paranoid about her opening it and daring to eat the cake in his spotless car now.

'Here, I'll pop that on the back seat. Save you holding on to it for the entire journey.' Holding his hand out for the box, Zac then leaned behind them and placed it neatly on the back seat.

Refraining from rolling her eyes, she reminded herself, however much he'd been coerced into this by Nicola, he was indeed doing her a favour, and this was his car, he had every right to have a no eating rule in place if he so wanted to.

Turning the ignition, Zac kept his eyes fixed on the rear-view mirror as he reversed out of the parking space. 'My mum has allergies. I try my best to avoid cross-contamination in here in case she needs a lift someplace.'

'Oh right.' Polly looked towards him as they pulled out onto the street. She hadn't been expecting an explanation, she'd just assumed he was being overly precious about his car. Was he showing her a glimpse of the Zac she used to know?

As they made their way through the small village of Meadowfield, Polly looked out of the window, the street lamps illuminating the chocolate-box thatched cottages before they gave way to fields; the white light from the car headlights now the only light source. Still, she continued to look out of the side window, in the hope that Zac would be too busy driving to question why she'd rather stare into the darkness than engage in conversation.

After a few minutes of silence, he reached out and turned the radio on, the quiet tones of Classic FM filling the air. Grateful for the distraction, Polly glanced across at him. He looked tired. Dark circles clung beneath his eyes. Not super obvious, probably not obvious to anyone but her, but she could see them. Maybe it was the dim light in the car. Yes, it could be. He had never been one to look dishevelled.

Apart from that time six months ago, when they'd both joined in a mud race to raise money for the trust. She smiled. He'd looked particularly cute then, what with his hair sticking up in all directions and dirt smeared across his face.

Glancing across at her, Zac met her gaze before frowning. 'Would you rather I turn it to a different station?'

'What?' Shaking her head, Polly fixed her eyes on the road ahead and leaned her elbow on the ledge of the door. He'd caught her staring. 'No, this is fine. It's your car.'

'Okay. Happy to change it if you want.'

'Thanks,' she mumbled. This was probably the most he'd said to her since they'd both started at Meadowfield Reserve and as they basically shared a desk, that was saying something. She tried to push Nicola's and Stacey's advice on speaking to him about the kiss out of her mind. Should she really speak to him? And if she did, would it actually clear the air or make each other's presence even less bearable?

Looking at him again, she drew her thumb to her mouth and began nibbling the cuticle. She did want the atmosphere between them to be less strained. And if it was, then these three months would be more enjoyable, but—

'Have you got something on your mind?' Zac turned the volume of the radio down slightly.

'I was just...' No, she couldn't do it. She couldn't bring it up. The kiss had ruined their friendship. Talking about it might just push him over the edge to ignoring her altogether. 'Nothing.'

Taking his eyes off the road for a second, he looked at her. 'There clearly is.'

Clasping her hands in her lap, she sighed. Now she didn't have a choice. If she didn't say anything now, he'd probably think she was staring at him because she was thinking about the kiss, not because she was thinking about talking about the kiss. She took a deep breath. 'I just think we should talk about what happened that night.'

Zac frowned slightly. 'What night?'

Polly widened her eyes. What if he'd been too drunk to remember that they'd shared a moment? What if he thought she was being weird? That it had been her fault that the friendship between them both had changed? If she was the only one that remembered, then it was her fault. She must have been acting differently around him.

'You mean...?'

'The kiss.' She bit down on her tongue. *Well done, Polly. A great way to approach the subject sensitively.*

Zac cleared his throat. 'Right, yes. I assumed that was the evening you were referring to.'

She looked across at him. He was still looking ahead, his eyes fixed on the road in front, but his knuckles had turned a greyish white as he gripped the steering wheel. This wasn't a conversation he wanted to have. She swallowed. Well, mate, it wasn't a conversation she wanted either, but here they were having to speak about the incident because, since he did remember it, it was obvious he couldn't have just carried on as normal. He'd had to try to freeze her out. 'Yes, of course. I just wanted to clear the air. Things have been weird, I mean, different between us and...'

Silence filled the car again as they approached a roundabout and Zac slowed to a crawl before speeding up again.

'We used to be friends, and now, since the... kiss, you barely speak to me.' She clasped her hands tighter together, digging her nails into her skin. Fab way to sound like a tormented teen with a crush. She tried again. 'What I mean is we used to talk, used to hang out both at work and outside of work and then Stacey threw that leaving party for me and—'

'I remember.' His tone was quiet, barely audible above the quiet roar of the engine and brusque too. He clearly didn't want to speak about the offending incident.

'Right, yes.' Of course, he remembered. He'd just said he knew what she was talking about. She closed her eyes. How was she supposed to save this conversation now? She'd made a complete mess of it. 'I guess what I'm trying to say is, it doesn't have to get in the way of us working together, of us living together at Pennycress, either. We're both adults and we can just put that stupid mistake behind us. Can't we?'

Releasing his death grip on the steering wheel, Zac dragged one hand across his face and muttered quietly, his words barely decipherable. 'It wasn't a mistake.'

Polly shook her head. Now she'd gone and insulted him, too. 'No, I didn't mean...'

The car slowed again as traffic built up and Zac turned onto a main road.

What had she been thinking? Bringing up such a topic when they were both confined in this small space with no chance of an escape for over an hour and a half. She looked back out of the window and watched longingly as they approached a lay-by, despondent that he hadn't decided to pull over and kick her out. 'I shouldn't have said anything.'

'You're right. I have been off with you, but that night, the kiss, that's not...'

Zac sighed as the loud ringtone of his mobile filled the small space. 'Sorry, I need to take this.'

Polly nodded as they slowed, and he bumped the car up on the grass verge before bringing it to a stop.

As soon as he'd pulled the hand brake up, Zac grabbed his phone and jumped out of the car, walking around to the back before bringing the mobile to his ear. So engrossed in the conversation he was having, he didn't even seem to notice the rain pelting down around him.

With the rhythmic click-click of the hazard warning lights, Polly couldn't hear a word he was saying, but looking in the wing mirror she watched as he paced along the verge, his hand gripping his hair as he spoke urgently into the phone. She frowned. Who was he on a call to? Clearly, it was a conversation he didn't want to have in front of her or else he'd have answered it in the car on speaker.

Perhaps it was his dad ringing back to confirm how much he was going to sponsor the reserve or someone from one of the other companies he'd reached out to. It made sense that he didn't want her to know how much he was raising, even though he'd heard her proposals and must realise there was no way she'd come close to raising even half as much as him.

She shrugged. She supposed that whatever it was, it was none of her business. She was doing what she could for the reserve and whether it was enough to secure the promotion, she wouldn't know until decision day. But what had he meant when he'd said the kiss hadn't been a mistake? Yes, he'd muttered those words and she may not have heard him right, but that's what he'd said. Or something to that effect, anyway.

Finally unclasping her hands, she relaxed back against the headrest. Whatever he had said, she was certain about one thing and that was that she wasn't about to bring up the conversation again in a hurry, so whatever he'd meant could stay a mystery. That short conversation had been the most uncomfortable few moments of her life. And that was including her ex-fiancé Ben's break-up speech. Zac could keep his secrets; he could keep his elusiveness. She just wanted to get back home and try to block her ability to feel anything until the weekend was over.

22

'You live here?' Pulling the car to a stop outside the block of flats, Zac leaned across the steering wheel and tilted his head to look up. 'Up there?'

'Yep, this is me. Thanks again for the lift.' Opening the door, Polly jumped out, a feeling of relief flooding through her body at finally being released of the stifling cage of his car. After Zac's phone call had ended the awkward conversation about the kiss, they'd travelled the rest of the journey in relative silence. He'd obviously had something on his mind, something he hadn't wanted to share with her, and so she'd let the gentle tunes of Classic FM wash over her whilst fixing her gaze out of the window. She looked upwards, the rain had abated, and the stark streetlights were doing their job in highlighting the row of empty beer bottles lining Mr Greene's balcony on the first floor, each one sporting a single white feather, as well as the discarded trolley and pile of bin bags outside the shared doorway.

Turning, she stifled a scream as she came face to face with Zac as he stood in front of her; her damp tote bag over his shoulder and the small Tupperware box Nicola had given them in one hand. 'I'll come up with you. See you to your door.'

She frowned as she closed the car door. He was fast. Shaking her head, she stuck out her hand, waiting for her tote bag. 'There's no need. I can carry that.'

Zac looked between her and the door to the block of flats and back again. 'All the same, I'd rather...'

Feeling her cheeks flush, Polly shrugged. Whatever. If it made him feel better, then sure, he could pretend to be her knight in shining armour. Although the truth of the matter was, she'd lived here the majority of her childhood. She'd grown up around here and, yes, it might not be all white picket fences and wheelie bins, but she felt safe here just the same. 'Fine.'

'This is all you had, is that right?' Zac patted her tote bag with one hand as he held out the plastic box with the other.

'Yep. I'm only here for the weekend and I've got a ton of stuff up in the flat still.' Polly nodded upwards before holding her breath as she walked past the overspilling bin bags, stabbed her code into the keypad in the wall and pulled the heavy door open. Taking a deep breath, she immediately regretted her decision as her lungs filled with the acrid smell of stale urine. Gina and Ken had been up to their old tricks again then, letting little Cloud, their toy poodle, into the stairwell to do her business. She glanced behind and couldn't stop herself from laughing at the look of disgust plastered to Zac's face. 'Don't worry, it's just dog pee.'

'Dog pee?' He scrunched up his nose as he carefully manoeuvred his way up the stairs, his eyes fixed on the floor beneath his smart leather shoes.

'Yep, our neighbours...' She swallowed as she corrected herself. 'My neighbours have a tendency to let their dog out onto the landing instead of taking her for a walk when she needs to do her business.'

'I see.'

'Uh-huh.' Sure you do. Polly ran her hand along the banister as she climbed the stairs. They had four floors to climb, but she figured this was safer than attempting to use the lift. She could only imagine the look of horror Zac would show if it was having one of its off days and got stuck between floors two and three again. Yep, although his reaction would be priceless, she didn't want him thinking any worse of her home than he likely already was. Besides, after escaping the confines of his car, she wasn't about to go willingly into the smaller confines of the lift with him.

'What floor are you on?'

'Four.' She paused and turned. 'If you're struggling, I'm happy to take those from you and make my own way up.'

'No, no, it's fine. I'm not struggling.' He glanced behind him as the door buzzed open, a waft of cold air filling the concrete stairwell.

'Okay, well, I can still go up on my own. Save you the trip.' She crossed her fingers behind her back. His reaction to this part was bad enough, she didn't want to see how he'd react if he saw inside her grandparents' flat. However garishly it was decorated, however cluttered it was, it had been her childhood home, and it was her sanctuary. Still.

'Nope, I'm seeing you to your door.' Zac jogged up to the step she was standing on before continuing past her.

'Hey, wait up.' Turning, she took her hand off the banister and began jogging up the stairs too.

Pausing five steps ahead of her, Zac treated her to one of his famous charming smiles. 'If you're struggling, you can always take the lift.'

'Oi!' Shaking her head, she smiled too as she quickened her pace and sped ahead of him. She could feel him close behind her, could hear his chuckle in her ear as he rounded the corner and raced in front of her. This almost felt like old times, before the incident she never wished to speak of again. They'd been friends then, had messed around like this. It was just as though he'd forgotten he was supposed to be treating her with indifference. Perhaps the talk they'd had in the car, however awkward it had been and however much she'd wished the ground had opened up and swallowed her whole, had been worth it. Perhaps following Nicola and Stacey's advice had done something after all.

As he rounded the stairwell again, Zac stopped abruptly.

'What?' Joining him, she held her hand up in acknowledgement as she realised the reason he'd come to a stop so suddenly was because Mr Greene was sitting on the top step, a cigarette hanging out of his mouth and a half-empty bottle of beer by his feet. 'Hi, Mr Greene. How are you today?'

As he saw her, a smile broke through Mr Greene's long and bushy beard as he gripped the banister above his head and pulled himself to standing. 'Miss Polly. What a sight for sore eyes you are. Are you moving back in?'

'Nope, afraid not. I'm back to do a spot of cleaning before another viewing on Monday.' Polly gave the older man a hug, coughing as he breathed out a lungful of cigarette smoke in her face.

'Sorry, love. This cough...' Sitting back down, he banged his chest with his fist as he hacked. 'You're still moving on, then?'

'I am.' Polly nodded. Mr Greene was another reason she felt so torn when thinking about the flat being sold. He'd lived here for as long as she could remember and after her grandad had passed away, he'd insisted on taking on any DIY her grandma had needed doing around the place.

'Well, good for you, girl. Get out and see the world. That's what I've always told you, isn't it?' Mr Greene picked up his half-empty beer bottle and held it up to Polly. 'Drink?'

'I'm good, thanks. I had a coffee before we left.' Polly held her hand up and smiled. He'd been offering her a sip of his beer since she'd moved in with her grandparents at age nine. She'd been tempted once, when she was thirteen and a group of her friends had stayed over, but after almost swallowing a stray beard hair, the experience had put her off beer for life.

'You, boy?' Mr Greene held his cigarette between his finger and thumb as he spoke, nodding towards his bottle.

'Thanks, but I'm driving.' Zac pointed his thumb in the direction of the road.

Pulling himself to standing again, Mr Greene peered through the large glass windows looking out onto the street below. 'Nice wheels. They must have been expensive.'

'Er... thanks. And no, they were a present from my parents and are pretty old now.' Zac shrugged, his ears pinking.

Pulling a face, Mr Greene sat back down before tugging on Polly's coat. 'You've done well with this one, then. Money in the family and all that.'

'Oh, we're not...' Shaking her head vehemently, it was Polly's turn to morph into a bright shade of cerise.

'No?' Mr Greene looked from Polly to Zac, who shook his head slowly. 'Right, well, I suppose the best relationships do indeed blossom from friendship.'

Keeping her lips tightly squeezed together, Polly refrained from telling him that, yes, indeed they had been friends, right up until the moment they'd shared that darn kiss and then, instead of blossoming, their relationship had dried up and died completely. 'I'd better get a wriggle on, Mr Greene. I've got a lot to get on with, but it was lovely to see you again.'

'And you, Polly, love. You'll pop by for a drink sometime?' Mr Greene lifted his beer bottle.

'I will. I promise.' Turning, Polly called over her shoulder, 'Take care, Mr Greene.'

'You too.' The older man locked eyes with Zac. 'And boyfriend or friend, you take care of that girl, okay? She's been through a lot and she's a special soul.'

Polly kept her eyes fixed on the stairs as she began to walk up slowly, desperate to eavesdrop on Zac's response. Only he'd either ignored the old man or else spoken so softly Polly hadn't heard a thing.

Rounding the stairwell, she paused, waiting for Zac to catch up. 'See what I mean? I'm perfectly safe here and don't need a chaperone.'

'I know, but I've begun the journey now and, besides, if I abandon you at this point, I don't fancy my chances of walking past dear old Mr Greene without being tripped up or else enticed into sharing his beer with him.' Zac shuddered.

'Haha, you're scared of him!' Leaning her hands on her knees, Polly laughed.

'Shush, he'll hear you,' Zac whispered as he cupped Polly's elbow and gently guided her further up the stairs.

'Oh, he won't. He's been hard of hearing most of my life. Whenever me and my friends would play music in the stairwell, he'd never complain.' Polly grimaced as she remembered the time Daphne from Flat 9 had appeared over her balcony railings shaking her fists at the group of three young teens when they'd been practising a dance for PE in the car park, even though Mr Greene, whose home was closer, had assured them he couldn't hear a thing.

'Well, he heard me perfectly well when I was talking to him, and I wasn't very loud at all.' Zac continued up the steps. 'I'd suggest he may just have a soft spot for you and didn't mind your music.'

'Huh.' Polly glanced behind her. That might be true. Her grandma had always said Mr Greene used to treat her like one of his own grandchildren. 'Sorry, Daphne.'

'Pardon?' Looking back at her, Zac frowned.

'Oh nothing. I just...' Polly shrugged. The last thing he'd want to listen to was her reminiscing over her childhood.

'It can't be much further now, surely?'

'Nope. Just one more flight.' Polly walked on, her legs feeling heavier the closer she got to the flat, and that wasn't due to climbing the stairs. She was used to that, but what she wasn't used to and didn't think she'd ever get used to was walking into an empty flat.

'What number did you say it was?' Zac called from above.

'Number thirty-one.'

'Oh, right.' Zac's tone was deep, different.

'Why?' Rounding the corner, Polly stopped short, her hand gripping tighter to the banister. This couldn't be happening to her. The first thing she'd noticed was the cracked glass in the small window in the door, a hand-sized hole in the corner. It took her a moment to take it in, to realise what she was looking at. The smashed glass, the door sitting ajar. 'I've only been gone a week.'

'Polly, I'm so sorry.' Zac walked towards her.

Coming to her senses, Polly pushed past Zac and made her way to the door. 'I don't understand. Why wouldn't Mr Greene have told me? He knows everything that goes on here.'

'Maybe he didn't know. This is the top floor, isn't it?' Zac looked around before continuing. 'And it doesn't look as though anybody lives next door. He'd have no reason to come up here.'

She nodded. He was right. Her immediate neighbours had moved out four months ago. Gone to live with their children apparently and had just seemingly abandoned their flat, and the flat opposite was between tenants. Zac was right. Her flat had been an easy target. No one around and whoever had broken in had likely gone for hers because of the original door and the lack of security. They must have slipped into the block behind someone who had known the code, and punched a fist through the glass of her door before unlocking it from the inside. 'What was I thinking?'

'What do you mean?'

'I should have upgraded the door. I should have—'

'Hey, it's not your fault. Good locks or not, no one should be breaking and entering into other people's homes.' Zac laid his hand on her forearm.

'But I...' She shrugged. It didn't matter now, what was done was done and she couldn't exactly go back in time and change the door, could she?

'You were lucky you weren't here.' Zac met her gaze.

'If I had been here, this wouldn't have happened.' Polly set her jaw before pulling her arm from Zac's touch and making her way towards the front door. Careful not to touch the broken window, she pushed at the open door and stepped inside, shards of glass crunching beneath her trainers. She closed her eyes as the tears began to fall. She didn't want to go any further. She didn't want to see what had been taken, what damage had been done. She couldn't do this. She couldn't. Her grandparents had poured their hard work and love into this place, and someone had just come along and barged their way inside, uninvited and unwanted. Why?

'Careful. You probably shouldn't go in. We should call the police.' Zac followed her into the tiny hallway before pulling out his mobile.

Opening her eyes, Polly scratched the cuff of her coat sleeve across her face, drying her cheeks. 'I need to see what's been taken.'

'But...' Zac lowered his voice as he began speaking into his phone.

Leaving him in the hallway, Polly pushed forward, forcing herself to inch open the hallway door into the tiny living room. Once inside, she walked into the middle of the room and turned slowly, conjuring up memories of how it had looked when she'd left it. The two shelves on either side of the small electric fire still housed her grandma's prized possessions, her collection of china dolls, which had always creeped Polly out as much as fascinated her. Her grandad's painting still hung above the short mantelpiece, forever preserving the day the three of them had spent down at the Witterings on the south coast the year she'd turned sixteen. They'd celebrated with flasks of tomato soup and cans of Coke before her grandma had pulled a small birthday cake, delicately decorated with dancing ballerinas cut from pink royal icing, from the picnic hamper and they'd sung 'Happy Birthday' as the sun set over the white sand and turquoise ocean. Her grandad had found the painting that day in a bric-a-brac shop and called it his 'lucky find'.

As Polly spun slowly around, her eyes rested on the small television set sitting upon the blanket box. The TV screen was cracked, the remote control lying on the rug in front of it. She didn't know whether to laugh or cry. Whoever had broken in had clearly expected something else. They hadn't figured they'd be met with such a lack of easy-to-grab technology.

'Is there much missing?' Zac came up behind her, one hand covering the mouthpiece of his mobile.

'Nothing. Not from in here, anyway.' Polly shook her head. Everything was just how she'd left it: the old Christmas TV guide her grandma had flicked through last December still sat on the coffee table, the clay flowerpot Polly had made in her first year of secondary school still held the carved wooden flowers her grandad had bought her grandma for the last wedding anniversary they'd shared, and the pack of cards which had been a favourite pastime over the years was still in its place next to the old carriage clock in the centre of the mantelpiece. She guessed whoever had forced themselves into the flat had had only one thing in their sights and that must have been something easy to sell, something they could flog to their mates in the streets or down the local pub. 'I'm guessing the TV was too old to bother with.'

'Right.' Turning his back on her, Zac spoke into the phone again.

Polly walked across to the fireplace and ran her forefinger along the edge of the painting before looking down at her feet. She rubbed the red and navy patterned rug with the toe of her trainer. There were crumbs of some sort, dropped here and there across the rug, across the floorboards too. She looked up at the walls at the red panelling her grandad had spent hours down the local DIY store having the paint mixed up for, to match the red of the rug perfectly, the cream woodchip above.

Hurrying back across to the other side of the room, she bit down on her bottom lip. There were greasy marks smeared across the walls, just as though whoever had been eating whatever was strewn across the floor had decided to wipe their hands across the paintwork for good measure.

Following the trails of crumbs, she walked through the small flat, first to her grandparents' bedroom and then her own, before finishing in the kitchen, where the source of the crumbs, two empty pizza boxes, still lay open on the kitchen counter. She shuddered, she wasn't sure what angered her more, that someone had broken into her home, into her safe space, into her grandparents' flat, or the fact they'd done so and then made themselves at home, ordered pizza and consumed it probably sitting on her sofa.

'They'll send someone out to take a statement when they can.' Zac spoke quietly behind her.

Jumping, Polly spun around, her heart hammering in her chest as though she'd expected to see one of the people who had broken in standing behind her in the kitchen. 'Sorry, I didn't hear you come in.'

'That's okay. I can imagine it must be a shock.' Slipping his mobile into the pocket of his jeans, he looked around the kitchen and pointed to the pizza boxes. 'The cheek of some people.'

Polly nodded slowly, her answer getting caught in her throat. 'Yep.'

'Have you got somewhere else to stay tonight? You can't stay here.'

'I'll be okay.' Polly waved her hand at him dismissively, despite a fresh surge of despair washing over her at the thought of spending the night on her own.

'No. There's no chance I'm leaving you here. It's not secure for one thing, not with the door as it is.' Zac shook his head.

Turning away, Polly blinked as tears began to flow again. The last thing she wanted to do was to hole up in the flat alone, but what other choice did she have?

Stacey. She could go to Stacey's. 'I'll go to my friend's house.'

'Well, give her a call and I'll drop you off once the police have been.'

'They might be hours yet.' Polly sighed as she rummaged in her pocket for her mobile. Where was it? Had she lost that now? What next?

'Are you looking for your mobile? I think it's in here.' Zac patted her tote bag he still had flung over his shoulder. 'I'm sure something was making a noise while I was on the phone with the police.'

'Oh, yes.' She'd completely forgotten he was still hanging on to her bag. Holding her hand out, she took the tote bag, pushed one of the empty pizza boxes to the back of the narrow work surface and placed her bag down before rummaging through her clothes, still damp from the earlier downpour she'd got caught in, until she pulled out her phone. Glancing at the screen, her heart rate slowed to normal as she saw a missed call from Stacey. She was probably ringing her to try to drag her out for drinks. That would be an offer she definitely wouldn't refuse right now.

'Sorry I'd best get this.' Zac held up his mobile as the screen illuminated before walking back through to the living room.

23

Dragging the back of her hand over her eyes, Polly squinted as she tried to focus on the small screen long enough to scroll through to Stacey's name and hit the Call button. Four rings later, and Stacey's cheerful voice filled her ear.

'Hey, Pols. So glad you rang back. I have so much to tell you right now. Mind you, though, I'm in the ladies' and have been for about five minutes, trying to call you.' Stacey took a quick breath. 'I don't want them thinking I'm escaping through a window or something worse.'

'Stacey, I—'

'It's cool. I'm only joking. Let them think what they want.' Stacey laughed.

'Who?' Polly managed to get out.

'The work crew, of course. We're out at the pub for Ben's leaving drinks. Remember I told you? Well...' Stacey paused as the flush of a toilet drowned her words. 'And you know we used to joke about him and Mrs Jedd?'

'Yep.' Polly held her hand over her mouth, willing herself not to burst out crying. She wasn't going to Stacey's then. Stacey rarely had a spare moment to go out and let her hair down, there was no chance she was going to get in the way of a night out for her. Knowing her old colleagues, they'd be out all night. By the sounds of it, dinner had already turned into drinks at the pub and later it would be the club. And had Stacey told her? She didn't remember, but Stacey tried her hardest not to speak to her about her ex in front of her, so it would be just like her not to mention it.

'It's not far off the truth. He's...'

Tuning out, Polly watched as Zac walked back into the kitchen. The furrows in his brow had deepened and his hair was dishevelled as if he'd been raking his fingers through it, just as he had when he'd taken that call on the way down here. Something was up with him, something was going on, and the more she thought about it, she wasn't so certain it was to do with the reserve and the money he was trying to raise.

She glanced at the clock by the door, for once regretting not replacing the battery when it had died three months earlier. It must be late, though. Nine o'clock. Maybe later. Would he even be taking calls about work this late?

Zac held his hand out, indicating her mobile, which she now held by her side, distracted by Zac's reappearance.

Turning her attention back to her phone, Polly cut across her friend. 'Sorry, I'd better get going.'

'Right, okay. I suppose I should as well. But I'll ring you later, right?' Stacey's voice suddenly sounded very far away.

'Yep.' Ending the call without letting Zac see, Polly gripped the phone closer to her ear. She had nowhere to go. She'd have to stay here. Trying her best not to let her voice wobble, she carried on speaking into her phone, her voice a little louder. 'Thanks, Stacey. See you in a few minutes.'

Waiting until she'd slipped her mobile into her coat pocket, Zac stepped a little closer. 'You can stay at your friend's house?'

'Yep, yes, I can stay. She's on her way.' Shoving her hands into her coat pockets, one hand gripped her mobile, the other the defunct key to the flat. 'Thank you for this evening, but you can go.'

'No, I'll wait.' Zac looked at his mobile as a message pinged through, the creases in his forehead deepening again as he read it.

'No, you've done enough. More than enough. And by the looks of it, you're needed elsewhere...' She nodded towards his mobile.

'Well, I...'

'Honestly, she's only round the corner. She'll likely get here before you've started your engine.' She swallowed. She hated lying, even to him, but he had things to do, places to be. He'd had to leave Meadowfield this weekend, just as she had. He had a reason, responsibilities too. 'Besides, Mr Greene will be sitting on the steps until at least midnight. And no one he doesn't know will get past him.'

Zac visibly relaxed a little. 'Yes, I suppose you're right. And you're certain she won't be long?'

'Nope. She'll be no time at all.' Polly shook her head, trying desperately not to give in to the stinging behind her eyes, willing the tears to stay where they were, hoping he wouldn't be able to hear the fear in her voice. 'Thank you for everything.'

'No worries, I'm just sorry this has happened to you.' Zac looked around the kitchen again. 'You'll ring me if I can do anything?'

Polly nodded.

'Right, okay.' Zac took a breath in before turning and leaving.

As soon as she heard the crunch of glass beneath his shoes and the feeble click of the damaged door closing, Polly slid to the floor, her back against the counter. Crossing her arms, she buried her face in the warmth of her coat sleeves. She was alone. Here alone for the night. The whole night. And yes, she hadn't been lying when she'd told him that Mr Greene would be perched on the steps for hours yet, but even he'd have to go to bed at some point, or else simply get too cold and venture inside to his flat.

She should have told Stacey what had happened. If she had, she knew her friend would have come straight over. But Stacey deserved a night out, she worked hard and needed to spend time with her colleagues unwinding. Besides, there was a small part of her that would be mortified if Ben found out what had happened. And he likely would if Stacey had to run out on his leaving drinks. He'd always been a snob about where she'd come from, about where her grandparents lived.

Pushing herself up to standing, Polly made her way back through to the living room, pausing just before entering the hallway. What if they – whoever they were – had watched Zac leave and decided to come back? The fact there hadn't been anything worth stealing in their eyes didn't matter. They'd still used the flat as a place to eat pizza. What if they assumed it was still empty and returned? Or decided to use it as a bolt-hole, somewhere to hide away, or simply just to eat and hang out?

She needed to do something. She had to somehow plug the hole in the window and barricade the door, make it impossible for anyone to enter. Yes, that's what she would do, and she had to do it fast, before anyone had a chance to make their way inside again.

First though, she'd turn the electric fire on, let it take the chill out of the air whilst she was doing what she could to secure the place.

24

Placing the last of her grandma's china dolls inside the large, battered suitcase they'd always taken on holiday with them, Polly lifted her forefinger to her lips, kissed it and placed it on the doll's forehead. Her grandma's prized possessions. She'd collected them for as long as Polly could remember, receiving one from Polly's grandad for every birthday, Christmas and wedding anniversary.

And now what? Polly had spent the last few hours packing them up, and what was she supposed to do with them? There were well over thirty which had been on display here in the living room and in her grandparents' bedroom, and more lovingly wrapped with tissue paper in boxes in the loft space above the flat – a perk her grandad had often reminded her of, always advising her to buy on the top floor if she ever moved into a flat.

For now, she could put the bulging suitcases in the loft, but when, or if, the flat ever sold, what then? She had nowhere to take the dolls and other things. Where would they go? She didn't think she was ready to sell or give her grandparents' belongings away. Besides, they'd always be pieces she'd want to keep, want to treasure. What did people do with such things?

Tucking the edge of a doll's satin dress into the suitcase, Polly carefully zipped it up. She'd have to look into storage solutions, those big containers or rooms you could hire in the large metal warehouses on the edge of town. Yes, that's what she'd do. For now, at least.

Slumping back on the floor, her back against the sofa, Polly closed her eyes for a second. She wasn't sure of the time – she'd taken the batteries out of all her grandma's clocks, leaving only the clock in the kitchen ticking because they usually had the door closed, when she'd first moved in to look after her all those months ago, and she'd left her phone on the mantelpiece on the other side of the room – but she knew it must be almost, if not past, midnight. Or at least it felt like it.

Ever since Zac had left, she'd been trying to keep busy, trying to distract herself from the creaks and noises from the flat below and she'd given up counting the number of times she'd been to check the door for any sign of someone trying to force entry again. She'd told herself a million times that now she'd covered the hole in the glass with an empty cereal box and enough duct tape to secure even the most valuable bank safe, she was secure. Not to mention the wooden chair she'd jammed up against the handle of the door leading from the tiny hallway into the living room. No one was getting in here, not without making a huge racket first, anyway.

Forcing her eyes open, Polly pushed herself up to standing. She couldn't sleep. Well, she could. She could sleep for an eternity the way she was feeling at the moment, but there was no chance she was about to let herself doze off when there was every possibility whoever had barged their way inside to lounge, eat pizza and do goodness knows what could come back at any moment. Nope, she needed to stay awake, which would be a good thing, because she had so much to do anyway.

Sleep could wait. She'd ask Stacey over to help later today if she wasn't too hungover and she'd perhaps sneak in a quick nap at some point, but not whilst she was alone. Besides, she still had so much more to pack away. Yes, the china dolls had been a large part of what she assumed David was talking about when he said viewers were struggling to see past the décor and clutter, but that was far from the end of it. If she was going to prepare the flat as best she could for a viewing, then she might as well go the whole hog and pack up the rest of her grandparents' belongings too.

And her own. Her bedroom, albeit being the box room, had both teenage paraphernalia stuffed in boxes beneath her bed and in her wardrobe, as well as knick-knacks she'd brought from her house-share with Stacey when she'd moved fleetingly in with Ben and then back in to care for her grandma. Yes, she was sure she must have broken some world record for the sheer amount of stuff that could fit into a box room whilst still allowing it to be useable.

Walking into the kitchen, she clicked on the kettle, not for the first time that evening wishing she'd thought to ask Zac to stop off at a garage on the way down here so she could grab some milk. Black coffee it was then. Again.

After she'd rinsed the mug she'd used earlier under the tap, Polly turned and caught sight of those darn pizza boxes sticking up out of the kitchen bin where she'd tidied them away. She shuddered. They served as a stark reminder of how vulnerable she felt at the moment and, for the first time since putting the flat on the market, she felt that she had made the right decision after all. If she stayed after this, she'd only be waiting for the next time some person decided to break in.

The kettle switched off, tearing her from her thoughts and making her jump. She couldn't wait to get back to Pennycress Inn now. Pouring the boiling water, Polly shook her head. She was being daft. She was probably the safest she'd ever been at the flat before. The burglars had been, gone and wouldn't be back now they knew there was nothing worth stealing. Bringing the mug to her lips she grimaced at the taste. No one—

A loud knock rang through the flat and Polly watched as her mug fell to the floor, coffee splattering up the doors of the old blue Formica kitchen units. Freezing, she held her breath. Waiting. But there was nothing, no sound, no hint of another forced entry.

Maybe she'd been hearing things. She'd been on edge ever since Zac had left, even before that. Of course her mind was playing tricks on her. That was normal. To be expected.

Kneeling down, she felt the hot liquid quickly soak through the knee of her jeans as she began collecting up the broken ceramic. She needed to sleep, that's what she really needed, but that wasn't about to happen, especially not now since her mind was playing tricks on her again.

With the pieces of mug picked up, she stood up and grabbed the tea towel just as another knock sounded through the flat. And again. And again. This wasn't her imagination. This was real. There was really someone here, someone standing outside her flat after midnight. And whoever it was knew she was inside. If they were the same people who had forced entry before, broken the TV and eaten pizza without a care in the world, then they knew someone had been back. They could see that from the stuffed hole in the window of the door.

Gripping the edge of the kitchen work surface, Polly held her breath. *Please go away. Please go.* She'd always felt safe here, always. Growing up here with her grandparents, knowing that there were people next door, opposite and below, had always comforted her, even on the rare occasions her grandparents had stayed away for the night at friends' houses or gone on holiday when she'd been out working. It was one thing she loved about this place – the community, the feeling of being cared for.

But now, everything had changed. She couldn't even solely blame the people who had broken in. Yes, the fact her home had been violated had made it worse, but before that, when the occupiers of the other flats on the floor had left, and she'd suddenly felt alone up here, that's when it had begun. Things had changed.

And now, now there was someone standing outside the flat, banging on the door.

Turning slowly, Polly lifted her chin. She might be selling soon, but at the moment, this was still her home. Her grandparents' belongings were still here, and she wasn't about to let anyone else come in and do whatever they pleased. Not again.

Stepping over the coffee splatters across the lino, Polly walked through the living room before shifting the chair which she'd pushed up against the door to jam the handle. Taking a deep breath, she inched her way into the small hallway and grabbed her grandad's large navy umbrella from the wooden stand by the door.

Raising the brolly above her head, she froze, suddenly unsure of herself. What did she think she was going to do? Open the door and invite them in? Or open the door and bash them round the head with the brolly?

She couldn't do this. She wasn't brave enough. She should just ring the police. Yes, they still hadn't come out after Zac had rung them, but this was different, she was trapped alone in the flat. They'd come out now.

With her hands shaking and the brolly still held above her head, ready to use if they forced their way inside, Polly began to back away slowly, trying her best not to make a sound.

She saw the end of the brolly get tangled in the heavy plastic 'gems' hanging from the lampshade before she heard the inevitable loud clinks as it broke free and the gems knocked together. Drat. With the brolly in mid-air and her hand on the living room door, Polly froze again. Whoever was outside would have heard that.

'Polly? Are you there? It's me, Zac.' His familiar voice filled the hallway.

'Zac?' It was Zac. No one was trying to break in. She was safe, her home was safe. Her grandparents' belongings were safe.

Stepping forward, Polly unlocked the door and pulled it open. Never more grateful to see him.

Zac frowned, his lips twitching in amusement. 'Death by brolly? That sounds painful.'

'Huh?' Blinking, Polly looked from Zac to the brolly still in her hand. Lowering it, she shrugged. 'I didn't know it was you banging on the door. I thought it was the people who had broken in again.'

Zac nodded slowly. 'I'm not sure they would have knocked. Possibly once to see if anyone was inside, but I don't think they'd have had the patience I did.'

Polly let out a small laugh, the relief flooding her body. 'No, you're probably right. What are you doing here?'

'I could ask you the same thing. You said you were staying at a friend's house tonight. I was driving past and noticed the lights were on, so thought I'd come and check it out.'

'To make sure the burglars hadn't returned?' Polly gripped the handle of the brolly a little tighter. It wasn't just her who had thought that was a possibility then.

'Exactly.' Zac shrugged and held out his hand, indicating the small hallway. 'May I?'

Backing into the living room, Polly nodded. 'Yes, of course. Come on in.'

'Have the police been round yet?'

Polly shook her head as she watched Zac lock the door behind him before slipping his shoes off to reveal bright purple socks with tiny hedgehogs scattered across them. She stifled a smile. She'd always assumed he was a grey sock guy, smart and businesslike. 'No, I don't think they'll be in any rush. Nothing was stolen.'

Zac followed her through to the living room and paused, looking around at the bare shelves and the suitcase sitting on the floor. 'You've been busy.'

Realising she was still gripping hold of the brolly, she leaned it up against the end of the sofa and looked at the chair she'd been using to jam the door shut. She couldn't really put it back in place now, could she? Not with Zac here. He'd think she was trying to imprison him or something. 'I've got a viewing on Monday and the estate agent advised me to declutter and redecorate.'

'A viewing? You're selling?' The muscle in Zac's jaw twitched. 'Where are you moving to?'

Polly shrugged. It wasn't rocket science. 'Hopefully to Meadowfield.'

'Oh, right.' Turning, Zac looked out of the living-room window.

Joining him, Polly frowned. Why had he reacted like that? Did he really think she was going to stay here and commute to Meadowfield every day once their three months were up at Pennycress? Or was he just so set on securing the promotion and then sacking her that it hadn't occurred to him that she might already be taking steps to move?

'I imagine this is a great view in the daylight.' Zac shoved his hands in his pockets.

And now a complete change in conversation?

She forced herself to focus on what he was saying. The view. 'Yes, it is. I used to spend hours sitting in that little chair as a kid, reading and looking out of the window.' She smiled at memories of watching the world go by whilst the flat filled with delicious smells wafting out from the kitchen before her grandad came home from work, usually with a comic rolled under his arm for her or a chocolate cake someone at the factory had made. Even if she did stay, take the flat off the market, give up on her dream of working in conservation so she could stay living in her childhood home, she knew it wouldn't be the same. She no longer had the unconditional love and support of her grandparents and after finding the flat had been broken into, she realised the burglars had stolen something after all. They'd stolen her misguided sense of safety.

'You grew up here?' Zac tilted his head. 'I didn't realise that. I knew you'd moved in when your grandma got sick, but I didn't realise you grew up with them.'

Why would he? Yes, before the whole leaving party incident, they'd been friends, they'd got on well, but they'd never really delved into their pasts. He'd always refrained from speaking about his upbringing, presumably because he didn't want to highlight to everyone the fact he'd had everything handed to him on a silver plate. 'Well, I did. Since the age of nine.'

'Right.' Looking at her, he held her gaze for the briefest of seconds before turning back towards the view.

Following his lead, she fixed her eyes on the yellow street lamps illuminating the town centre, the blinking of the traffic lights as they turned from red to amber to green, and the ebb and flow of the headlights from the few cars which were meandering along the road. Most of them were probably taxis taking people home after an enjoyable Friday night out, just like Stacey and her colleagues, celebrating the end of the working week. Huh, it was all right for some. Maybe one day she'd get to that point – where she didn't have a ton of work to complete over the weekend or a flat to declutter and decorate. One day.

Polly glanced across at Zac. He was almost entranced by the light show going on below them. 'So, what were you really doing, coming up here?'

Blinking, he ran his palm across his face, his eyes still fixed to the window. 'As I said, I happened to drive past and noticed your lights were on.'

Pulling her sleeve over her hand, she scrubbed at a smear on the window. He'd just driven past, what, with his head hanging out of the car window and straining his neck to look up? She wasn't buying it. The only way he'd have noticed if her lights were on – or indeed, that any lights were on four floors up – was if he'd been looking intentionally. 'Did you have a nice evening?'

That gained his attention. Turning to face her, he frowned. 'A nice evening?'

She shrugged. 'I mean, I'm assuming you've been out to the pub or somewhere to be driving through town at this time?'

'I was visiting...' He shook his head. 'Look, have you got any coffee? Or tea? I'm parched and could really do with something.'

'Sure, I'll grab you one. No milk though, so it'll have to be black.'

She walked through to the kitchen, glancing behind her as she got to the door. He was standing back at the window, transfixed, by the looks of things. So, he'd been visiting someone. Someone he didn't particularly want to talk to her about. A girlfriend maybe? She clicked the kettle on before turning and leaning her back against the work surface. She could still see him from here, through the open doorway. Yes, a girlfriend. That would make sense. That would be why he didn't want to enlighten her, but why keep it quiet? The kiss. That was why. She slapped her forehead. Of course, it all made sense now. He had a girlfriend. A partner. Someone he had been seeing since before they'd shared that moment, or whatever it had been. No wonder he didn't want to dwell on it, no wonder he never brought it up and that he'd clammed right up when she'd tried to discuss it with him during the car journey.

And it was why he'd been acting so weird towards her, too. He was scared she'd put two and two together and search the girlfriend out, tell her what had happened. Looking down at the floor, Polly sighed as she spotted a pizza crumb she'd missed with the vacuum. Bending down, she picked it up and put it in the bin. Did he really think she'd do that? Try to break up his relationship because of a stupid kiss?

'The kettle's boiled.' Striding into the kitchen, Zac reached behind her and took down two mugs from the wooden mug tree sitting at the back of the work surface.

'Right. Thanks.' Stepping back, she watched as he made the coffee, his black, hers with one sugar. Taking it, she wrapped her hands around the searing ceramic. 'Thanks.'

'No problem.' Walking to the other side of the small room, he leaned against the wall. 'So, are you going to answer my question and tell me why you didn't go to stay with your friend in the end?'

Umm, like he'd answered her questions. She shrugged. She had nothing to hide. 'She's on a night out and I didn't want to tear her away.'

'How come you didn't just say that then instead of pretending you were going?' Zac took a sip of his drink, wincing slightly at the heat.

'Because you clearly had somewhere to go.'

'I could have stayed. Or found you somewhere safer to stay for the night.'

'This is safe! It's...' She let her voice drift off. It wasn't safe. Or it hadn't been, and it probably still wasn't, what with that cereal box-covered hole in the door. 'You were busy. You had that phone call...'

Zac nodded and shifted his stance against the wall. 'So, your plan is to sleep here alone?'

Polly blew on her coffee, her breath creating small waves on the surface of the liquid. 'I wasn't going to sleep, just get stuff done.'

'Right, I can see you've been busy decluttering. How much more do you have to do? I can give you a hand if you like?'

Polly took a sip of the sweet coffee before shaking her head. 'No, don't worry. I've got a fair amount left to do, but I'll start again with that in the morning because I don't want to disturb downstairs. I was going to take a look at that leaflet for the reserve tonight.'

'Great. I'll help.' Zac pushed himself away from the wall and looked around.

'My laptop is in the living room.' Brushing past him, she led the way back into the room they'd just left and called over her shoulder, 'You don't need to stay, though. I'll be fine.'

'Yes, you have the brolly.' Zac chuckled.

'And you must have places to be yourself. A bed to sleep in.' She sank to the sofa in front of the coffee table and placed her mug down before pulling her laptop towards her. The last thing she wanted was for him to feel forced into staying. She didn't need him here and she certainly didn't want to endure hours of awkward small talk or worse, silence. She'd had enough of that in the car. 'You go. I'll survive.'

Shaking his head, Zac joined her on the sofa, stretching his long legs beneath the coffee table. 'I'm good. Besides, it'll be nice to be able to have an input on the reserve leaflet.'

'It would? You don't want a break from the job for the weekend?' Why did he want to have an input? Didn't he trust her to do it right? To include all that was needed? Or did he just think he could do a better job? Nah, he wanted some of the credit for it. Not only did he want to bring the most money in, but he also wanted to make sure he was contributing to the reserve in other ways. It was all an act, an act to secure the promotion. 'Actually, I'm tired. I'm not sure if I'm going to be able to focus enough after today, to be honest. I might just leave it.'

'Sure thing. Let's relax and watch something then.' Unperturbed by her words and also the broken TV, Zac flipped open the laptop lid and navigated his way to the TV apps.

Watching him scroll through the choices each channel had to offer, every so often he looked across at her and raised an eyebrow questioningly before continuing. The truth was, she wasn't really bothered about what they watched; she was more interested in the reason he was here. Why was he determined to stick around despite her lying and saying she was fine? Did she looked that terrified that he didn't feel he could leave or was there a reason he didn't want to? Perhaps he wanted to be portrayed as the knight in shining armour who had made sure she was okay after the break-in?

What could she do? She had only two choices, to kick him out and spend the rest of the night willing the sun to rise and being terrified at every slight noise. Or let him stay, let him believe he was doing her a favour, but perhaps be able to relax a little. Or as much as she *could* relax in his presence, anyway. She looked across at him as an overwhelming tiredness rolled over her. Perhaps she should just let him be the hero.

She reached out and pointed to the comedy series she'd watched over fifteen times before. 'Are you happy with that?'

'Yep.' Hitting the Play button, Zac settled his back against the sofa cushions.

'Great.' As Polly watched the familiar characters move across the screen, she let herself zone out for a while. She knew the script exactly. It had been her grandma's favourite series, and they'd watched it on repeat while Polly had been looking after her. Leaning back against the sofa too, she picked up her mug. Whatever his reasons, she had to admit she was more than a little grateful he'd insisted on staying.

25

'You're not being serious?' Stacey glared at her from her vantage point at the top of the ladder, a paintbrush full of white paint threatening to drip across the old sheet Polly had laid to cover the floor. 'You fell asleep on him? On THE Zac Sinclair? The fittest guy in town?'

'Hey, you can't say that! What would Freddie say if he could hear you talking about another man like that?' Polly laughed as she brushed paint across the wall, leaving a satisfying streak across the red panelling. Polly was both pleasantly surprised and shocked her friend wasn't curled up on the sofa suffering a hangover after her night out. And, of course, she was grateful she'd shot round this morning to help.

'Haha, Freddie knows he's the one for me.' Stacey grinned as she twisted around and perched on the top rung of the stepladder. 'But seriously, Zac slept over? Here?'

'Yes, but not like that.' Polly shook her head. 'Definitely not like that. In fact, I don't know if he actually got any sleep at all.'

'But you did?'

'I did. I didn't think I'd ever be able to sleep here again, not knowing that one or more total strangers have been in here and especially with that measly cardboard covering the hole in the door, but I did. I woke up with my head on his chest.' Polly grimaced, her cheeks flaming the hot red they had done when she'd woken up to find herself lying against the blue cashmere of his jumper, saliva drooling down her chin. 'I don't think I'll be able to ever face him again. I probably snored too.'

'Oh, you definitely snored. Your snoring has woken me up on more than one occasion.' Stacey's expression was serious before she burst out laughing.

'Oi! If I wasn't worried about dripping paint everywhere, I'd be throwing this at you.' Grinning, Polly pointed her paintbrush at her friend. She probably had snored. Yikes. He hadn't mentioned it, though. When she'd woken up, he hadn't complained about the fact she'd fallen asleep on him, or her snoring. He hadn't even acknowledged the drool stain on his jumper. Thinking about it, he'd been quite relaxed about the whole situation. Yes, he'd had to rush off, but he'd appeared to be quite content. Definitely less stressed than he'd been when he'd first arrived at the flat. Not that any of that would make a jot of difference to the sheer humiliation she was feeling right now. 'I'm literally going to have to quit my job, aren't I?'

'Nah, don't be daft. He could have walked out at any point, remember, and he didn't. He stayed.' Gripping the edge of the ladder, Stacey stood up again and began painting the woodchip above the panelling. 'I think it's rather sweet, actually. Him checking up on you in the middle of the night like that and making sure you were safe.'

'He was just passing and noticed the lights on, that's all.' Polly dipped her paintbrush back into the pot, reloading it.

'Uh-huh, like anyone's going to believe that.' Stacey nodded dramatically.

'It's true. He said he was passing and saw the lights on. That's exactly what he said.'

'You mean he was driving with his sunroof open in the middle of the night and happened to glance up to look at the stars and instead of catching a glimpse of Orion, he noticed your lights were on.' Stacey raised her eyebrows. 'If you say so.'

Polly shrugged. 'Well, that's what he said.'

'Go on, spill.'

'What?' Frowning, Polly glanced around the room. They had only just begun and if they were going to get this room and the kitchen done, it'd take all day. And then another coat tomorrow, probably.

'Look, Pols, I know you. You've got something on your mind and it's not just the fact you're worried you might have snored in front of him.'

'Okay... I just don't understand why he popped round. I'd told him I was going to yours, so he'd have had no reason to check up on me, and like you say, it's pretty impossible to see if the lights are on up here or not without intentionally looking up.' She smeared the white paint on the panelling again, being careful to wriggle it so the bristles got in the dips and grooves of the wood. 'No, I think he came here to try to get in on the work I'm doing for the reserve.'

'The leaflet you were telling me about?' Stacey frowned. 'Why do you think that?'

Polly shrugged. 'Why else? It explains why he popped round on the off chance I was here. Besides, when I mentioned that I was going to work on it last night, he jumped right in and offered to help.'

Stopping, Stacey climbed down the ladder again and swirled her paintbrush in the tin. 'But he stayed anyway. Even after you told him you'd changed your mind and weren't going to work on it, he stayed, and he stayed all night. I don't think that sounds as though he was after any glory from work about helping with the leaflet. I think it shows he cares about you.'

Polly scoffed. Zac care about her? As if. Zac was Zac, and being indifferent towards her had become the norm since the kiss. Before that, though, she may have been inclined to believe Stacey, may have even come to the same conclusion herself, but now, after how he'd acted towards her... 'Nope, he's made it clear that he doesn't give two hoots about me anymore. That's been pretty obvious from the way he's reacted since the leaving party.'

Wiping her brush off on the edge of the tin, Stacey climbed back up the ladder, looking down on Polly before continuing. 'I still maintain you've got him all wrong. You're just being cynical.'

'Can you blame me?'

'No. No, but he's probably got his reasons. I'm not saying it's right, but there must be a reason.'

'I know he has his reasons. It hit me last night that he probably has a...' Polly stopped mid-sentence as someone hammered on the front door.

'That might be the police again. Maybe they've come back to collect some evidence or something?' Stacey glanced towards the hallway door.

'I doubt it.' Polly carefully laid her brush on the lid of the tin. The police visit that morning had been brief, and they'd basically told her they'd ask around but not to hold her breath. She'd known she was destroying any evidence by cleaning up after the break-in yesterday, but she hadn't been able to stand staring at the pizza boxes and the crumbs – a stark reminder of her sanctuary being invaded by strangers. Besides, she'd known the break-in wouldn't have been a police priority, especially as nothing had been stolen and the only thing, apart from the front door, that had been damaged was a twenty-year-old TV worth close to nothing.

Polly stepped into the hallway and, despite the fact it was only the early afternoon, and the stairwell would be flooded with autumn light, grabbed the brolly with one hand as she opened the front door. 'Zac?'

'Hi, how are you? I've finished with my... thing and wondered if you needed a hand?' Zac held up a brown paper bag and a cup holder with two takeaway cups. 'I brought lunch too.'

'Oh right, I...' Polly stammered as she lowered the brolly back to the umbrella stand. What was he doing back here? When he'd left this morning she'd assumed she wouldn't be seeing him again until she returned to Meadowfield.

'Pols...' Stacey appeared behind her, her coat carefully hooked over her arm, away from the splatter of paint down her top. 'Oh, hello. Lovely to see you again, Zac.'

'Afternoon, Stacey. Good to see you too.' Zac held up the cup holder. 'I can go and grab another coffee if you're hanging around?'

'I'm not. I have to get off. Sorry I couldn't stay any longer.' Stacey glanced back at Polly, a mischievous grin spreading across her face.

'I'll go in and pop these down then.' Zac sidled past Stacey.

Waiting until Zac had stepped into the living room, Polly pulled the hallway door shut while whispering to Stacey, 'Why are you going? You told me you were free all day.'

'I was. Until now.' Stacey smiled sweetly. 'I have to go and—'

'Go and do nothing more like,' Polly hissed under her breath. 'Don't walk out on me. It's going to be super awkward.'

'Nah, it won't.' Reaching out, Stacey rubbed the pad of her thumb across Polly's forehead. 'Let's just get that off, though.'

'Get what off? What is it?' Polly scrubbed at her skin.

'Just a bit of paint.' Stacey tilted her head. 'Actually, it looks kind of cute. You go and have some fun.'

'Fun? I—' Too late. Her friend was walking towards the stairwell. 'Stacey...!'

'Sorry, can't hear you...' Shrugging her shoulders, Stacey disappeared around the corner.

'Great, thanks. Some best mate you are,' Polly muttered before closing the door softly. What was she supposed to do now? It had been awkward enough when she'd woken up and Zac had legged it out of the flat on an 'errand', but now? Now would be even worse. And why had he come back again, anyway? He knew she'd be painting all day. Unless he thought she'd been lying and just wanted to get him out of the way so she could work on the leaflet alone. Now, that wouldn't have been a bad idea...

Taking a deep breath, she plastered a fake smile to her face and opened the living room door, her smile fading as she realised Zac had made himself at home and it looked as though he was planning on staying a while too. His coat was draped across the back of the sofa, which she and Stacey had pushed into the middle of the room, and he was wearing old jeans and a stained grey T-shirt. They might be old, but he definitely looked better in them than she did in her ancient leggings with a hole at the knee and an oversized T-shirt of Ben's she'd found stuffed in the back of her drawer. Not that it mattered what she looked like. She was dressed for painting, not for impressing anyone. Plus, Zac was the last person she'd want to impress anyway. She shook her head slightly. What was she even doing wasting time thinking about how she was dressed? 'Thanks so much for stopping by.'

'No problem.' Zac released the cups from the cup holder and held one out to her.

'Thanks.' Taking it, she took a sip. Yep, he'd remembered the sugar. Again.

'Here you go. Grilled cheese and tomato with mustard. That's what you like, isn't it?' Zac frowned.

'Wow, yes, yes it is.' Taking the sandwich, she perched on the sofa, careful to leave an almighty gap between them. Not many people knew she liked mustard with her cheese. In fact, the only people had been her grandparents and Stacey, and even then, Stacey almost always forgot to add it. She must have ordered it for lunch sometime when she'd been working at HQ.

'It's looking good in here.' Zac nodded towards the half-painted wall opposite.

'Is it?' Polly frowned. It was just going to look like a white plain box by the time she'd finished it. At least her grandparents' décor had given the place character. They could be anywhere, in any home, with the white. She sighed.

It didn't really matter what it ended up looking like. She was only painting it to sell and it wasn't as though she'd be hanging around here.

'Yep. It looks fresh.' Zac sank his teeth into his sandwich, a string of melted cheese dripping down his front.

'Careful.' Automatically, she reached out and brushed her finger against his T-shirt. Pulling her hand back, she murmured an apology and bit into her own sandwich. She didn't want to scare him away again with her physical touch.

'I think I owe you an explanation to your question yesterday.' Lowering his sandwich to the coffee table, Zac looked at her.

'My question?' Great, her touch had scared him and now he was about to bring up the one subject she'd hoped had been well and truly buried.

'When you asked about why I began acting differently towards you after we'd shared that kiss at your leaving party.'

Yep, there it was. Polly dug her fingers into her sandwich, the heat of the cheese burning her skin. He was scared she'd got the wrong impression after him coming round last night. He was likely terrified she'd read something into it which wasn't there. 'You don't need to give me an explanation.'

'I think I do.' Zac nodded slowly.

'Okay.' Closing her eyes momentarily, Polly placed her feet flat on the floor, willing a crack to appear in the floorboards so she could slither through it and land on the sofa in the Tylers' living room in the flat below.

'I should have said something earlier, but I couldn't find the right moment.' Zac shifted position.

'Should have said what?' This was it; this was where he was going to tell her he had a partner and he was worried she'd spill the beans and ruin everything.

'I knew the truth about the promotion. I found out the day after the party that both of us were being put forward for it. That's why I distanced myself from you.' Zac rubbed his palm across his face.

Polly opened her mouth before closing it again, the words failing her. Her brain failing her. How was she supposed to respond? He'd known she'd been put forward for the promotion? He'd known that he had too, and they'd be competing for it?

She lowered her sandwich to the coffee table, not caring that she'd missed placing it on top of the paper bag and it would likely leave a greasy mark on the wood. 'Why on earth didn't you tell me?'

'Honestly? I just didn't know how.' Zac picked up his coffee cup before lowering it again without taking a sip. Twisting the cardboard cup in his hand, he shook his head. 'No, that's not true. I know I could have told you. I know I should have warned you.'

'Yes, you should have done. I changed my entire life for this opportunity and if I'd known...' Polly shook her head. What would she have done if she'd known? If he was telling her the truth, by the time Zac had found out they'd be competing, she would have already given up her teaching job. But still, if she'd known, she would have been able to make that decision herself, she would have been able to decide whether to stay around here and look for another teaching job or relocate to Meadowfield on the off chance she was the one who was promoted. 'I've risked everything.'

'I know. I know you have.' He rested the cup against his knee. 'But when I found out, you'd already given up your job, you'd already gone all in with the job at the reserve. I didn't know what to do.'

'So, you just decided to freeze me out?' Polly felt a fierce heat growing in the pit of her stomach. He'd played with her life! 'You just decided to make me feel as though that moment we'd shared, that stupid kiss, was the reason you suddenly hated me?'

'I never hated you.' Looking at the floor, Zac spoke quietly. 'But I also knew I couldn't begin a relationship with you without telling you about the promotion.'

Begin a relationship? Now he was just playing with her. How could she have been so stupid? 'You never wanted a relationship with me. You realised the kiss had been a drunken mistake, and you panicked. You didn't tell me about the promotion because you needed a reason to keep me at arm's length.'

'That's not true.' Standing up, Zac walked across to the end of the living room and stared out of the window.

'Then what is?' She sighed heavily. Why were they even having this conversation? It didn't change anything. It didn't make anything any clearer. In fact, it just made her question what to believe or not even more. She slumped back against the sofa cushions.

'I needed to fight for that promotion. I need it.'

Leaning forward, Polly looked across at him. She could barely hear him, he was speaking that softly. 'I do too and if I'd known it wasn't a sure thing, I'm not sure whether I'd have taken the job.'

'I'm sorry.'

'Why do you need the promotion? To prove something to your parents? To continue the Sinclair legacy at the trust? I think you can see why I need it.' She swept her arms in front of her, encompassing the room. She needed the promotion for the money, and he needed it for what? Validation?

'Legacy? No. I have nothing to prove to anyone.' Shoving his hands in his pockets, Zac turned around to face her. Standing beneath the light, she could see the dark circles beneath his eyes again. What wasn't he telling her?

'Zac?'

Glancing down at the floor, Zac took a deep breath in, his chest rising beneath the grey T-shirt. 'I need the money too, but that's no excuse. I should have told you. I just thought...'

Wait, what? He needed the money? Zac Sinclair, the only son of the Sinclair family who had enough money to plough thousands into the trust every year up until a short time ago? What did he need the extra money for? To buy another ten vintage Porsches? 'You thought what?'

He dragged his fingers through his hair. 'I thought if I didn't tell you that we were both up for the promotion, then I'd be able to prove myself.'

'Huh, you thought you'd keep me in the dark so you could get one step ahead without me knowing.' Polly clenched her fists. What gave him the right to think he could play with her life like this?

'No.' He shifted on the spot. 'Yes, I suppose so. Something like that. Not that I had thought about it in that way, just that—'

'Right. Just in what way, then? What possible way could you have thought that you keeping quiet about us both competing for the promotion was fair?' Jumping to her feet, she strode to the opposite end of the room. She didn't want to be near him. She could barely look at him. 'You had no right.'

'I know. I didn't.' He held his hands out in front of him, palms forward. 'I had no right at all to keep it from you and I had no right to treat you as I did, to make you feel as though the way I was acting was because of the kiss. In truth, I just had to distance myself from you because I was feeling guilty.'

'Yeah right. I don't believe for one second that you felt guilty for not telling me. I bet you were as pleased as punch when you realised I didn't know about it. I bet you thought you could get ahead without me knowing, without me realising.'

'Look, it wouldn't have changed anything, even if you'd known. You wouldn't have done anything differently, would you?' He spoke hesitatingly, unsure of what he was implying.

She frowned. Would she? She was trying her best as it was and she would have done if she'd known Zac was competing for the promotion or not. 'That's not the point. You kept that from me and you made me feel as though I'd done something wrong.'

'I'm sorry, that wasn't my intention.' Zac walked towards the middle of the room.

Turning to face him, Polly bit down on her thumbnail. Whether he'd meant to hurt her or not didn't matter. He'd still done it.

'I really am sorry. I know I was in the wrong keeping it from you like that, and I should have been honest with you. I wish I had, because maybe if I'd been honest from the start, I wouldn't have messed up what there was between us.'

Polly took a step closer to him. 'What do you mean?'

'Please tell me you felt it too?' Zac grimaced. 'If not, then I really have messed everything up.'

Polly froze. Was he saying what she thought he was? Had he really felt something between them that night? No, he couldn't have. If he had, then he certainly wouldn't have prioritised the promotion over her. 'What are you saying?'

'I'm saying I felt a connection that night, at your leaving party. I felt something between us.' Taking another step towards her, Zac paused again.

'No, you didn't. If you had, then you definitely wouldn't have pushed me so completely away as you did, promotion up for grabs or not. We'd always got on until that night and then after it was as though you couldn't stand to be around me.'

'That was because I didn't know what to do. I was torn.' He took another step until he was standing right in front of her. 'I didn't know how to act.'

'Because you were trying your best to swindle me out of a promotion?'

'No, because I had to put the chance of me getting that promotion ahead of my own feelings, ahead of how I feel for you.' He held out his hands towards her.

'And now what?' He wasn't making any sense. It was as though everything he was saying was in some cryptic language she was trying to decipher without the secret code. 'You suddenly don't need it?'

Zac shook his head ever so slightly as he reached out to take her hands in his. 'I'm afraid I do, but after working in the office together and then the car journey yesterday and...' He nodded towards where they'd fallen asleep on the sofa. 'I can't keep lying to myself and I need to find out if you feel something, too.'

His skin felt warm against hers, her fingers tingling with electricity. She looked down at their hands, his gently encompassing hers. Did he really feel it too? Did he feel the electricity between them?

'Do you?'

She blinked, pulling her gaze away from their hands to look him in the eyes. She thought she knew what he was referring to, what he was asking her, but so much had changed between the two of them in such a short space of time, she couldn't be sure. 'Do I what?'

'Do you still feel it? The connection we had at the party? How close we were before?' He kept his eyes upon hers, his gaze steady.

'I...' Breaking the moment, Polly looked away. What was happening? This was what she wanted. She'd felt the same connection he said he did since the moment she'd laid eyes upon him two years ago and their friendship had begun. She'd dreamt about there being more between them, but after the way he'd pushed her away? She wasn't sure. Did he expect her to just shrug her shoulders and say no worries and jump into his arms? She pulled her hands away and walked back to the sofa, sitting heavily upon it. 'I can't. I'm sorry, but after the way you've been around me, after the way you've treated me with such indifference, as if you hardly even knew me? How can you just suddenly turn up and say you feel a connection now? It doesn't work like that. You can't just switch to hating me and then liking me again.'

Looking at the floor, Zac reached his hand behind his neck, dragging it across his skin before walking towards the sofa. 'May I?'

She nodded. She wasn't about to tell him he couldn't sit down now, was she?

'Thanks.' Sitting, he leaned forward, lacing his fingers together. 'You'd be right, feelings don't change overnight like that, but that's what I've been trying to tell you. The only person I was lying to when I was pushing you away was myself. I've always had feelings for you, you must know that. You remember how close we used to be?'

She nodded. 'I remember, but I also remember that literally the day after we'd kissed, you went weird on me, and you treated me as though we were strangers.'

'I know I did and I'm sorry.' He kept his eyes fixed on the floor in front of him. 'The only reason I did that was because I felt guilty about keeping the fact we'd both been promised a chance at the promotion from you.'

Polly pulled a cushion onto her lap, hugging it to her middle. She had so many questions. 'So, did you and Mr Bob work together to keep me in the dark? Did you ask him not to tell me?'

Zac turned to glance at her. 'No, I didn't. Mr Bob just forgot to tell you. You know what he's like. He'd forget his head if it wasn't screwed on. But, I admit, when I realised he hadn't told you, I didn't and I should have.'

'You didn't even tell me you were getting a job at Meadowfield.' It wasn't just the fact he had chosen not to mention the issue with the promotion, but the job, too. That he was coming to Meadowfield with her. Why hadn't he told her?

Zac shrugged. 'I didn't tell many people. I had a lot going on at home. Not that that is any excuse. I should have found the time to tell you, the right moment, but I knew if I did, then I'd end up telling you about the promotion, too.'

Polly leaned her head back against the top of the sofa and closed her eyes. 'But why couldn't you? What's this big secret? There's something you're not telling me. And before you say it's nothing, I'm not daft, you know. Despite what you think.'

'I don't think that. Far from it, actually.'

Opening her eyes, she looked at the back of his head. He was still gazing at the floor, his neck bent. 'The phone calls, leaving yesterday just to come back at midnight, being out of the office constantly. There's something going on and if it isn't a secret partner...'

'It's definitely not a partner. I don't have a girlfriend, I haven't for years.' A hollow sound escaped the back of his throat as he let out a lone chuckle.

'Then what? What it is?'

With his elbows on his knees, Zac lowered his head, pulling his fingers through his hair. 'My family are broke. My dad lost the company last year.'

Polly gasped. Broke? His family had always been wealthy, but if it was true, if what he was telling her was true, then it did make some sort of sense, even if it was the last thing she'd expected him to say. Leaning forward, she spoke quietly. 'Right about when they stopped sponsoring the trust?'

'Yep, and right about the time my dad told me he wished I'd never moved my career away from the corporate world.' Zac still had his fingers in his hair, his shoulders slumped.

'Oh, Zac. I had no idea.' Reaching over, she laid her arm gently around his shoulders.

'You wouldn't have. It's not exactly something to shout about.' Turning his head, he looked at her. 'I couldn't exactly write it in a company email that my family had no money, and my dad was disappointed in his only son.'

'No, I don't suppose you could.' Polly frowned. 'But if this happened a year ago, we were still friends then, still talking. You could have told me.'

Zac nodded. 'I know and I should have done. I see that now, but at the time I just felt I had to keep it to myself. My family used to sponsor the trust, my parents still attend the fundraising events, they still dress up to the nines to keep up appearances. If the truth had got out, they'd have never forgiven me.'

'I wouldn't have said anything.'

'I know, but...' Straightening his back, he ran his palm across his face. 'I guess it's been engrained into me that I need to put on this front, and when my dad lost his company, the responsibility fell to me. It was – it is – my job to provide for my family.'

'You were embarrassed?' Why? Why would he be? But that was how he was acting.

'I felt as though it was my fault. I mean, if I hadn't quit my corporate job and started working at the trust, then I would have been able to save my dad's company and we wouldn't be in the mess we're in.'

Looking across at him, Polly's eyes filled with tears. He looked so broken. Reaching forward, she stroked his cheek. 'This isn't your fault and your parents' finances aren't your responsibility.'

He gave a small smile as he covered her hand with his, leaning his cheek into her palm. 'They are. They need my help.'

'What I don't understand is that if all this happened a year ago, what's changed now? How come you didn't go for another promotion?' Not many, but a few promotions had come up across the Cotswolds within the trust.

And he could have always applied for similar roles within different charities.

'Because my gran hasn't been well. My parents had been caring for her at home until a few months ago, but now we need to cover the costs of her nursing home too.' He took a deep breath, filling his lungs. 'That's where I rush off to. When she's having a bad day, I sit by the side of her bed and work from there. And that's why I haven't taken a different promotion. Meadowfield is close to her home.'

'Oh, I'm so sorry to hear that.' Polly blinked back her tears. Her grandma had ended up in a nursing home for the last few months of her life and that was the worst time of Polly's life. Each time her phone had rung, dread had filled her, and every free moment she'd had, she'd just wanted to spend with her. 'That's where you had to go last night.'

Zac shook his head. 'No, I had to go back to my parents' last night. They had a meeting with a financial advisor today and needed me to look through a few things before he came.'

Polly nodded. She could feel the coarse stubble on Zac's cheek beneath her palm. Everything suddenly felt clear. He was allowing her to see beneath the shield he'd put up to barricade her out and, for the first time in months, she was seeing him for who he was. Really seeing him. More so than he'd ever let her see before, even before the kiss, the promotion, everything. 'I think I understand now. I understand why you felt you had no choice but to keep quiet about your move to Meadowfield, about everything.'

'I'm sorry, I just...' He shrugged.

'It's okay.' She smiled softly at him. And it was. It was okay. He was just trying to do his best for his family, for his gran. And she understood that. He'd put his gran first, and it had nothing to do with her. Not really. He hadn't meant to hurt her. He'd just been trying to cope, trying to do what he thought was best. Keeping her palm nestled between his cheek and his hand, she leaned forward, waiting for him to meet her before touching his lips with hers. They were softer than she remembered.

Pulling back slightly, he searched her eyes. 'You want this? After everything I've told you?'

Brushing away the unruly tuft of hair from the middle of his forehead, she nodded. 'I do.'

Zac leaned in again, bringing his free hand around the back of her neck as he kissed her.

Pulling away, Polly took his hands in hers and searched his eyes. Was this really happening? Her feelings for him had literally gone from one extreme to the other. No, that wasn't true. She realised now that she'd been suppressing her feelings for him because she'd been hurt and angry. She realised now that she'd felt this way all along. She'd always remembered how well they used to get along, how kind he'd always been to her. Before. But now, now he'd opened up, and she'd seen a side to him she hadn't even seen when they'd been friends. And she understood. Kind of. She understood how trapped in the middle he'd felt between his feelings for her and his loyalty and responsibility towards his family. She got that, but despite all he'd told her, she was still left with questions. 'So, what happens now?'

Grinning, Zac nodded towards the paintbrushes. 'We paint.'

Polly laughed. Okay, that wasn't what she'd meant, but he was right about one thing. She did need to get the painting done and perhaps they'd had enough of the deep conversations for the time being.

26

Walking down the staircase at Pennycress Inn, Polly picked at the flecks of dried paint around her cuticles. After painting all weekend, all she could see when she closed her eyes was stark white walls. She grinned. And Zac's face, of course.

'Welcome back, Polly. You look happy. How was your weekend?' Laura paused at the bottom of the staircase and looked up at her.

'It was good, thanks. Great, even.' Stepping into the hallway, Polly noticed a bundle of wedding magazines in Laura's arms. 'Ooh, are they what I think they are?'

'Haha, yes. And these are just the tip of the iceberg.' Laura grimaced. 'You should see the pile I have up in our little flat. Jackson's threatened to fashion them into some sort of coffee table, there are that many.'

'Ah, weddings are fun to plan and there are so many options. You need all the inspiration you can get so you can choose what's right for you.' Polly laughed. She remembered only too well the excitement of planning her wedding to Ben, although at the time she'd been more sure about what colour napkins to have on the tables in their reception marquee than the groom himself. And look how that had turned out.

Laura glanced towards the kitchen and lowered her voice, 'To be perfectly honest with you, I think I know exactly what I want, but I'm having too much fun looking through the magazines and reading up on other people's big days to want the planning stage to end.'

'What is it you've decided on? Or is it top secret?'

Laura looked around the hallway wistfully. 'I want to get married here. We hosted our first wedding earlier this year, and it was so nice. Everyone had a wonderful time and I just think it would make so much sense for me and Jackson to get married here, at Pennycress. Well, to have the reception here at least.'

'Aw, that would be really special.' Polly smiled. The inn was such a beautiful place and the large garden at the back was stunning, even in the dreary depths of autumn, so she could only imagine how gorgeous it would be in the spring or summer. Plus, it was clear how much Pennycress meant to both Laura and Jackson. 'It sounds like the perfect solution.'

'It does, doesn't it? Although I'm not sure how I'll get the time to plan and organise it all, what with the day-to-day running of the inn. We're busier now than we were when me and Nicola pulled off hosting our first wedding here.' Laura wiped a finger beneath her eye. 'Sorry, I'm getting all tearful just thinking about it, about marrying Jackson and everything.'

Reaching out, Polly rubbed Laura's forearm. 'You'll find the time. I'm sure of it. And it's understandable to get teary over it all, getting married is a big deal.'

'Yes, it is, isn't it?' Laura patted the bundle of magazines in her arms. 'I'll still keep looking through these, though. I might get some inspiration on how to decorate or something.'

'And ideas for your dress.' Polly grinned.

'I literally have no idea what dress to get. I don't normally wear dresses, so I don't have a clue what shape suits me or anything.' Laura grimaced.

'Ah, you'll know when you try it on.' Polly had. She'd loved her wedding dress, ivory and flowy. She shook her head. She still had it boxed up in the loft of the flat somewhere. She'd kept that longer than her fiancé.

'I hope so.' Laura nodded towards the kitchen. 'Are you coming for a coffee? I promise we'll take a break on the wedding talk.'

'Haha, no it's okay, thanks. I'm going to get some work done in the sitting room.'

'Ah.' Laura glanced towards the closed sitting room door. 'Just to warn you, Zac is in there.'

'That's okay. We've got some work to do together.' Polly automatically grinned. She couldn't help herself, but since their conversation on Saturday, she and Zac had been inseparable. He'd not only helped her paint and finish decluttering the flat, but he'd also given her a lift back here.

'Oh, really?' Laura raised her eyebrows. 'Judging by your smile, I'm guessing work isn't the only thing you're sharing?'

Polly felt the heat of self-consciousness flush through her cheeks. Was it that obvious things had changed between them? She nodded. 'We've made up.'

'Uh-huh?' Tilting her head, Laura raised one eyebrow higher before grimacing. 'Sorry, I shouldn't be so nosey!'

'Haha, that's okay. It's no secret.' Polly laughed. In truth, she didn't see Laura or Nicola as her landladies, or whatever she was supposed to call them, she viewed them as friends. She might not have been staying at the inn that long, but they'd spent enough time together chatting to get to know each other.

'Oh good.' Relaxing, Laura smiled. 'In that case…?'

'Okay, okay, we kissed. We've decided to start seeing each other and see how things go.' Polly laughed as she held her palms against her cheeks, the cool of her hands soothing her flushed face.

Laura grinned. 'I'm really pleased for you. For both of you. It was obvious something was there between you.'

'Really?' Polly hadn't realised Zac felt the way he did until he'd told her. How could anyone else have guessed?

'Yep, running this place you see a lot of different people come through these doors.' Laura nodded towards the front door. 'And I'd go as far as saying I'm a bit of an expert at reading people now.'

'I can imagine.' Polly smiled. Maybe Zac's admission shouldn't have come as much as a surprise to her after all then.

'Anyway, I'll let you get on with your work.' Laura pulled a knowing face. 'And I'll bring some coffee and cake through.'

'Okay thanks.' Polly watched as Laura disappeared into the kitchen before she raked her fingers through her hair and pulled open the door.

'Hey, you.' Zac looked up from the laptop he had perched on his knee.

'Hi again.' Walking across to the sofa, she sat down next to him as he inched closer to her and pecked her on the lips. 'Right, shall we get this leaflet planned out then?'

'Yep.' Zac nodded without taking his eyes off her.

Laughing, Polly picked up her own laptop from the coffee table and pulled the screen open. 'Come on, as much as I'd prefer to spend the evening curled up with you watching a movie, this leaflet needs to be ready to go to the printers tomorrow.'

'I know. Give me one second though and then I promise I'll concentrate.' Zac reached behind her, resting his hand on the nape of her neck as he dipped his head, their lips touching.

Holding her laptop steady with one hand, she cupped his head with her other. This was happening. However many times she questioned herself, questioned whether they should be getting into a relationship whilst they worked together, whilst they were still both vying for the same promotion. She just couldn't push these feelings away. She'd felt a connection with him for so long now. From the moment they'd met two years ago, she'd felt something for him, and it had taken long enough for them to kiss on a drunken night out, that she wasn't about to push him away now. The promotion thing, they'd work out. They'd have to. It hung in the air between them and they'd have to face it and talk about it at some point. However difficult it would be. But for now, she just wanted to enjoy what they had together. She just wanted to enjoy this.

Reluctantly pulling away, Zac reached his arms out in front of him, lacing his fingers before cracking his knuckles. 'Okay, let's crack on.'

'Yes, let's.' Polly grinned as she watched him open up the program on his laptop and began writing, his forehead creasing in concentration. Running the pad of her index finger over her lips, she resisted the urge to reach out and try to tame his unruly tuft of hair. Shaking herself, she turned to her own laptop, trying to focus on the screen rather than watching Zac.

27

'Fantastic. Absolutely fantastic. Don't we all agree?' Declan looked away from the screen on the wall showing the leaflet Polly and Zac had created and glanced around the small meeting room as Art, Dennis and Vicki gushed their approval.

'I love it. It's informative as well as being colourful and easy to read at a glance.' Vicki nodded enthusiastically.

'Thanks.' Polly looked at Zac, who was sitting next to her. 'Me and Zac worked on it together, so it's very much a joint project.'

'You did?' Declan looked from Polly to Zac and back again. 'That's great. I do like to see our team working together.'

Polly nodded.

'I've got the printing company on standby, so I'll email it over to them now.' Vicki clicked on her computer, opening the file Polly had sent everyone before the meeting and then clicking away again. 'There. Sent.'

'That's great. Thank you, Vicki.' Polly smiled before turning to the rest of the group. 'I spoke to Jarvis and Helena when I arrived this morning, and they're all set for this weekend. They've hired a food truck for the evening and are just making the finishing touches to their menu.'

'Excellent.' Declan rubbed his hands together. 'And the competition? You mentioned we'd be running a competition on our stall to reel the public in, so to speak.'

'Yep. I thought a raffle?' Polly waited for Declan to nod his approval before continuing. 'I've ordered the raffle tickets which will be delivered tomorrow, and I'll pop to the shops after work to buy some prizes. I thought some small prizes and then a big bunny soft toy or something as the main prize.'

'Well, it sounds as though you have everything under control.' Declan scribbled in his notebook before glancing around the table again. 'Is that the last of the updates?'

'I think so, boss.' Art glanced at the clock. 'In fact, I'd better get going. I've got that meeting to get to.'

'Yes, of course.' Standing up, Declan bundled his papers into his arms. 'Okay, good work, everyone. Let's make this a fantastic week.'

'You bet.' Vicki grinned as Rolo crept out of his home in the sleeve of her sweatshirt and ambled across the table. 'Not here, Mister.'

'He's getting a little livelier now.' Polly waited until Vicki was holding Rolo in her hands before stroking his tiny, soft nose.

'Oh yes. He's certainly coming out of his shell.' Vicki rolled her eyes. 'I'm just glad Betty's taken Nutkin back or I'd be run off my feet just with the two of them.'

'Aw, he's so cute though.' Polly smiled as Vicki stood up.

'Haha, looks can be deceptive. Especially when it comes to this one, unfortunately.' Vicki laughed as she followed Declan, Art and Dennis out of the room.

Leaning across the arm of his chair, Zac nudged Polly gently with his shoulder. 'So, shall I be putting a pet rat on your Christmas list this year?'

Grinning, she shook her head. Was he really thinking that far ahead? Okay, it was only a couple of months away, but they'd literally only just started this thing between them and they still had so many battles to get through. She looked across at him. It would be nice if their relationship did go from strength to strength, but there was so much which could go wrong.

She looked away and closed her laptop. One day at a time. That's what she needed to do, that's what she'd told herself she'd do.

'That's not a no then?' Zac pulled out his mobile and began writing 'Polly's Christmas List – rat', in the Notes app.

'You're not seriously writing a note about that?' She rolled her eyes. 'But if you are, could you add a buyer for the flat while you're at it?'

Lowering his mobile to the table, Zac grimaced. 'What time is the viewing today?'

'Twelve fifteen, although if I know anything about David, it's that he'll leave the potential buyers hanging around, which won't be a good thing.' She'd been in the flat for one of the first viewings he'd organised and she'd ended up showing the couple around herself as they'd been waiting for him to arrive. Which he had, when she was showing them out of the door.

'I'm sure it'll be fine.'

'Umm, I wish I had your confidence.' Polly ran her index finger along the edge of her closed laptop. She knew the block of flats wasn't in the best of areas and first impressions counted. Really counted when someone was looking to buy a property. 'I'm just worried that if they're left to their own devices, they'll go looking around the block and might see Gina and Ken letting their dog out to pee in the hallway.'

'Or Mr Greene's rather impressive beer bottle collection lining his balcony?' Zac chuckled.

'Ah, yes, or that.' Polly twisted in her chair to look at him. 'Although there's a really sweet story behind his collection. You see, his wife passed away years ago and each year, on the anniversary of her passing, he searches for a white feather and that's where he keeps them, in beer bottles on his balcony.'

Zac covered her hand with his. 'Oh, that is a sweet sentiment.'

Polly nodded. 'Although I guess it still doesn't change things. The people viewing aren't going to know that, are they? And then there's the small matter of the flats on my floor looking derelict.'

'That might be a good thing, though. They might think to enquire about purchasing them too. Besides, at least the glazers were able to fit you in on Saturday.'

'True.' Polly nodded. That had been one expense she'd rather not have had, getting the glass in the door window replaced, and paying well over the odds for the privilege of securing her property at short notice. Still, the insurance should pay out for that. Eventually. Polly closed her laptop screen slowly, remembering how bland and unwelcoming the flat had looked after they'd finished painting. Yes, some would say it was fresh, and she could see it could be viewed in that way, but it hadn't looked anything like her childhood home anymore. The trinkets had gone, the boldly painted walls, the very essence of her grandparents had been erased. She pinched the bridge of her nose. She guessed that was a good thing perhaps. Yes, maybe it was a good thing she, Zac and Stacey had transformed her childhood home into a blank canvas, maybe it would make it slightly easier for her to say goodbye to it when it did eventually sell. 'And hopefully they'll be impressed with how clean and tidy it looks inside.'

'I'm sure they will.' Zac lifted her fingers, white paint still engrained around her nails, to his lips.

Glancing behind her, Polly checked the meeting room door was still shut. 'Careful, we don't want anyone seeing.'

Zac shrugged. 'Would that be so bad?'

'I... I don't know.' Would it? They were only a small team here at Meadowfield Reserve and she was just worried it might... She shrugged and laughed. 'I guess I'm just worried they'll think things will be awkward if we break up.'

'You're thinking about breaking up already?' He frowned.

'No, no. I just mean, if we do, then they'll worry things might be strained in the team, that's all.' Polly gripped his hand tighter. Breaking up was the last thing she wanted to think about.

'Okay, well, we can keep it quiet for now, if you'd prefer?'

'Thanks.' Polly reached out and cupped his cheek. 'I promise you one thing, though, and that's that I'm not thinking about breaking this off. We've only just started and I'm excited to see where things go.'

'Me too.' Zac grinned.

Hearing the creak of the door, Polly jumped back, her hand whacking the edge of the table as she did so. Grasping it in her other one, she looked behind her. 'Everything okay, Declan?'

'Yes, yes. I just seem to have misplaced my pencil somewhere. You've not seen it, have you? The blue one with the little rubber unicorn on top. My granddaughter gave it to me for my birthday and every time I see her, she asks if I still use it at work.'

'Do you mean the one behind your ear?' Zac pointed to his own ear.

Bringing his hand to the side of his head, Declan found the pencil. 'Ah, that's where it'll be, then. Thanks.'

'No worries.'

Holding the pencil up, Declan nodded before leaving again, closing the door quietly behind him as he did.

Still gripping her hand, Polly laughed. 'Ow, that hurt.'

'I bet it did. It did make quite a crunch.' Zac chuckled as he held out his hand for hers before lifting it to his lips.

'I guess that'll teach me for trying to keep secrets from the rest of the team.' Polly grinned. Perhaps she was being overcautious, but only time would tell, she supposed.

28

'Polly, can you grab Rolo before he gets to the door, please?' Vicki screeched as she ran across the office.

Looking down, Polly watched as Rolo sped across the threadbare carpet before dropping to her knees and cupping her hands around the small creature.

Rolo, who had grander adventures on his mind, jumped over the wall of her fingers and continued to head for the open door.

'Not today.' Taking two great strides, Zac reached the door before Rolo and shut it quickly before squatting down and picking the small rat up. 'One day, but you're still too young to be able to fend for yourself in the big wide world.'

'Thank you, Zac! I tell you, this little one is going to turn my hair grey if he carries on like this.' Vicki walked across and held her hands out as Zac carefully transferred the little Houdini. 'Come on, Rolo, Uncle Zac is right. You're still too little to go and live in the reserve. Not much longer though, I promise.'

Polly turned as her ringtone rang through the office and, seeing David's number rolling across the screen, she snatched it up. Standing up, she walked towards the door. 'Sorry, I just need to take this.'

'Estate agent?' Zac mouthed at her.

Nodding, Polly slipped outside into the foyer and held the mobile to her ear. 'Hi David. How did it go?'

'Ah hello, Polly. I've got to say I was rather impressed by the amount of work you've done this weekend. The decluttering and the decorating are excellent and it's made all the difference.'

'So what did they say? How did the viewing go?' Polly crossed her fingers, hardly able to breathe.

'Good, good. They've only gone and put an offer in on the place, haven't they?' David's voice boomed down the line.

Biting down on her bottom lip, Polly grinned. 'They want to buy it? The flat has sold?'

'They've put an offer in.'

An offer, of course. Which meant they'd not wanted to buy it for the full asking price, didn't it? Polly felt her heart sinking again. 'How much for?'

'Five thousand under the asking price.'

'Right.' Five thousand. 'That sounds like quite a bit being as we've already lowered the price twice before.'

'Would you like me to ring them back with a counter-offer?'

'You don't think it'll scare them away?' They'd been waiting so long for this viewing, she wasn't sure if she was brave enough to go down the route of counteroffering but five thousand pounds was a heck of a lot of money and could make all the difference to her if she was ever able to buy here.

'I think we can give it a go. They liked the space the flat offered and, as I think I mentioned, they're building a portfolio of rental properties, so the location being so close to the town centre is a big plus for them.' David tapped something against the phone. 'I think it's a gamble worth taking. We'll tell them we can go down two grand and see what happens.'

'Right, okay. I'll go with what you think.' Polly took a deep breath. It was worth a go, wasn't it? They wouldn't just walk away because she'd asked for more money, if they wanted the flat enough to put an offer in, they wouldn't want to lose it even if Polly had to agree to the lower offer after all.

'They seem quite eager to get this wrapped up, so I'll give them a call and ring you straight back.' Without waiting for Polly to confirm, David ended the call.

Pulling her mobile away from her ear, Polly looked at the blank screen. How long would it take? She might be waiting hours, days even, for an answer. Walking across to the large glass doors, she pushed them open and stepped outside. Pulling the sleeves of her sweatshirt over her hands, she breathed in the fresh crisp air before watching as her breath turned to an icy cloud as she exhaled. She loved autumn days like this, when the fragrance of rain and foliage hung in the air but the sun peeked between clouds promising a clear day ahead.

She should probably go back into the office. There was definitely enough work to be getting on with, but there was no chance she'd be able to concentrate. Not right now. She'd leave it for a few minutes, take a quick walk and clear her head before going back.

Turning, Polly walked across the narrow bridge and into the reserve. A couple of gulls dived and skidded across the water of the lake, causing a stir amongst the ducks who were swimming serenely towards the small island in the middle of the water.

Just as she stepped down from the bridge and joined the gravel pathway which wound its way around the reserve, her mobile rang again. She frowned. It was David. That was quick. Answering it, she lifted it to her ear. 'They weren't in?'

'They were and they accepted our counter-offer. You've got a sale! They've agreed on the new price.' David's voice was triumphant.

'Wow. They're buying the flat? It's really sold?' The questions tumbled from her mouth.

David's loud chuckle sounded down the phone. 'Yes, it's sold, Miss Burrows. And the best thing is, they're eager for a quick sale.'

A quick sale? It was really sold. 'Thank you, David.'

'My pleasure. I'll get things moving my end and be in touch shortly. Speak soon.'

'Bye,' Polly whispered into the quiet phone. That was it. All done.

Walking across to the bench by the side of the path, she sank onto the cold wood. Her grandparents' flat was sold. Shortly, it would no longer be hers. Everything her grandparents had worked hard for, all the love they'd put into their home, it would soon belong to someone else. Their memories, their ties with the flat, would be extinguished.

She stared at the ducks as they glided across the surface of the water, dipping their beaks below the surface every so often. She wouldn't be able to go back there. Well, she would, but only to clear it out. She'd no longer have her bolthole, her sanctuary, the place she felt closest to her grandparents.

Leaning her elbows on her knees, Polly covered her eyes with the heels of her hands and pushed, waiting for the stars to appear in the blackness before her vision turned red. This is what she'd wanted. She'd wanted to sell the flat. That had been the end goal. It had been a stepping stone to securing her future here in Meadowfield, her new life, but now David had uttered those words she'd begun to suspect she'd never hear, now he'd told her it was sold, she wasn't sure what to think.

She felt guilty. An immense tug growing in the pit of her stomach. What if she'd done the wrong thing? What if she should have kept the flat? What if she should have lived in it, been happy with her old life? What had she been thinking coming here, taking such a gamble, and at the expense of losing her grandparents' beloved home too?

She felt someone sit down next to her and pulled her hands from her eyes, straightening her back. 'Zac.'

'Hey, are you okay?' Draping her coat around her shoulders, he shuffled closer to her. 'Don't worry. There'll be more people looking for a flat in that area. You never know, someone else might come along tomorrow and put an offer in.'

She smiled weakly at him. 'It's sold. The people who viewed today put an offer in, we countered it and they accepted.'

'Oh wow. Congratulations!' Zac frowned. 'Or not?'

'I don't know.' Slumping back against the hard wood of the bench, Polly gripped the edges of her coat around her. 'I should be celebrating, shouldn't I? Shouting from the rooftops or something, but all I feel like doing is crying.'

'That's understandable.'

'It's not. It's pathetic. I'm the one who put it on the market. I knew what I was doing, so why do I feel like this?' She shrugged. She didn't even understand herself anymore.

Placing his arm around her shoulder, he leaned down and kissed the top of her head. 'It is understandable. It's a big deal. A really big deal. You grew up there, didn't you?'

Leaning against his arm, Polly nodded. 'I did. And I keep reminding myself that my grandma literally told me to sell it and use the money towards a new place. She made me promise to go for my new start, but I still just feel... guilty. I feel as though I shouldn't be doing it. That doesn't make sense, does it?'

'It does. But it's what she wanted. That's worth remembering.'

Dragging the back of her hand across her face, she dried the tears. 'I know. I know I need to remember that. It's just...'

'You feel as though you're closing the door on that part of your life? On the memories of them?' Zac pulled her closer.

Polly nodded. That was just it. That's exactly how she felt. She so desperately wanted this fresh start, the chance to follow her own dreams and make the changes in her life she'd longed for, but now it was about to become a reality. She wasn't quite sure she was ready to let go. 'Yes, exactly that.'

'Growing up, I used to spend a lot of my time at my grandparents' house. My parents were often away for weeks at a stretch, on business or going to this charity event or that, so I'd go to my grandparents'. I had my own room there and, to be quite honest, I often felt more wanted, more nurtured by them than my own parents. When my grandpa passed away, their house was sold, and my gran moved into an annexe at my parents' place.'

Twisting in his embrace, she looked at him. There was so much she hadn't known about him. 'So you understand then?'

'Yep, I do. To a point, anyway. Even though it was me dealing with it all – the estate agents, the solicitors and then the builders at my parents' place – the driving force behind the sale of my grandparents' home was my dad.' Settling back against the bench, he took her hand in his free one. 'So, I understand, to a degree. It was just after I'd quit my job in the city, but if I'd had the money, I'd have snapped up their house.'

'So, you think I should pull out of the sale?' Polly watched as another duck swam furtively towards the small group she'd been watching.

'Nope. That's not what I think. If I'd had the money, I would have brought my grandparents' house, and I'd have lived in it, quite happy surrounded by the memories of my childhood and the time I had with my grandparents.' He smiled at the memories.

'But you said you think I should sell?' Polly frowned. What did he mean?

'Yes, if I'd bought the house, then I'd have been surrounded my grandparents' things, but I'd also have been...' He shifted a little on the bench. 'Stuck, I guess the word is. I'd never have wanted to get rid of it, to sell it on and I think that would have ended up limiting what I felt I could do and that's not what my grandparents would have wanted.'

'I see.' She nodded. She thought she understood. 'So, you're glad you weren't in a position to buy it?'

'Yes, I think so. It took me a while to come to that realisation though. To begin with I just felt anger towards my dad for forcing the sale. Of course, I wasn't aware of just how much trouble his business was in at the time, which is why I couldn't understand why he just didn't keep it, rent it out to me, maybe.'

Polly felt his shoulder shrug beneath her cheek and waited until he continued.

'I have all the memories I could ever need up here.' He lifted the hand he was holding hers with, drawing both their hands to his head before lowering them again. 'I've come to realise I don't need the physical stuff to remember them by and to remember the times we shared whilst I was growing up. No one can take those away from me.'

'That makes sense.' Polly sighed heavily. 'Deep down, I know it's the right thing to do and so I guess I've just got to get through it.'

'Unfortunately, yes. Any change is difficult, even more so than when a loved one has passed and you're faced with making decisions like this, but your grandparents' hard work and the hours they spent decorating and making their flat a home, they did that for you. And this, selling it, it's not getting rid of all of their efforts, they wanted their life's work to do good for you, they wanted to make a difference to your life, and this is what the money you'll get from the sale will do.'

Polly laced her fingers through his. 'So, I just need to remember that their work still goes on. It's still making a difference to me?'

'Exactly. Try not to feel guilty for selling the flat, because ultimately that's what they wanted. They wanted you to go on and live your life.'

Polly smiled. Her grandma had said those exact words. She'd made her promise to sell. 'Thank you. I needed to be reminded of that.'

'So, how do you fancy going out for dinner to celebrate? The sale of your flat and the success of your leaflet idea.'

'I'd like that.' Polly slapped her forehead. 'Although I need to go and buy those raffle prizes.'

Zac chuckled. 'Right, shopping first, dinner after?'

'Sounds perfect.' Leaning back into his arm, Polly closed her eyes. She listened to the clucking of the ducks on the water and the crunch of fallen leaves as someone ambled past. The flat was sold, and that was a good thing. It really was.

29

'How about this one?' Zac called across the aisle of the toy shop as he threw something towards her.

Polly screeched as she caught the large, hairy stuffed spider toy. 'Jeez, for a moment I literally thought that was real!'

Placing his hands on his knees, Zac let out a belly laugh. 'Your face was priceless!'

'Haha, thanks so much!' Polly tried her best to keep her voice serious before her own laughter broke through her scowl. 'You know what, I think this one might actually be a good shout. It looks pretty realistic, which the kids will probably love.'

'As realistic as a thirty-centimetre fluffy spider can look, you mean?' He chuckled.

Holding it up, she stared back at the eight large eyes looking at her. 'I think I'd run a mile or burn the place down if I found a real one of these.'

'Nah, I'd protect you.' Walking across to her, he took the spider from her before putting it into the trolley he was pushing.

'I believe you, thousands wouldn't.' She grinned as she watched him continue to the next shelf and pick up toy after toy, inspecting them. They'd come straight from the office and after hurrying to the local shopping precinct only to find the toy shop had closed down months ago, they'd driven past a retail park with one of those giant supermarket-sized toy shops and forty-five minutes later they had chosen the majority of the toys they'd need for the raffle. 'I remember one of your first days working at the trust when you screamed because you'd found a spider's nest by your desk.'

'Oh, I'm sure I wouldn't have screamed.' Zac grimaced.

'Haha, it was definitely a scream.'

'Wasn't it more like a tiny, terrified exclamation?' Zac paused in front of her, turning so his back was against the trolley, his lips twitching as he tried not to laugh.

She grinned. 'You can call it that if you like. Yes, a terrified exclamation, but not tiny. It was loud. In fact, I wouldn't be surprised if Mr Bob almost called the police.'

'Okay, a terrified exclamation it is then.' Chuckling, he wrapped his arms around her, pulling her closer. 'Is that when you first realised you wanted to get into a relationship with me?'

'Haha, nice try. It was when I realised how much fun it would be to hide a plastic spider in your drawer.' Polly laughed at the memory. She'd spent almost an hour searching through the nursery classroom at school for a plastic toy spider after teaching one day, but it had been worth it. His reaction had been almost as priceless as his reaction to the spider's nest.

Dropping his arms, he covered his mouth with one hand. 'That was you?'

'It was.' She nodded.

'I blamed Mr Bob for that. For almost two years I blamed him.' Shaking his head, Zac grinned. 'Wow, my respect for you has just multiplied by a million or so.'

'You forgive me, then?' Batting her eyelids, she tilted her head.

'Umm, let me see.' Tapping his cheek with his forefinger as he walked backwards, pulling the trolley along, Zac looked at her. 'Perhaps I will, if you play your cards right.'

'And what might that look like?' Stepping towards him, she took his hand in hers as she tried to keep her tone serious.

He lowered his voice, talking softly, the laughter and fun of a few seconds ago dissipating. 'You forgive me for acting like a complete eejit and making the worst mistake of my life by pushing you away?'

Scrunching up her nose, Polly nodded. 'I've already forgiven you.'

'Then let's call it a truce.'

'A truce it is, then.' Polly leaned forward and kissed him before spotting a large soft toy squirrel on the shelf behind him. Stepping away, she pointed. 'Look, a super-sized Nutkin! How perfect will that be for the main raffle prize?'

'Now, Vicki will love that.' Zac turned.

'She definitely will.' Picking up the large stuffed squirrel, Polly laughed as the bushy tail tickled her nose. 'This will be our main attraction at the raffle.'

Zac began pushing the trolley again. 'Time for some dinner?'

'Yes please, I'm starving. I think I still need to make up for all the calories I used up painting over the weekend.' Pushing the other toys to one end of the trolley, Polly sat the squirrel down, facing Zac.

'At least it was worth it. The viewing went well.'

'Absolutely. I think I'd have cried if it didn't.' Pulling her hair over one shoulder, Polly ran her nails over the blobs of paint in her hair. 'I'm still covered in the stuff.'

'You still look beautiful. Paint or no paint.' Zac grinned before raking his fingers through his own hair. 'I think I got splattered too, but then again, I might just be greying.'

Shaking her head, Polly stood on her tiptoes to take a look. 'Umm, maybe a mixture.'

'Oi!' Turning to her, he tickled her under the arm.

Flinging her arms down to her sides, Polly pursed her lips, trying her best not to screech as a parent and toddler walked by. 'Nope, nope, nope. Don't you dare tickle me, not unless you want me to go round the reserve tomorrow and find a real spider to stick in your drawer.'

'Haha, fair enough.' Smiling, Zac led the way to the cashier and joined the small queue. 'Everything's sorted for Bonfire Night, then?'

'Yes, I think so.' She began counting on her fingers. 'The leaflets will be ready to pick up on Thursday, the raffle tickets will be delivered tomorrow, Helena and Jarvis have secured the food truck and now we have these.'

'Great. You'll have nothing to do but sit and relax for the rest of the week until your first event, then.' Zac began placing the soft toys on the conveyor belt. 'You've done great with this. I'd never have even thought to use a village event like this to raise awareness of the reserve and to raise some money, too.'

'Ah, I know it won't raise much. I mean, the sales from the food truck have to cover the product costs, the hire as well as Helena and Jarvis' overtime, so I'm guessing we'll break even at worst, or else make a small profit at best, but

I'm hopeful the raffle will raise something. I mean, everyone loves a raffle, don't they?'

The young boy standing in line in front of them tugged his mum's hand before pointing behind them towards the toys. 'Mum, look at how cool that spider is.'

'Wow, it is, isn't it?' The mum smiled and mouthed at Polly, 'It looks very realistic.'

'We're from Meadowfield Nature Reserve and if you're coming to the Bonfire Night celebrations at the school, we'll be giving this scary spider' – Polly raised her eyebrows at Zac – 'and the other toys away in a raffle.'

'Aw, can we go, Mum? Can we?' The boy looked up at his mum.

'We certainly can.' The mum ruffled her son's hair as they were called to be served.

'That's one definite customer, then.' Zac leaned in closer as he spoke.

'Yep.' Polly took a deep breath. Now everything was planned, the nerves over whether this would work were beginning to creep in. From what Jill had said, there'd be lots of stalls, mostly craft stalls and the like, so theirs might be easily overlooked. And as for food trucks, well, if she'd learned anything about events like this, then there would likely be an abundance of those. If Helena and Jarvis lost money...

'Evening, folks. Wow, someone likes our cuddly wildlife selection.' The cashier smiled at them as she began scanning the toys.

'Haha, they're prizes for a raffle in aid of Meadowfield Nature Reserve.' Placing her tote bag on the end of the counter, Polly rummaged inside, looking for her purse with the reserve's payment card inside.

'Ooh, now that's exciting. It's not for Jill's Bonfire Night celebration she's organising, is it?' The woman tucked her hair behind her ears as she totalled up. 'Of course, I know it's not just Jill on the Community Hub team, but, hey, everyone knows she's the driving force behind the Meadowfield events.'

Pulling the card out, Polly smiled. 'Yes, it is. We've got a stall and a food truck too.'

The woman nodded. 'Fantastic. It'll be a great place to drum up awareness of the reserve.'

'I'm hoping so. Do you go to the reserve a lot?'

'I sure do. Me and my dog, Pebbles, absolutely love it up there. It's always so quiet, though, and I often think it's quite sad people seem to forget about the place. After all, it's right on their doorstep, if not a short car journey away.' The woman held out her hand. 'I'm Freda. I live in Meadowfield and I can see you work at the reserve?' She pointed to the embroidered motif on Polly's sweatshirt peeking out from under her open coat.

'Hi, Freda. It's lovely to meet you and great to know you utilise the reserve.' Polly turned to Zac. 'This is Zac. He works there too.'

'Fantastic.' Freda shook Zac's hand, too. 'Well, I'll be sure to come along to your stall at the weekend.'

'Thanks.' After tapping the card against the machine, Polly began to bundle the teddies into her arms.

'Do you want a bag for those?' Freda began pulling a large paper bag from beneath the till.

'No, we're good. Thanks though.' Poking her face through the mound of teddies, Polly said her goodbyes before following Zac, who was carrying the enormous squirrel back to his car. Well, that was two confirmed customers they'd have at the stall at least.

30

'Two pie and mash.' Jackson lowered the plates onto the pub table in front of them. 'It's good to see you both in here.'

'Thanks. We thought we'd best check out the local.' Zac grinned as he pulled his plate towards him. 'No rest for the wicked, hey?'

'Haha, nope. Not that I mind it and I only work a few shifts in here nowadays. What with helping Laura with the inn, too.' Jackson glanced behind him and lowered his voice. 'Besides, I'm pretty sure the Community Hub is meeting there this evening, and knowing them, they'll be there for hours, so I'm safer here, where Miss Cooke can't rope me into all sorts for the good of the village.'

Polly laughed.

'Not that I mind it usually. I've moved around a fair bit, as I used to do a spot of property developing, you know, buying somewhere run-down, refurbishing it and selling it on again, and I've got to say, Meadowfield is the only place I'm happy settling in.' Jackson smiled. 'Of course it helps that Laura moved here too.'

'I hear wedding plans are being made?' Zac took a forkful of mash.

'They are, mate, yes.' Jackson crossed his arms, the tea towel he was carrying hanging from his hand. 'I'm hopeful we'll get it organised for next spring or summer at the latest. No need to wait, is there? Not when you find the right one?'

'Wow, that's not long to get everything organised.' Polly raised her eyebrows. Had Laura mentioned to her that the wedding would be so soon?

'It's not, but I think we'll be having the reception at Pennycress, so at least we won't have to worry about booking the venue.' Jackson chuckled. 'And anything else, well, Nicola and Jill are star organisers, so I'm sure with a little help we'll get everything covered. Hopefully.'

'That's true.' Polly nodded.

'Right, well, I'll let you two eat in peace. Just shout if you need anything.' Jackson turned and headed back to the bar.

Picking up her fork, Polly stabbed at the mash. It looked delicious, but she couldn't help but wonder how Zac's funding plans were coming along. They'd both been so focused on the Bonfire Night event, even during the day at the office, and although she'd seen him on the phone a few times, he'd not spoken about his work.

'Everything okay?' Zac shovelled another forkful of mash into his mouth before pointing at it. 'This is the best mash I've tasted in a very long time.'

'It is nice.' Taking a small mouthful, Polly swallowed. 'Umm, I was just going to ask how your fundraising was going? You've done a lot to help with the Bonfire Night event and I've not really asked you.'

Zac shrugged. 'Oh, it's going okay, thanks. I had confirmation back from the company I used to work for that they're willing to sponsor the reserve.'

Placing her fork back on her plate, Polly reached across the table and laid her hand on his forearm. 'That's fantastic news! Congratulations for sealing that deal!'

'Thanks.' Zac mumbled as he shifted in his seat.

Frowning, Polly picked up her cutlery again. 'Zac?'

Lowering his fork, Zac met her gaze. 'Yes?'

'I don't want this promotion to become something weird between us. We should be able to celebrate each other's wins. You suggested having dinner to celebrate the sale of my grandparents' flat and getting organised for the Bonfire Night, but we should be celebrating your wins too.'

Zac gave a short smile. 'What I've done is nothing. I got in touch with a few contacts with a sponsorship proposal, that's all. What you've done, coming up with these ideas to raise awareness of the reserve and to raise money, it's much more.'

Polly shook her head slowly. She wouldn't have had the first clue how to approach companies to ask for sponsorship deals, let alone what to write in a proposal to entice them or how to draw up contracts. 'No, it's not. What you're doing for the reserve is amazing, and the amount of money you raise will make a huge difference to what we can offer our visitors and the rewilding projects we'll be able to invest in.'

Tilting his head from side to side, Zac sighed. 'Maybe, but what you're doing will make a difference to the lives of people who begin coming to the reserve, as well as make sure there are funds in place long term.'

Reaching across the table again, Polly held her hand up, waiting until he'd taken her hand in his before carrying on. What she wanted to say was important, and she wanted him to realise it too. 'Zac, I really don't want this promotion to come between us. I know it's super early days and either one of us could walk away tomorrow...'

'I hope not.' Zac gave her hand a squeeze. 'We may have only just got together officially, but we've both felt this, certainly since the night of your leaving party. Or I know I have.'

'I have too.' And before. 'Which is why I want to make sure we talk about it, that we can celebrate each other's wins.'

'Okay.' Zac nodded.

'So, no more talking down your own achievements?'

'I won't. I promise.' Zac ran his palm across his face. 'It's just difficult, isn't it? It feels so wrong to compete with you.'

'But we're not.' Polly moved the salt shaker an inch. 'Not really. I mean, I know only one of us will be put forward for the promotion, but what we're doing at work, what we're doing for the reserve, we'd be doing even if there wasn't a promotion available. We'd be doing our best for the reserve and the animals and nature there, wouldn't we?'

'Yes, you're right. We would be.'

'So, we don't need to feel guilty about our own wins.' Polly hoped it had come across as a statement rather than a question because, she, for one, knew she felt guilty. Yes, she wanted the promotion, she needed the money, but so did Zac and she could see how much it meant to him too. They were in an impossible situation and the only way through she could think of was to pretend as though it wasn't happening and that meant cheering each other on just as they would be if the promotion didn't exist.

'Hey, Declan might choose someone from outside the team, anyway.' Zac raised his eyebrows. 'So there's literally no reason for us to be tying ourselves up in knots, feeling happy for each other when things go right, but feeling guilty when we get the win.'

'Ha, true.' She smiled. He was right. All of this might be for nothing, anyway. She swallowed. She wasn't sure what that would mean for her and her future here in Meadowfield, but at least it meant Zac wasn't her only competition and she could hopefully push the promotion to the back of her mind when she was with him and focus on their fledgling romance instead. 'No more thinking about the promotion, then?'

'No more thinking about the promotion.' Picking up his glass, he held it up towards her. 'Here's to focusing on us.'

'To us.' Taking her own glass, she clinked it against his and grinned, suddenly feeling a little lighter.

31

'Zac, what do you think of these for the new display in the foyer?' Wheeling her chair across to Zac's desk, Polly placed her laptop on his desk.

'The information boards?' Zac began scrolling through the photographs on the screen.

'Yes. I found them in the trust's archives and thought they might be a good focus. I was trying to find the most interesting examples of how the reserve has changed and big events here.' She'd spent the last two days trawling through photographs and articles about the reserve, struggling to find anything much to write about. That was until she discovered a huge fire had taken hold in the visitor centre fifteen years ago and destroyed much of the natural habitat around the building. Not that anybody would realise if they visited now, as the ranger and team had done an amazing job of bringing the reserve back to life.

'Well, these are certainly interesting, for sure. I wasn't aware of half these things – the fire, the rewilding scheme of native trees, the fact the Queen had visited.' Zac widened his eyes. 'I think they're fab. I can't wait to read what you write about them.'

'You definitely don't think these topics will bore visitors?' Polly chewed on her bottom lip. This was her chance – *their* chance – to help the reserve come alive to the visitors, their chance to instil pride in the local community, and she really didn't want to mess it up. 'I know not everyone who comes in here will read them, but I'm just hoping a few will glance at the photos and want to find out a little more.'

Zac smiled. 'I think they're great. Really great. You've definitely got an eye for this, and I think the majority of people will want to read more.'

'I hope so.' Taking her laptop back, Polly closed the screen but stayed where she was. 'How about you? How are you getting on?'

'Good, thanks.' He shrugged. 'Well, okay anyway. I had two "thanks but no thanks" this morning but have set up a telephone conversation tomorrow with another firm. I used to work closely with them when I was in my marketing job, so I'm hopeful.'

Polly crossed her fingers. 'That's great. You'll get it.'

'I hope so.' Zac nodded.

Leaning forward, Polly kissed him before pulling back quickly and glancing around the office, relieved to see that everyone else had their heads buried in their laptops. 'Sorry, I completely forgot where I was then.'

Grinning, Zac raised his eyebrows. 'No need to apologise to me. I'd be happy to shout it from the rooftops.'

Smiling, Polly tapped her laptop. 'Best get back to it.'

After wheeling her chair back, Polly opened her laptop again, pretending to concentrate on the screen in front of her whilst she glanced at Zac. Maybe she was being paranoid. Perhaps there wasn't any reason their relationship would be frowned upon by their colleagues. Besides, they were working and basically living together, being as they were both staying at Pennycress, so spending their whole time together, there were bound to be more slip-ups like that one. It was only a matter of time before one of their teammates found out.

'No, no, no.' Wheeling her chair back from her desk, Vicki began pushing her collection of photo frames to the side of her desk.

'Everything okay?' Art called across the office.

'No, I can't find Rolo. He was here, literally just sleeping in my sleeve as he always does, and now, I can't find him.' Vicki dropped to her knees and crawled under her desk.

'Don't worry, we'll find him. He can't have got out.' Polly glanced behind her, checking he wasn't behind her chair, before pushing it back and standing up.

'Dennis and Declan went out a few minutes ago, though, and I don't know when he went missing.' Vicki scraped her dark hair back into a ponytail before crawling around the floor.

'I'll go outside and see if he's in the foyer. He'll be scared if he's got out and I'm sure he won't have got far.' Zac stood up and headed for the door, cautiously pulling it open and slipping through.

Slowly walking around the edge of the room, Polly ducked her head to look beneath the desks and bookcases. Rolo could be anywhere. Literally. He was fast, super-fast, and he could climb too.

'I can't believe I let this happen.' Vicki placed her hands over her face. 'They trust me at the sanctuary and now I've gone and let them down, but, more importantly, I've put a defenceless baby in danger.'

Making her way across to Vicki as Art continued searching the office, Polly knelt down and wrapped her arms around her colleague. 'Hey, you've let no one down. What you do for those animals is amazing. This is just a glitch and something we'll all be laughing about in a few minutes when he's found.'

'But he's so fast. And sneaky too. I caught him on top of one of my kitchen cupboards yesterday evening after I'd let him out of his enclosure for a little runaround. I thought he'd be safe in there and now, now I've not even learned from that mistake. I've let it happen again. I can't be trusted.'

'You can. You can be trusted more than any of us here.' Polly rubbed Vicki's back.

'She's right. Can you imagine how long Dennis would last looking after a baby rat?' Art chuckled as he ran his hand over the tops of the books on the shelves. 'He'd have lost Rolo in a day, and I wouldn't have done much better.'

'Nor me. You're doing a fab job with him, with all the animals you care for, and it's only a matter of time before we find him.' Polly leaned back as Vicki wiped her sleeve across her eyes.

'Okay, okay, let's find him.' Standing up, Vicki began searching again.

Polly walked across to the meeting room door, slipping through it before looking beneath the table and chairs and behind the small refreshment table. There was no sign of the small furry creature.

Heading back into the office, Polly was careful to keep her eyes on the floor as she shut the door. The last thing they needed was for them to think the meeting room had been searched and then Rolo to have sneaked in as she walked out. She glanced around the office. Both Vicki and Art were still searching, one either side as they made their way methodically down the room. 'I'll go and help Zac out in the foyer.'

'Thanks,' Vicki called as she scrambled across the floor, running her hand beneath the photocopier.

Making her way into the foyer, Polly closed the office door quietly behind her and watched as Zac looked beneath the benches on either side of the large foyer. 'Any luck?'

'Not a sign.' Shaking his head, Zac stood up and walked towards the glass doors leading outside.

'Do you think he may have got out into the reserve?' Polly joined him, watching as rain lashed against the window. If Rolo had ventured outside for the first time today, he'd have been petrified at the vastness and at the weather too. He'd had an easy life growing up with Vicki caring for him and he wasn't anywhere near being ready to be released.

'I hope not.' Zac shook his head. Then a screech from Vicki filled the room. 'Let's hope that means she's found him.'

Polly nodded as they both made their way back to the office, Zac holding the door open for her. 'Thanks. Have you found him, Vicki?'

'Yes, he's here. Art found him nibbling at the bag of sugar on the work surface.' Grinning, Vicki held the small rat aloft before tucking him in her sleeve. 'I'm going to have to make him an enclosure here from now on. I don't think I can cope with this stress every day.'

'That's a good idea. I'm sure we can find something to use. In fact, I'm sure I saw an old fish tank in the classroom when we were shown around?' Zac glanced towards the door.

'Ah yes! That would be perfect! Thank you. I'll go and grab that.' Vicki began walking towards the door.

'I'll help.' After letting the bag of sugar drop into the bin, Art joined her.

'Oh actually. Could one of you look after him for me? It's probably not a great idea taking him into the classroom after the stunt he's just pulled.' Vicki grimaced as she turned back towards Polly and Zac.

'I'll take him.' Holding his hands out, Zac waited until Rolo had scurried out from Vicki's sleeve and into Zac's cupped hands before he gently closed them.

'Thank you, Zac. You're a star.' Vicki jogged across to where Art was standing in the open doorway. 'We'll be quick, I promise.'

Sitting back down, Polly watched as Zac took his seat again and held open the sleeve of his sweatshirt for Rolo, who immediately ran up and curled up in the crook of his arm. 'Aw, he likes you. He feels safe.'

'You think? Or maybe he's just tired after all the excitement and chaos.' Zac grinned.

'No, he definitely likes you. He wouldn't have gone straight to sleep if he didn't feel comfortable.' Polly leaned across and touched Zac on the arm. The last few days had been perfect, a mixture of working at the reserve, going out for dinner and generally spending as much time together as they could. They were definitely making up for lost time.

'You look deep in thought.' Zac smiled as he settled back against his chair, careful not to bend his arm or disturb Rolo.

'I'm just thinking about how everything's turned out. When I saw you here on our first day, I've got to admit I didn't relish the thought of working with you...'

'Charming!'

'No, you know what I mean. Things were... odd between us.' Polly glanced out of the large window in front of them as Harold strode through the rain with his hood down, as though he hadn't even noticed how bad the weather was today. 'You know, since the kiss. And I just never thought we'd be in this position.'

'You mean in a relationship?' He looked across at her, his lips twitching into a smile.

'Yes, exactly.' She nodded.

'I did. Or, what I mean is, I hoped we would be some day.' Zac stroked Rolo through the fabric of his sweatshirt as the little animal squirmed in his sleep. 'I hoped we'd be able to get to the point we're at today, although I wasn't sure how, seeing as I'd gone about this whole job thing the wrong way and the fact I'd kept you at arm's length because I just couldn't see what else to do.'

'I know.' Polly leaned back in her chair and picked up her cold coffee from earlier, taking a sip. 'If Nicola hadn't basically strong-armed you into giving me a lift back to Featherford, do you think things would be like they are now?'

Zac shook his head. 'Honestly? I'm not sure I'd have let you in, told you what was going on in my life.'

Polly smiled. 'In that case, and I never thought I'd ever say this, but I'm glad my flat got broken into and you came round to check on me.'

'Me too. Although I think something a little less extreme than a home break-in would have done the trick. I'd have probably caved and admitted my feelings on the car journey back, anyway.'

'Oh, I assumed you wouldn't have given me a lift back.'

'Of course I would have. Well, I'd have offered anyway, whether you'd have accepted or not is another matter, I'm guessing?'

Polly laughed. 'I'm not sure. I think I would have, although after the journey down there and my lame attempt to clear the air, I think I might well have walked back to avoid another conversation like that.'

'Haha, I don't blame you.' Zac held his breath as his mobile rang, vibrating across his desk. Keeping his eyes fixed on the small bump beneath his sleeve, he quickly picked it up, silencing it before bringing it to his ear and speaking quietly.

Standing up, Polly picked up her mug before grabbing Zac's and heading into the small kitchen area in order to give him some privacy. Switching the kettle on, she leaned against the counter and grinned. Since their conversation in the pub, she'd even managed to put the worry of the looming promotion out of her mind. She knew how she felt about Zac was an accumulation of her feelings towards him as they'd worked together over the years, and she knew she could feel comfortable with him. She could be herself and she didn't have to prove anything to him. He'd said he'd had feelings for her since before the kiss and she certainly hadn't been trying to be anything other than herself back then.

Yes, that was what was special about what they had, and probably why they'd slipped so easily into this relationship, too.

She shook her head. No, it hadn't been easy, but now they'd both spoken about things, spoken about the past few months and cleared the air. It was easy now. And she couldn't wait to see what lay ahead for them together.

Turning back to the kettle as it boiled, she picked it up and filled their mugs. They'd planned on the cinema after work. A film and then a few drinks and she was looking forward to being able to relax before the Bonfire Night celebration. Not that she wasn't looking forward to it, she was, but she couldn't help feeling nervous too. She didn't want to mess up the first event she'd organised.

'Polly.'

Replacing the kettle, she glanced over her shoulder before turning around.

Standing in the doorway, Zac shifted on his feet, his face ashen. 'What's happened? Are you okay?'

Zac shook his head. 'I have to go. My gran's had a fall at the nursing home and been rushed to hospital.'

'Oh no.' Dashing towards him, she threw her arms around him, before hurrying towards her desk and grabbing her and Zac's coats. 'I'll come with you, you can't be driving there on your own.'

'Thanks.' Zac carefully shook his sleeve until little Rolo slid down his arm to his hand.

Passing Zac his coat, Polly took Rolo in her hands just as the door to the office was swung open and Vicki and Art shuffled in, carrying the large glass fish tank between them as they laughed and joked about who was doing all the heavy lifting.

Stopping in the middle of the room, Vicki frowned. 'Is everything okay?'

As Zac stood there distractedly, running his palm over his face, Polly walked across and waited until Vicki and Art had lowered the fish tank to the floor before passing Vicki little Rolo. 'Zac has a family emergency and I'm going to go with him to the hospital. Can you let Declan know we'll be back as soon as possible, please?'

'Of course.' Taking Rolo, Vicki looked across at Zac in concern. 'I hope everything's okay.'

'Yes, take care, mate.' Art retraced his steps and held the door open for them.

'Thanks.' Taking Zac's arm, Polly led the way outside. It was times like this that she wished she hadn't given up on learning to drive, but at least she could be with him. She remembered how much it had meant to her having Stacey by her side when her grandma had been at her worst; if she could give Zac half the support Stacey had given her, it would be something.

32

Hurrying down the hospital corridor, Polly tried to match Zac's long strides, keeping her eyes focused on him in an attempt to block out the familiar smell of disinfectant and sickness. Just stepping back inside the hospital was bringing back memories of the last time she'd seen her grandma. Shoving her hands in her pockets, she tried to suppress the memories. She was here to support Zac, and that's what she'd do. She wouldn't allow the past to consume her.

Zac pushed open the door to the ward his parents had told him his gran had been taken to and came to a stop by the nurses' station.

Coming up a few steps behind him, Polly paused next to him as the nurse indicated the family room to their left.

'Thank you.' Nodding, Zac turned and walked across to the family room before waiting at the door. 'Polly, my parents will be in here. Are you sure you want to stay? I wouldn't blame you if you didn't.'

Reaching out, she pushed the tuft of hair from the middle of his forehead before cupping his cheek with her hand. 'I'm here for you, Zac. I'm going to stay.'

'Thank you.' His expression suddenly relaxing a little, Zac nodded before pushing open the door.

Taking a deep breath, Polly followed him inside. An older couple, presumably his parents, were the only ones in the family room, and as they entered, his mum stood up and hurried across to Zac before giving him a quick hug, whilst his dad remained on the chair in the corner, one leg crossed over the other whilst a newspaper lay open on his lap.

'So glad you could come, Zachary.' His mum glanced across at Polly. 'Are you two together?'

'Yes, she came with me.' Zac cleared his throat. 'Mum, this is Polly. Polly, this is my mum, Miranda.'

'Hi.' Holding her hand up in acknowledgement, Polly noticed his dad glance up briefly from his paper.

'Lovely to meet you, dear. I'm so pleased Zachary has someone to support him at such a difficult time.' Miranda sat back down, lifting her handbag from the floor and perching it on her lap.

'Nice to meet you too.' Polly spoke quietly, darting her eyes towards Zac's dad, who made no move to greet her.

'Dad, this is Polly. Polly, my dad, Alan.'

'Hello.' Polly shifted on her feet before following Zac's lead and sitting down next to him on the opposite side of the room to his mum, his dad having not even acknowledged her.

'The nurse said Gran is still being stabilised on the ward. Do you know what happened and have you been told anything else?' Zac looked at his mum.

'She's fine. It was just a tumble.' His dad spoke gruffly, his eyes fixed on his paper.

Polly noticed the muscle in Zac's jaw jump. She'd gathered he didn't have a very good relationship with his dad through the conversations they'd had, but she hadn't expected his dad to be quite so... cold. She reached out her hand and laid it briefly on Zac's arm before pulling away again and clasping her hands in her lap. She wasn't sure what he had told his parents about them, probably nothing being as their relationship was so new, and this wasn't the time or the space to announce they were seeing each other.

'Apparently, she fell as she was going back into her room from the dining hall. The nursing home staff were concerned she'd broken her hip, but the doctors don't think so.' His mum spoke quietly. 'Your dad's right. She'll be fine. A little bruised, but she'll survive.'

'Right.' Letting out a long breath, Zac leaned back in his chair.

Polly swallowed. The relief in his face was clear and he looked a little less broken. Even if he hadn't told her about his childhood, she'd be able to tell how close he was to his gran by his reaction.

'How are things with you, Zachary?' His mum smiled at him.

'Good. A little better now I know Gran will be okay.' He leaned forward, resting his elbows on his knees and clasping his hands between his legs. 'She's getting on okay, though? Apart from the fall? I've not had a chance to visit her since Monday.'

'Yes, she's fine.' His mum nodded and crossed her legs, her handbag still sitting on her knees.

'And how are you, Mum? How are things at home?'

'Fine, all fine. Your father had the estate agents round to take photos today.' Miranda glanced towards her husband. 'He thought it was best. We both did.'

'So soon? I thought you were going to wait a while?' Zac clasped his hands tighter, his knuckles whitening.

'No point in waiting, son. It's this or we move Gran to a cheaper home.' Alan spoke up from the corner.

His mum glanced towards the closed door as if she were worried Zac's gran might be able to hear them talking.

Zac shook his head, his voice coming out as a croak. 'We can't move her. She loves it there. She's settled. But the house…?'

'We just need to get things moving. Just in case…' Miranda's voice trailed off.

Shaking out his newspaper, Alan's voice was clipped. 'It won't come to that if you get the promotion, son.'

Polly gulped. The promotion. She'd known Zac had worked towards the promotion to help his family, but she hadn't realised it was this extreme – he got the promotion, or his parents lost the house and his gran risked her place at the nursing home. She tugged at the collar of her sweatshirt, the room suddenly feeling stiflingly hot.

Zac glanced across at her and shook his head slightly before pushing his hands against his knees and standing. 'We'll get some coffee.'

Standing up, Polly kept her eyes fixed to the floor as she followed Zac out of the room, thankful for the distraction and the opportunity to see if he was holding up okay under the scrutiny of his father. As soon as the door closed behind them, she slipped her hand in his. His skin was clammy against hers. He wasn't okay.

Squeezing her hand gently to let her know he was thankful she was there, he led them down the corridor towards a coffee machine by the nurses' station. Letting go of her hand, he turned to face her. 'I'm so sorry about that. I've not told them I'm guaranteed the promotion or anything. I don't want you to think I assume it's mine. I know you have every chance of getting it. Jeez, you deserve it.'

'Hey, don't worry. That's not what I thought.' No, the only thing she'd thought when his dad had said what he had was that he was putting too much pressure on his son, that he was taking him for granted. 'I'm glad your gran is going to be okay.'

'Yes, me too.' He rubbed the back of his neck. 'It gets me every time. Every time I get a call from the hospital or the home, I think the worst.'

Taking his hands in hers, she nodded. 'I know.'

Zac looked around the ward. 'I'm sorry, this must be so difficult for you to come in here. I mean, I'm assuming this is where...'

Cutting him off before he could finish the sentence, Polly spoke quickly. She needed to drive the conversation away from her. She couldn't think about the last time she'd been in here, not now, she just couldn't. 'Let's get that coffee, shall we? I know I'm parched.'

'Yes, good idea.' Nodding slowly, Zac leaned forward and kissed her on the forehead before turning towards the machine.

Polly smiled sadly. He realised she couldn't talk about it now. But she knew she'd have walked across burning coals to be with him today, to support him. Glancing away, she pinched the bridge of her nose, forcing herself not to let the tears run. As she watched him take cup after cup from the machine and place them on the small table next to it, she felt her stomach flip. She was falling for him.

33

The tick of the cheap white clock on the wall was the only sound filling the small family room as the four of them sat sipping their scalding-hot coffees from the plastic cups. Polly glanced across at Zac's dad as he still sat reading his paper, every so often placing his cup down on the window ledge and turning the pages dramatically. Why couldn't he see Zac for who he was? For the kind, caring man he'd raised? It seemed as though he couldn't even give his son the time of day.

She dipped her head and looked at the white scum floating on the surface of her coffee where the milk powder hadn't fully dissolved. She knew why, because he hadn't raised him. From the little Zac had told her, it had been his grandparents who had cared for him, who had moulded him into the man he was today. Not his parents.

Looking across at Zac now, she caught his eye and gave him a small smile.

Reaching across the gap between their chairs, Zac held his hand open, nodding to her.

Polly looked over at his mum, who seemed engrossed in whatever she was doing on her mobile, and took his hand, feeling herself relax as his skin touched hers and she felt the strength of his fingers interlace with hers.

A short knock on the door sounded before a nurse peered through the door and smiled brightly. 'She's ready for visitors now. Two at a time, please. Who wants to come first?'

Still holding her hand, Zac made to stand up before leaning back in his chair again as his dad folded his paper slowly and stood up.

'Let Zachary and his friend go first, Alan. They need to get back to work after all.' Miranda smiled at Zac and held her hand out, indicating to the door. 'Go on. Off you go.'

Nodding his thanks, Zac stood up and waited for Polly to join him by the door.

Following him outside, Polly tugged on his sleeve. 'Hey, do you want me to wait outside?'

Looking back at her, Zac shook his head. 'No, I think my gran would like to meet you. If that's okay with you, of course?'

Polly smiled. 'Yes, it is.'

'Just through here. She's in the bed at the end by the window.' The nurse paused and indicated down the ward.

'Thank you.' Taking Polly's hand again, Zac led the way quietly through the aisle between the beds until they reached the end of the row. Giving her hand a quick squeeze, he let go and drew the blue papery curtain aside.

Polly waited by the foot of the bed as Zac hurried towards his gran, leaning down and kissing her cheek. 'You gave me a fright, Gran. How are you feeling?'

'Oh, what a lot of fuss over nothing. I'm fine. Just tripped over my own darn feet, that's all.' His gran shook her head, her white curls bouncing across the stark white pillow as she took his hand.

Polly let out the breath she hadn't realised she'd been holding. She was okay.

'I think it was a little more serious than that, Gran.'

'No, no. I told them not to bother with an ambulance. They blue-lighted me all the way here. Anyone would have thought I was about to pop my clogs the way the paramedics were fussing over me.' His gran chuckled quietly before looking at Polly and tapping her grandson on the hand. 'Aren't you going to introduce your old grandmother to this beautiful young lady?'

'Sorry. This is Polly and, Polly, this is my gran, Maeve.'

Holding her hand up, Polly smiled. 'Hi, Maeve. It's lovely to meet you. Zac's told me a lot about you.'

'Come on here, Polly, love, and say hello properly.' Patting Zac's arm, Maeve batted him away and held her hand out towards Polly.

Tucking her hair behind her ears, Polly approached the bed and took Maeve's hand. 'I'm glad you're okay.'

'Ah, like I say, all a fuss over nothing.' Maeve patted her hand. 'Now, tell me, are you the young lady my grandson has been pining over all these months?'

'Sorry?' Polly frowned before twisting around and searching Zac's expression. What was she saying?

Pulling a face, Zac shrugged.

'Oi, Zac, I saw that. And don't you go pretending you don't know what I'm talking about.' Maeve pointed at her grandson, stabbing her finger in the air. 'Is she the one you've been telling me about?'

Running his hand across his chin, Zac gave a quick nod.

Smiling, Maeve turned her attention back to Polly. 'Well, I'm pleased then. I'm glad my Zachary has someone nice to look after him.'

Polly bit down on her bottom lip as she felt the rush of embarrassment flood her face. He'd been talking about her to his gran? So it was true what he'd said about pushing her away because he hadn't wanted to hurt her.

'And I hope he's taking good care of you, too. If he doesn't, send him my way and I'll sort him out for you.' Maeve glanced at Zac and gave him a nod.

'I will.' Polly laughed.

'I'm being serious, love. I want my Zac to be happy and with happiness comes responsibility. I hope he's been buying you flowers.'

Zac cleared his throat. 'Not yet, Gran. It's kind of early days for us.'

'Don't take that for an answer.' Maeve patted Polly's hand again. 'It's never too early for flowers.'

'I won't.' Polly smiled as Maeve let her hand go and turned back to her grandson.

'I'm proud of this boy, I am. He gave up a job in the city, a big wage, a nice apartment, to work towards his dream in conservation.' Maeve indicated Polly's sweatshirt. 'I can see you're a kind one, too. You work for the same trust as him.'

'I do.' Polly nodded.

'That's good. I knew you were a good'un when Zac began talking about you.' She pointed at them both. 'I have a good feeling about this. I think you'll be as happy as me and my Ned.'

'Gran, we've really not been together long.' Zac turned to Polly and mouthed, sorry.

'Oi, don't you go apologising for me.' Maeve tutted and looked back towards Polly. 'I've not embarrassed you, have I, love? I've not scared you away?'

Polly grinned. She'd done nothing of the sort. She could see where Zac got his kindness from now. 'Not at all.'

Nodding, Maeve clutched the sheets as she shifted further up the pillow. 'Good, because I'm never wrong when I have one of my feelings. Now, go back to work and keep that wildlife safe.'

'Are you sure, Gran?' Zac took Maeve's hand in his. 'Do you need anything before we go? A drink? Magazine?'

'Unless you're offering me a stiff port, I'm fine, thank you. Go on, loves, be off with you and send those parents of yours in.'

Leaning down, Zac kissed his gran on the cheek before walking to the end of the bed and indicating Polly to go ahead.

Polly waved at Maeve before heading through the curtain and towards the door. She smiled as she felt Zac's hand on the small of her back. Turning, she whispered to him, 'She's really lovely.'

Zac grinned. 'She is. Even if she is a bit full on. Sorry about what she said.'

Polly looked at him sidelong and smiled. 'You mean about you talking about me to her?'

Running his fingers through his hair, he dipped his head to the floor as they walked out of the ward. 'Ha, yes, that too.'

'I think it's really sweet. It shows you do actually care.'

Halting in his tracks, Zac turned to face her, waiting until she was looking at him before continuing. 'I care. I really care. In fact, I can feel myself falling for you and I know that sounds daft because of everything that's happened between us, but—'

Polly lifted her finger to his lips, placing the pad of her index finger against his soft skin. 'It's not daft.'

'You mean...?'

'Where is she then?' Zac's dad's voice sounded behind them, and Polly dropped her hand and turned around. Sure enough, Alan was walking towards them, his newspaper tucked beneath his arm as his wife walked beside him, her mobile clutched in one hand whilst she carried her handbag in the other.

'In the bed at the end,' Zac answered before turning to his mum. 'We're going to get back to the office now. You'll let me know if there's any change, won't you?'

'Of course.' Miranda nodded before giving him a quick goodbye hug.

As they continued out of the ward, Polly slipped her hand into his. Now they knew his gran was safe and on the road to recovery, all she wanted to do was to get out of here, out of the hospital and away from Zac's parents who didn't seem to realise just quite how brilliant their son was.

34

'I love this time of the year.' Polly grinned as she looked across the green towards a small coffee shop, which, if the A-frame sign advertising their specials standing proudly on the path below the Victorian-style street lamp was anything to go by, was still open despite the fact it was now early evening. After spending the day working hard in the office, she was glad they'd decided to wander into the centre of Meadowfield. Not only was it a good way to break up the working week, but it also meant spending some alone time with Zac. 'Do you fancy grabbing a drink?'

'Good idea.' Pausing at the edge of the path as a car crawled past, Zac then took her hand as they crossed. 'I honestly think this is my favourite time of the year. It's cooler, the colours are beautiful and, of course, there's Christmas just around the corner.'

'Ah, yes, Christmas.' Polly nodded. If she was honest, she'd not given it a moment's thought. She'd spent last year by her grandma's side... She gripped Zac's hand a little tighter.

After stepping onto the path weaving its way across the green, Zac paused, bringing them to a halt, and turned towards her, concern etched across his face. 'Sorry, I can only imagine how painful last Christmas was.'

Taking a deep breath in, Polly scrunched up her nose. Christmas had been both her grandparents' favourite time of the year and she knew they'd want her to find new traditions and try to enjoy the season again. It would be difficult, but she knew she owed them that much. And after the urgent hospital trip last night, she was only too aware this year would be difficult for Zac too.

Reaching out, Zac tucked his forefinger beneath her chin and gently tilted her head so she was looking at him. 'Sorry, I shouldn't have brought that up.'

Bringing her hand to his, Polly smiled. 'No, it's fine. It will be difficult... different, but Christmas was always such a big celebration in our home and I know I need to carry on my grandparents' love of it.'

'What did you used to do?'

As they began walking again, she felt his arm around her waist, pulling her to his side. 'Ever since I moved in with them, every Christmas Eve, Mr Greene and his wife would host a party. They'd invite everyone from our block of flats and have Christmas music blaring whilst people chatted over mini quiches and trifle. Then, at midnight, my grandad would suddenly look out of the window and declare he'd spotted the glow from Rudolph's nose in the sky as he pulled Santa's sleigh towards us. Of course that had the desired effect and any children present were quickly bundled back home to bed.'

Chuckling, Zac shook his head. 'I can imagine.'

'Yes, and then on the big day itself, I'd wake up to find a stocking on the end of my bed and huge white boot prints leading to more presents under the Christmas tree.' She smiled as she crunched through a pile of fallen leaves, their colours bright beneath the streetlamp. 'The rest of the day would be filled with my grandad getting increasingly frustrated as he tried to put together whatever toy I'd been desperate for that year before the three of us curled up on the sofa and watched back-to-back Christmas movies.'

Pulling her towards him a little more, Zac planted a kiss on the top of her head. 'That sounds perfect.'

'How about you?'

Glancing away, Zac shrugged slightly. 'Christmas Eve and Christmas Day were filled with family dinners and charity events. It was Boxing Day and the day which followed which have always been my favourite. My parents would leave for some engagement or other and drop me round my grandparents' house. Of course, they knew how my parents celebrated, so they'd put on another Christmas especially for me. A traditional Christmas, complete with a stocking, board games and movies. And, of course, chocolate for breakfast the next day.'

Stopping, Polly twisted in his embrace so she was looking at him. 'Maybe we could begin our own traditions this year?'

Zac grinned as he wrapped his other arm around her waist too. 'I'd like that. I bet Jill and the community hub here put on some amazingly Christmassy events.'

'Yes, I bet they do.' Standing on her tiptoes, Polly pecked him on the lips before nodding towards the café as she spotted a woman clearing tables. 'We should probably hurry, they look as though they're beginning to close up for the evening.'

Taking her hand, Zac waited until they'd both turned back towards the café before glancing down and kicking at the leaves beneath his feet. 'Just so you know, I really am glad the last few months are behind us and we can focus on our future.'

Snapping her head towards him, Polly widened her eyes. He'd said 'our future'. Yes, they'd just been speaking about making Christmas plans, but this... What he'd said was something else entirely. The words 'our future' meant he viewed their relationship – however ridiculously new – as something special, as something more. She grinned as she felt the flutter of excitement in the pit of her stomach. He felt the same way she did. After knowing him for over two years, she supposed it was only natural that now they'd finally got together, it wasn't a surprise that they both knew they wanted to be in it for the long haul. Still, to hear him say it was special.

She swallowed. 'Me too.'

* * *

As they made their way through the garden gate towards Pennycress, Polly gripped her takeaway cup in one hand, the comforting cinnamon aroma of the pumpkin spice being carried on the slight crisp breeze, filling her lungs with the signature autumnal fragrance. After he'd closed the wrought-iron gate behind them, she slipped her hand in Zac's again and was grateful as he tucked their clasped hands into the pocket of his coat, the thick fabric warming her skin. She took a sip of her latte as she glanced around them. With the light from the street lamp out on the road and the low hanging moon in the sky illuminating their garden, she grinned. She wanted to remember this evening for the rest of her life. The evening Zac had said he could see a future with her.

After walking up the steps, Zac gently took his hand from hers and pulled open the door, the warmth from inside escaping.

'Thanks.' As soon as the front door had closed behind them, Polly heard Laura's voice call out from the kitchen.

'Polly? Zac? Is that you two?' Appearing in the open doorway, Laura gripped a cake tin between her oven-gloved hands. 'I've just taken an apple and caramel cake out of the oven, would you both like some?'

'Ooh, sounds good. And it smells delicious.' Polly grinned. Dinner suddenly felt like a long time ago and the cake would be a perfect complement to their lattes.

'Great. I must warn you though, it's a bit of an experiment. It's the first time I've made it and although I followed Nicola's mum's recipe to the letter, I can't promise anything.' Laura grimaced. 'So if you have an important meeting tomorrow or something, it's probably best you decline to avoid all risk of food poisoning.'

Shaking his head, Zac chuckled. 'I'm sure it'll be great. Polly's right, it smells good.'

Laughing, Laura turned away again before calling over her shoulder. 'Okay, you have been warned. I'll bring some through.'

Walking across the hallway towards the sitting room, Polly paused. She was sure she could hear voices, and as if to prove she wasn't mistaken, Miss Cooke's voice boomed through the wooden door. She glanced at Zac and frowned. Did they really want to disturb Miss Cooke?

'Oh, sorry I forgot to say...' Laura hurried back into the hallway, the cake tin still in hand, and lowered her voice as she nodded towards the sitting room. 'Miss Cooke called a last-minute community hub meeting. Of course you're more than welcome to go in too, but I thought I should let you know.'

'Thanks. We'll head upstairs, I think.' Zac raised his eyebrows slightly, looking towards Polly for confirmation.

'Yep, definitely.' She nodded. Miss Cooke had been welcoming enough, but she wasn't unaware of the village gossip about Meadowfield's mayoress and she didn't fancy trying their luck and interrupting. Or spending the evening being drawn deep into village discussions.

'Good choice. I'll bring the cake up,' Laura whispered before turning again.

As she followed Zac up the stairs, Polly groaned. 'That's reminded me. I bet their meeting is about the Bonfire Night celebrations and you know what I haven't done yet?'

'What's that?' Pausing on the landing, Zac looked back at her.

'I haven't designed the posters for the stall and food van. I wanted to put some information up, something to show what we were raising money for.' How could she have forgotten? Yes, she could probably get them done tomorrow at work, but she'd already planned her tasks for then.

Zac smiled and shrugged. 'Come on through to mine, we'll pop a movie on and get designing. It'll be fun.'

Breathing out a sigh of relief, Polly grinned. She'd hoped he'd offer to help. The last thing she wanted was for this evening to end prematurely and for her to slink back into her own room, cutting their time together short. And besides, he was right, it wasn't as though they would be filling in spreadsheets or anything, designing posters would hardly feel like work. 'Okay, sounds good.'

'I'll take your drink through whilst you grab your laptop.' Stepping towards her, he took her takeaway cup before pausing and bringing his lips to hers.

Kissing him back, Polly reached behind his head, pulling him closer before stepping away again. 'Thanks.'

'See you in a few moments.' Keeping his eyes fixed on hers for a while, he then smiled and turned, walking across the landing.

With her fingers wrapped around her door handle, Polly watched as Zac juggled the lattes as he slipped into his own room. After this evening's discussion, perhaps they might get to a point where they could tell Laura to let out one of their rooms sooner than she'd hoped.

35

'Okay, are we all set?' Polly looked at the stall in front of her. Raffle tickets? Check. Prizes? Check. The grand prize of the giant stuffed squirrel? Check. And most important of all the leaflets to hand out to anyone who came within five feet of the stall? Check.

Polly glanced around the school hall. Stalls lined the large room, selling a mixture of home-made crafts, cakes and jewellery.

'Ah, not quite all set.' Declan tapped his mobile against his palm as he walked towards them.

'No? Why not?' Polly asked, the nerves in her stomach threatening to explode.

'Jarvis has twisted his ankle and Helena needs to take him to Urgent Care to get him checked over.'

'Twisted his ankle?' Polly gripped hold of the edge of the stall in dismay.

'Ay, that's right.' Declan nodded, seemingly unperturbed by the unravelling disaster.

'Don't worry, I'll go and collect the food truck and, all being well, we can rustle up something to sell in time, even if we end up just serving hot drinks.' Leaning down, Zac pulled his car keys from his coat pocket.

'No need. The van is here. The person they hired it from has just delivered it and Helena and Jarvis fully stocked it before Jarvis had his accident. Everything's ready to go.' Declan pointed his phone out towards the large windows surrounding the hall.

'Really? Okay, that's great. That's great.' Polly nodded. It would be fine, she reassured herself. Everything would be fine.

'Why don't you two go and make a start out in the van and I'll hunt Art, Vicki and Dennis down and we'll man the stall?' Declan looked around the vast hall.

'Good idea. We've got this, Polly.' Zac grinned.

'Yes, yes.' Nodding, Polly followed Zac out of the hall.

'Hey, it'll be fine. Disaster averted.' Pausing, Zac turned to face her.

Polly grimaced. 'Is it that obvious that I'm panicking?'

'No, not at all. You might be panicking on the inside, but on the outside, you're as cool as a cucumber.'

'A cucumber. Haha.' Polly laughed before shaking her arms and taking a deep breath. 'Okay, we're fine. We've got this. Please tell me we've got this.'

Zac grinned. 'We've got this. How hard can mac and cheese and chips be?'

Polly widened her eyes. She hadn't even thought about the fact they'd have to cook. 'You're kidding, right? I've got no idea how to make the mac and cheese they serve in the café.'

'I'm pretty certain Jarvis mentioned that he was prepping it all earlier today. I think we've just got to serve.'

'I hope you're right.' Shoving her hands in her pockets, Polly looked around her. There were five other food trucks, all standing along one side of the playground, each and every one of them manned by people who looked as though they knew what they were doing.

Trying to calm her nerves, she turned her attention to the playing field to the side of the playground. A large pile of wood had been collected and positioned in the middle of the field and metal railings had been erected at the edge of the grass to stop anybody wandering too close once the bonfire had been lit.

Stopping in front of a smart green van, Zac smiled as he opened the door and held his hand out towards Polly. 'We'll find out soon enough.'

Taking his hand, she stepped into the van and shrugged out of her coat before moving across to the counter. It certainly smelt as though the food was ready to be served. Lifting the lids on two huge bowls, she relaxed. 'You're right, it's all done.'

'Excellent. Here.' Stepping behind her, Zac lowered an apron over her head before tying the apron strings around her middle.

Looking over her shoulder, Polly smiled. 'Thank you.'

'You're welcome.' Leaning over the counter, Zac swung the hatch open and nodded towards the school gate opposite. 'Are you ready? Because here they come.'

Looking up, Polly watched as a swarm of people filed through the open gates, some meandering into the hall and others heading towards the food trucks. This was it. There was no reason to be nervous now. What would be would be as her grandma had always said. She couldn't change anything now.

'Hey, we've got this.' Zac repeated to her, as he turned to their first customer. 'Good evening. How can we help you?'

'Hi, could I have two helpings of mac and cheese, please?' the man standing in front of the van asked.

'Coming right up.'

Biting down on her bottom lip, Polly widened her eyes. She'd known she'd forgotten something. Placing her hand on Zac's arm, she lowered her voice, 'I haven't put the signs up on the outside of the van so people can see we're serving what they can get at the reserve's café. Will you be okay for a few minutes while I go and grab the posters? I think they're behind the stall.'

'Yes, of course. You go while I serve.'

'Thanks.' Pulling her apron over her head, Polly hung it on a hook by the door before climbing down the two steep steps. How could she have forgotten?

Hurrying across the playground, she weaved her way through the crowds of people walking around the hall until she arrived at their stall. Slipping behind, she grabbed the posters from the box sitting by the wall before pausing and watching a long queue form at the stall. She caught sight of the mum and the boy who they'd seen at the toy shop and waved as they caught her eye.

While people waited to pay for raffle tickets, they picked up the leaflets, flicking through and chatting with the people in front or behind them, pointing at the photos and looking at the map.

'A good start, hey?' Declan nudged her shoulder and raised an eyebrow.

'Yes, it is, isn't it?' Polly grinned before shaking herself and looking down at the posters in her hands. 'I'd better get back to Zac.'

'Good luck.'

'Thanks.' Taking a final look at the crowd gathered around the stall, Polly hurried back outside as relief flooded through her body. Zac was right. Tonight was going to be a success. They were raising awareness of the reserve and, if the stall was as busy all night as it was now, they should make a tidy profit too.

36

Locking up the door to the food truck, Zac passed Polly her coat before shrugging into his own. 'I'm shattered after that.'

'I know exactly what you mean.' Polly laughed. They'd sold out of both chips and mac and cheese so when they'd spotted Miss Cooke standing in the middle of the playground ringing an old-fashioned school bell, they'd decided to join the crowds for the bonfire and fireworks display rather than keep the food truck open just to serve the few drinks they had left. 'And I don't think I'll want to eat mac and cheese for months to come.'

'Haha, I think I could. I actually wish I'd kept a bowl aside.' Zac chuckled as he led the way towards the metal railings before taking Polly's hand and manoeuvring her in front of him. Wrapping his arms around her waist, he pulled her back towards him and whispered in her ear, 'I think this is definitely a success.'

Polly grinned as she watched Miss Cooke slip between the panels of railings, pick up a microphone and position herself in front of the gathered crowd. Zac was right. Judging by the comments she'd had from people she'd served asking her about the reserve, she was happy that they'd managed to get people talking about it and hopefully that would mean a few more visitors too.

'Good evening, folks.' Miss Cooke's voice projected through a microphone across the playground as the crowd continued to grow. 'We're in for a treat tonight! Have you seen how big this year's bonfire is?'

A loud cheer erupted from the crowd.

'Exactly. Well, to light the bonfire tonight we have our very own Jill Davies, who has worked tirelessly to organise this event for us all, so a big round of applause for Jill.' Lowering the microphone, Miss Cooke clapped. After a few seconds, she stopped and brought the microphone to her lips again, searching the crowd in front of her. 'Jill? Jill Davies, are you here?'

Polly frowned. It wasn't like Jill to be late, especially to an event she'd organised. People around them began shuffling as they turned to look for Jill. 'I wonder where she is.'

'I don't know.' Zac frowned before pointing towards where the mound of wood stood waiting to be lit. 'What's going on over there?'

Straining her eyes into the dark field, Polly could just about make out the flashes of torches being swung from side to side. 'It looks as though someone is looking for something. Or a few people are.'

One of the lights began making their way towards the front of the field and slowly Jill's silhouette became visible as she reached the lights from the flood-lights set up around the playground. A few seconds later and she was speaking with Miss Cooke.

Bringing the microphone to her lips once more, Miss Cooke addressed her audience again. 'It transpires that we have a small complication. It seems that a certain sheep which was terrorising this village up until a short time ago has escaped her new home at Little Mead Farm and come in search of an adventure once more.'

A resounding groan filtered through the crowd and Polly twisted in Zac's arms to look at him. 'A sheep? Did she say a sheep?'

'I think so.' Zac shook his head as confusion swept across his face. 'Unless we misheard.'

'Yes, maybe.' They must have misheard, the words sheep and terrorise surely couldn't come up in the same sentence, could they? One lone sheep terrorising an entire village? She laughed. 'Yep, I bet we're hearing things.'

Settling back against Zac's chest, Polly squinted into the darkness of the field again as someone ran up towards her. It wasn't until they'd almost reached them that she realised it was Nicola.

Straightening her back, Polly leaned on the railing and called towards her, 'Nicola? Is everything okay?'

'Polly, Zac. Hi.' Nicola paused to catch her breath. 'Claudette, the sheep

Charlie rescued up at the farm, has broken free and was last seen squeezing through the hedge into the field. We can't find her anywhere but need to catch her before the bonfire or fireworks are lit.'

'Do you need a hand?' Reaching into his pocket, Zac pulled out his mobile and switched on the torch app.

'The more help, the better. Thank you.' Turning again, Nicola ran off back towards the middle of the field.

Taking her own mobile out, Polly turned on the torch app as she and Zac squeezed between two panels of railings and headed in the direction Nicola had gone. They hadn't been hearing things then. There was a sheep on the loose. A sheep.

'There's something over there. Something white,' Charlie called across the field.

Shining her torch in the direction of Charlie's voice, Polly jogged towards where everyone else was running and, sure enough, she could see a glimpse of the animal amongst the undergrowth beneath the hedge encircling the school playing field.

As he neared the hedge, Charlie turned to face the group of people helping. 'I think we've got one chance at this before she bolts off into the middle of the field again, so can I have everyone make a circle behind her, please?'

Stepping back, Polly joined the circle forming around the fluffy white animal and grinned across at Zac. He wouldn't be able to see her face in the dark, but she could almost feel him meet her gaze. She'd never heard about a sheep being on the loose before, let along encountered one, but it couldn't be that hard to catch, could it? Even in the dark, the sheep's brilliant white fleece should stand out, so surely it was just a case of walking across to it and, what? Hooking a lead around its neck or something?

'Right, everyone in position? If she comes towards you, stand your ground. She's a soft little thing, even if she is an expert escapee. Just hold your arms out and kneel down and she's unlikely to try to push past you.' Charlie waited until people were in position before turning and inching his way towards Claudette.

'Quick, Charlie. She's looking like she's going to make a run for it.' Nicola's voice was carried across the circle.

'Good spot,' Charlie whispered as he changed direction.

In a flurry of activity, Polly was unsure whether Charlie had run at

Claudette or Claudette had run at Charlie, but when she shone her torch in their direction, Charlie was on his knees in the grass with his arms wrapped around the fluffy sheep. Huh, maybe she'd underestimated the fluffy creature after all.

'Well done, mate.' Jackson's voice reached them through the dark.

'Thanks for your help, everyone. Me and Nic will get this one back to the farm and let you carry on with the firework celebrations.' Charlie thanked them before he and Nicola led Claudette away.

Walking across to Zac, Polly grinned. 'That's two escape artists this week. Maybe Rolo and Claudette could become best pals.'

'Oh no, imagine the two of them swapping tips.' Zac chuckled as he shone his torch onto the ground as they made their way back to the playground and the crowd waiting patiently for the bonfire to be lit and the firework display to begin.

'True, they'd never be found, would they? You're right, we should keep them as far away from each other as humanly possible.' Slipping back through the gap in the railings, Polly turned her torch app off, slipped her mobile back into her pocket and turned to face Miss Cooke, once again feeling Zac's touch as he reached around her middle and pulled her back towards him. Smiling, she held Zac's hands, lacing their fingers together. Perfect.

'Well, I would give Charlie a cheer, but I don't want us frightening Claudette and her escaping again.' Disaster averted, Miss Cooke's voice boomed through the microphone.

As Laura and Jackson came to stand beside them, Laura whispered, 'Charlie can get away with anything in her eyes.'

'She definitely has favourites in the community.' Jackson chuckled.

'And you're no better. You're like her golden child, too.' Laura batted his arm playfully.

'What can I say? I can't help my natural charm.' Jackson wrapped his arm around Laura's shoulder, pulling her close, and kissed her on top of the head.

'Haha, true.'

Polly watched as Jackson and Laura gently teased each other before turning back to see Jill running across the field to light the bonfire as the people gathered clapped. Yes, Meadowfield was perfect. She already felt at home far quicker than she'd ever thought possible. 'How did the mulled cider and sparklers go down at the inn?'

Laura grinned, her eyes shining in the glow from the floodlights behind them. 'Great, thanks. Everyone seemed to enjoy the mulled cider and I think most people said they were bringing the sparklers here to light after the display.'

'That's brilliant.' Polly smiled back.

'I may have saved some mulled cider for us all when we head back too.' Jackson chuckled.

'Perfect.' Polly turned back to look towards Miss Cooke as her microphone crackled to life again.

'Thank you, Jill. And now for our display!' Miss Cooke waited until Jill had raced back around the railings before joining her and pointing to whoever was in charge of the microphone.

Much to Polly's surprise, music began to play through the speakers and the fireworks were lit and popped, fizzed and banged their way into existence perfectly to the beat of the music.

Glancing behind her, Polly watched as Zac rubbed at his eyes before turning back to the display. He was tired. After waking up at 5 a.m. to find his side of the bed empty, she'd caught him downstairs in the kitchen, unable to sleep and he didn't look as though he'd had a solid hour's kip since his gran had been rushed to hospital.

As he placed his hand back in hers, she gripped it tighter. He was worried. He was worried about the promotion, about the money, about the consequences if he didn't get it. And she didn't blame him. He had a lot riding on it. The future of his parents' house, as well as his gran's nursing home.

Leaning back against his chest, she lifted her head, staring at the bright colours filling the dark sky. Tonight's event had been an accumulation of everything she'd learned about Meadowfield since arriving. The readiness to accept and welcome newcomers, the pulling together of one community for the good of the village, and the shared celebrations. Not to mention the way people had flocked towards Charlie and Nicola when they'd needed help with capturing Claudette and getting her back to safety. This is what she wanted. This is the exact place she had longed to be.

But she couldn't have it. Sighing, Polly dragged the sleeve of her coat across her eyes. She couldn't have any of it. But that was okay. The one thing she needed more than Meadowfield, more than her fresh start or her career change, was for Zac to be happy. She needed him, and she wanted him to be happy.

And in that moment, she knew what she had to do.

'You okay?' Leaning down, Zac whispered to her, his breath tickling her ear.

Twisting in his arms as the light show continued above them, Polly placed her hands on either side of his face and kissed him squarely on the lips before answering him. 'I am. I'm more than okay.'

37

Polly twisted in her chair as Declan walked into the middle of the office and clapped his hands.

'Can I just have everyone's attention for a moment please, folks?' Declan lowered his voice as Zac, Art, Dennis and Vicki all looked at him expectantly.

'What is it, Declan? You're giving us all a raise?' Art called out.

'Haha. I wish. Believe me, I wish.' Declan shook his head and held up a sheet of paper. 'Afraid not, but I have just had an email through from HQ congratulating us on the astounding success of our presence at Meadowfield's Bonfire Night celebrations.'

'Ooh, and that's really from HQ?' Vicki leaned forward, Rolo in her arms.

'It certainly is.' Declan waved the paper in the air. 'It seems Miss Cooke, the mayoress, reached out to them to sing our praises.'

'Fantastic. It's nice to be recognised.' Dennis stood up and held his mug in the air. 'I think we should raise a glass to Polly, without whom we wouldn't have even been participating in the Bonfire Night event.'

'Hear, hear.' Zac held up his mug too and grinned across at her.

'To Polly,' Dennis said loudly as the room echoed in response.

'Ah, no. None of it would have worked out if we hadn't all pulled together.' Polly could feel the heat of embarrassment prickle her skin.

'Don't be so bashful, Polly. Dennis is right, without your idea of having a stall and food truck, we wouldn't have even been there.' Declan grinned.

'Thanks.' Mumbling, Polly turned back to her desk as the room quietened down again.

Leaning across his desk, Zac squeezed her arm. 'Well done.'

Polly glanced at him and smiled before standing up. 'I'll be right back.'

Polly hovered, placing her pens back in the small metal pen holder until she was sure Zac was once again engrossed in his work. It would be easier if he didn't see what she was about to do, if he didn't start asking questions. Satisfied he wasn't going to look up again for a while, Polly grabbed the envelope she'd stashed in her desk drawer and walked across the office to Declan's desk and lowered her voice. 'Do you mind if we have a quick word in private, please?'

Looking up from the papers he was reading, Declan smiled and stood up. 'Of course.'

Following him through to the meeting room, Polly closed the door quietly behind them before standing there and clasping her hands in front of her.

'What can I do for you, Polly?'

It was now or never, and she was ready for this. She took a deep breath before speaking. 'I'd like to hand in my notice.'

Blinking, Declan ran his fingers through his beard. 'I beg your pardon?'

'Just that, I'd like to hand in my notice.' She passed him the envelope, holding it between them until he reluctantly took it.

'But you've been doing so well. You've made such a difference here already. Why would you want to throw all that away?' Declan looked down at the envelope and turned it over in his hands, making no effort to open it.

Polly chewed on her bottom lip before answering. She didn't want to lie to him, but she couldn't go into details either. 'Personal reasons.'

'I see.' Leaning against the edge of the table, Declan looked shocked. 'I must say, this is somewhat of a surprise. Is it because of the mix-up with the job roles?'

Shaking her head, Polly shoved her hands in her pockets. She'd surprised herself at how much she was enjoying the new role and if circumstances were different, if there was any way she could stay on here without needing the money the promotion would bring, she'd be more than happy continuing in her current job. 'No, not at all. I've actually really enjoyed working on the fundraising and development side of things.'

'Then I must ask again, why?'

Polly glanced behind her towards the closed door. She couldn't tell him the real reason. She couldn't tell him that she was doing this for Zac, that Zac needed the promotion more than her and even though she had no reason to believe she'd win it over him, she wasn't going to take that risk. She wasn't prepared to put him through the pain of her getting the promotion when he needed it more or him being given it and feeling guilty for it. They both needed the extra money and one of them wasn't going to get that. She might as well swing things in Zac's favour as well as safeguarding her future, even if it was one she didn't particularly want. Nope, the last thing she wanted was for her reasoning to get back to Zac. She'd figure out something to tell him when the time came. 'Honestly, I just need to do this.'

'I still don't understand.' Declan ran his finger and thumb around the edge of the envelope. 'Is it the team? Me?'

'No, no. I've loved working with you all. I just miss my old teaching job.' As she blurted out the words, she hoped they sounded more sincere than they did to her.

'Right, okay.' Declan nodded. 'The team are going to be devastated you're leaving us. And so soon too.'

'Sorry, I'm going to miss you all.' Polly shifted on her feet. She hadn't realised quite how hard this would be, but it was for the best and now she'd made her decision official, she felt a weight lifting from her shoulders. Next would be a conversation with David, the estate agent, to tell him she wanted to pull out of the sale of the flat. Another conversation she wasn't looking forward to, but that one could wait. It could wait until she knew whether she'd secured a job at her old school or not. And it wouldn't be long to wait, being as Stacey had managed to slip her in for an interview tomorrow. Polly had known interviews were already scheduled to take place, but it had been a stroke of luck one of the other candidates had dropped out and Stacey had been able to get her in.

'You will be missed, too. Very much so.'

'And I'm sorry to ask so soon after handing in my notice, but would I be able to have tomorrow off please? I have an interview at the school I used to teach in.'

'Right, well, yes, of course.' Declan nodded.

'Thank you. I know it's short notice.'

'Shall we?' Declan held the envelope out, indicating the door.

'Yes.' Polly began pushing the door open before pausing and looking back at Declan again. 'Can we keep this between the two of us for the time being, please?'

'Of course.' Declan folded the envelope, still unopened, and slipped it into his pocket before holding out his hand and indicating her to go through.

Walking back to her desk, Polly breathed a sigh of relief. That had been harder than she thought it would be, but now she'd done it, now she'd officially given up on her dreams, she felt okay. She felt at peace. There were more important things going on in her life right now, namely her new relationship with Zac, and all she wanted to do was to protect that. She didn't want the promotion hanging over them, threatening to pull them apart. And she wanted to make things easier for him, too.

Zac glanced up as she sat back down. 'All okay?'

'Yep, all good.' Polly smiled across at him, hoping that Declan could keep this promise of not saying anything. She would tell Zac, but not now. When the time was right.

'Shall we catch that film at the cinema we missed last week?' Zac grinned.

'Umm, I can't tonight.' Polly wheeled her chair in closer to her desk, keeping her eyes fixed on the screen of her laptop. 'I've got to go back to the flat. Sort some things out.'

'Oh, is the sale moving that quickly? I can run you there straight after work, and we should easily have three or four hours before coming back to Meadowfield.'

'No, because I...' She pulled her laptop closer and opened a new window on the screen. She hated lying, and she was sure he could see straight through her, but it was for the best. It was the only way. 'I've arranged to have tomorrow off.'

'That's a good idea. I can see if I can get it off too.' Pushing his chair back, Zac stood up.

'No!' Polly steadied her voice as she took hold of Zac's hand. 'No, it's fine. I've arranged to meet Stacey.'

'Is it a teacher training day tomorrow?' Zac smiled as he sat back down.

'Er, no, but I'm going to catch up with her after school.' Now that wasn't a lie. She would catch up with her when she finished work, but to dissect the interview rather than anything else.

'That'll be nice, then. I know I kind of got in the way of you both catching up when we were decorating.'

Polly shook her head. 'You didn't. I really appreciate everything you did for me that weekend. You know that, don't you?'

'Of course I do. You've told me enough times and, like I've said, it was my pleasure.' Zac looked down at his phone as it began to ring. Holding it up, he stood up before whispering, 'Wish me luck. We might just have another sponsorship deal if this call goes right.'

'Good luck,' Polly whispered before turning to look out of the window. How was she going to get through until tomorrow without blurting something out? She would because she was doing this for him, for their relationship, and if he found out, he'd likely quit on the spot to save her from walking away.

38

'Eek, this is so exciting! I still can't believe you've decided to come back to us!' Stacey waited until Polly had clicked her seatbelt in before starting the engine.

'Thanks again for convincing Mrs Jedd to fit me in for the interview today.' Polly pulled down the sun visor and checked her reflection. She hadn't slept much at all last night, and it hadn't been because it was the first time she'd been in the flat alone since the break-in. But she still hadn't changed her mind. She knew this was the right thing to do, the right thing for her relationship with Zac. She just needed to get through today, to get through the interview. That was all. Once the interview was over and she'd secured the job, she knew she'd feel better. 'Does this look okay? I'm so used to wearing sweatshirts around the reserve, it feels odd to wear something smart again.'

'You look fab. Very professional.' Pulling out of the car park next to the block of flats, Stacey joined the slow queue of traffic. 'And you know Mrs Jedd, she jumped at the chance of interviewing you. She knows you're a great teacher and today is just to tick a box. You've got this job.'

'I wish I could be as confident as you are. I've not done a teaching interview for over ten years, and I've only had a couple of days to prepare a sample lesson.' Polly pulled her tote bag up from where she'd placed it on the floor and checked she had her folder containing the copies of the lesson plan and the resources she'd managed to print off at work without Zac noticing.

'Honestly, Pols, you literally have this, and the best thing is, Ben isn't going to be interviewing you. He's gone to his new school for some taster day or something.'

'Really? That's a relief.' Letting her tote bag slip to the floor again, Polly leaned her head back against the headrest. At least she wouldn't have to contend with her ex's smug face, thinking she couldn't hack it in the 'big, wide world', as he used to refer to life outside of teaching. Plus, she had been worried that he'd have chosen someone else to give the job to just out of spite, as she'd always got the feeling he'd assumed she'd left because they'd split. Which, of course, she hadn't. Yes, working in the same school had been difficult for a while, but once the new school year had come around and Mrs Jedd had shifted them around year groups, things had become easier.

'Haha, thought it might be.' Stacey glanced at her before clicking on her indicator. 'So, are you going to tell me the real reason you've decided to move back? You and the lovely Zac haven't split up already, have you?'

Polly opened her eyes and shook her head. 'No, we're still very much together.'

'Then why? I thought that was what you wanted, the new start in a nice little village, a job in conservation? You worked hard enough for it, and what? Now you're just going to quit and come back home, back to your old job? Your old life?'

Polly looked out of the windscreen, watching the rhythmic swoosh of the windscreen wipers displacing the rain. 'Something like that.'

'Umm, I don't believe you. You were so set on making this change.' Stacey held her fingers up, away from the steering wheel. 'Not that I'm complaining. I want nothing more than to have my bestie back in town and back at work, but something's going on.'

Polly kept quiet, focusing on the windscreen wipers. She knew that whatever she said, Stacey would see right through her, she always did.

'This has something to do with Zac. I know it does.' Finally reaching the roundabout, Stacey turned onto a quieter street as they made their way further from the town centre. 'It does. I just don't understand what.'

'It's nothing,' Polly mumbled, hoping Stacey would drop the conversation.

'No, it isn't nothing.' She tapped the steering wheel before glancing at her. 'This is about the promotion, isn't it? Did he get it?'

'Nothing's been decided yet. The decision won't be made until Declan retires.' At least she was on safe ground now. She didn't have to attempt to spin anymore lies.

Indicating, Stacey swerved the car and pulled up on the side of the road as the car behind them sounded its horn.

'What are you doing? We can't be late.' Polly frowned. They were nowhere near the school.

'We won't be late. This is me. I'm never late for anything.' Unclicking her seatbelt, Stacey turned to face Polly.

'What? Have I got lipstick on my teeth or something?' Pulling the visor down again, Polly pulled her lips back and scrubbed at her teeth. Not that she could see anything on them. She looked back towards Stacey.

'No, you do not have lipstick on your teeth.' Stacey rolled her eyes.

'Then what? And why do you suddenly look so mad with me?' Polly frowned. The last thing she wanted to do was to upset her friend. Zac was going to be annoyed with her when he found out what she'd done. She needed Stacey in her corner.

'I am mad at you because I've just figured out what you're playing at.'

'I'm not playing at anything.' Polly tried to look away, but Stacey caught her gaze again. Great, this was it. She'd had a feeling she wouldn't be able to keep this from her.

'You're quitting so Zac can take the promotion. I can't believe that man! And to think I thought he was good for you.' Stacey shook her head vehemently and brushed her hair from her face. 'What a low-level rat.'

'No, he's not. You've got it all wrong.'

'Huh, not from where I'm sitting.' She held out her hand. 'Here, give me your phone. I want to give him a piece of my mind.'

Gripping her mobile tightly in her hand, Polly shook her head. She'd have to come clean now. 'It's not what you think. Zac doesn't know I've quit.'

Dropping her hand to her lap, Stacey stared at her. 'You're making no sense. No sense at all.'

'He has a lot more riding on this promotion than I do. If he doesn't get the rise, his gran will have to move nursing homes or else his parents will have to put the family home up for sale.' She spoke quietly, hoping Stacey would understand.

'But you're missing out on what you wanted? Why? He's a grown man. He can sort things out for himself.'

'I know, but I...' Polly whispered the rest of the sentence. 'I think I love him.'

Sitting heavily back in her seat, Stacey let out a long, slow breath. 'You think you love him?'

Polly shook her head and looked out of the window, watching a cyclist mounting the path to cycle around them. 'I know that I love him, and I don't want him to go through what I had to with my grandma. I don't want him to have to worry about money like I did. I want him to be able to enjoy the time he has left with her. And if I still worked at the reserve, and he got the promotion, I know he'd feel bad for me and that would come between us. I don't want anything to ruin what we have. It's taken us long enough to get here.'

'Oh, Polly.'

She glanced across at Stacey. 'You're not going to have a go at me?'

'Would it do any good?'

'No.'

'Then there's no point. But I'm warning you, he'll find out and he's not going to be happy about it either.'

'I know.' Polly took a deep breath in. She'd have to cross that bridge when she came to it. She just needed a little more time to think of a way to present this to him, to show him she'd done it for the both of them and that she'd be happy teaching again. Because, given time, she was sure she could be. If she just didn't let the unnecessary paperwork and politics stress her out this time round, she could be. Things would be better. Yes, the reserve would always have a special place in her heart but she was doing this for the right reasons and she'd learn to live with the sacrifice. She knew she would. 'Now, can you please start driving again before I'm late for my interview?'

'Fine. Whatever.' Stacey clicked her seatbelt back on. 'I still think this is a mistake.'

'I know.' Polly nodded. 'I'll ply you with coffee and cake as an after-school snack whilst we mark together and I know you'll come round.'

39

Letting the heavy door to Daisy Chain Primary click shut behind her, Polly made her way through the car park and down to the street, thankful that the schoolchildren had long since disappeared home.

Sinking to the wooden bench on the edge of the grass verge, Polly slumped her shoulders. Stacey had warned her the interview process had changed since she'd last got her teaching job, but being on show all day had been gruelling. First a lesson observation, followed by being scrutinised as she spoke informally to a group of children about their visions for the school and what they were looking for in a new teacher and then the actual formal interview and all that between endless hours of waiting around.

Watching the wind drag a leaf across the pavement, Polly pinched the bridge of her nose. Stacey had told her to go straight into her classroom to tell her she was done, but she'd just needed to get out, to get away from the people she used to work with, who were now sitting around discussing her flaws and imperfections and deciding on her future.

At least it was done now. They'd promised her they'd let her know the outcome of the interview process later today, so she wouldn't have to wait long. Pulling her tote bag onto her lap, she wrapped her arms around it. And then more interviews would come if she didn't get the job, or, if she did, she'd have to have the worst conversation with Zac.

Pulling her mobile from her pocket, she scrolled through her apps, leaving the messages from Zac unopened. She couldn't face reading them. She knew what they'd be saying. He'd be asking her how things were going and whether she'd managed to get everything done she'd needed to sort. He'd likely be offering her a lift back to Pennycress, too. But she couldn't face lying to him. It had been hard enough when she'd said goodbye yesterday and she'd had to make something up again and, now after feeling drained from the day of relentless questions and judgements, she really didn't think she could face trying to evade more questions, not when she didn't even have the answers herself.

No, she'd wait until she'd heard the outcome of the interview and then she could be honest with him. Once she'd accepted the position – if she was even offered it – then it would be done. He wouldn't be able to talk her out of it. Swiping away as a missed call from him flashed up, she clicked on Tetris and settled back against the hard wooden bench, looking forward to zoning out whilst she waited for Stacey. Looking forward to not thinking.

She heard a car pull up on the road in front of her and kept her eyes fixed on her screen, guiding a purple block into the perfect space. She didn't have the energy to make small talk and she couldn't risk looking up and one of her old pupils' parents recognising her or anything. She watched as the row of tiny bricks flashed on her screen before disappearing and began guiding another block down into position.

'Polly.'

Dropping her phone, Polly leaned forward and grabbed it just before it landed screen-down on the tarmac. Looking up slowly, her eyes locked with Zac's. She swallowed. What was he doing here? What would she say to him? Tell him she was waiting for Stacey? It was true, but it wasn't the whole truth.

'Zac, what are you doing here?'

Widening his stance in front of her, he frowned. 'I could ask you the same thing.'

'I...' She looked down at her phone, closing the app of the game before she mumbled her reply. 'Declan told you?'

'He did.'

Feeling the seat of the bench shift under his weight as he sat down next to her, she forced herself to look at him, to see the hurt in his eyes. 'I'm sorry I didn't tell you. I just—'

'The problem is, you quitting has left poor Declan in a bit of a sticky situation.' Zac held out his hand.

Placing her hand in his, she immediately relaxed as she felt his touch, the stresses of the day melting away, and this confirmed she'd done the right thing. Only, what was he saying?

She shook her head. 'What do you mean? What situation?'

'Well, last week he had two potential successors to train up to take over his job from him and now he has none.' Zac smiled.

'You've quit too! Why did you quit?' Snatching her hand back, she tucked her hair behind her ears.

'The same reason as you, I should think.' He shrugged nonchalantly.

'No, you can't. I quit for you, so the stupid promotion didn't come between us. You didn't need to as well. What's the point in us both handing in our notice?' This couldn't be happening. It made no sense. Why did he have to do this after finding out she had? It was madness. Utter madness.

'Not much point, really.'

'Then take it back. Take back your resignation.' She widened her eyes. All of this had been for nothing.

'You take back yours.' He met her gaze again, challenging her.

'No! I quit first! You do it. You go back.' She crossed her arms. What was he trying to prove?

Zac shook his head slowly, a smile tugging at the corners of his lips. 'I phoned Declan up when we got back from the hospital. I handed in my resignation before you.'

Slumping her shoulders, Polly opened her mouth, ready to speak before closing it again. How was she supposed to respond to that admission?

'You blew me away at the hospital. The way you were there for me. You even hung around after having the displeasure of meeting my parents. Not many people would have done that,' he chuckled quietly. 'It was then when we were driving back to Pennycress after our dinner that it hit me.'

'What hit you?' She searched his face. What was he trying to say?

He shrugged. 'That I love you and I have for a while now. I pushed you away before because I had feelings for you and I didn't know how else to cope having to compete for the promotion, but what I didn't realise, not until that weekend at your flat, was quite how much I felt for you, and I wasn't about to let anything have a minuscule chance at coming between us.'

'Say it again.' Shifting on the bench, she turned to face him.

'I don't want anything to jeopardise our relationship.'

She shook her head. 'Not that bit, the other bit.'

Zac broke into a grin. 'The bit about me loving you?'

Polly nodded, unable to form any words.

Turning, he faced her before taking her hands in his. 'I love you, Polly Burrows.'

He loved her. He had actually said he loved her.

'I love you too.'

Bringing his hand to the nape of her neck, he leaned forward, their lips millimetres apart. 'Then follow your dreams. Tell Declan you don't want to resign. Accept the promotion.'

Pulling back, Polly shook her head. Didn't he see that him telling her how he felt didn't change anything? Not anything to do with the job, it only made her even more sure she'd done the right thing. 'No, you take it.'

'I can't. I've already accepted a position back at HQ. They're looking for someone to run the sponsorship accounts.'

'No.' Jumping to her feet, Polly began pacing up and down the path. This couldn't be happening. He wanted her to go back to Meadowfield whilst he moved back here, back to Featherford, to work at HQ? He'd just told her he loved her and yet he was quite happy to live a two-hour drive from her? But then, if she took this teaching job, and he stayed in Meadowfield, they'd end up in the same position, both of them living at opposite ends of the Cotswolds. How was this going to work? She sat back down and sighed. 'We'll only see each other at weekends.'

Zac scrunched up his nose. 'Apart from the fact that I made being able to work out of the Meadowfield Reserve offices a condition of me taking the job. Plus, the pay rise is enough to cover my gran's nursing home fees so my parents don't have to sell up.'

Turning to look at him, Polly grinned. 'Seriously?'

'Seriously. We'll still both be working in Meadowfield. If you're happy having me under your feet and taking up one of your desks, that is?'

'Happy?' Polly shook her head. 'I can't believe it. Everything is coming together. Is this even real?'

'It sure is.'

Lifting her hand to his face, she cupped his cheek as she looked into his eyes. It felt real, he felt real, but... 'Pinch me. Let me see if I wake up.'

Chuckling, Zac shook his head. 'I'm not going to pinch you, but this should work just the same.'

Feeling his hand come to the nape of her neck again, this time she didn't pull away as he leaned in, their lips touching as he kissed her. Bringing her hands to his head, she ran her fingers through his hair before resting them against the back of his head.

Yep, this was definitely real.

EPILOGUE

Weaving in and out of the people sitting on picnic rugs in the garden of Pennycress, Polly checked everyone had blankets and flasks of hot chocolate to hand before walking towards the back of the group.

'Come on, sit down. Everyone's okay.' Shooting his arm up from where he was sitting on a picnic rug, Zac took her hand and nodded to the spot next to him.

Taking a final look around the small gathering, Polly nodded and sat down. Everyone looked happy and warm enough too, and Brian, the astronomy expert she'd sourced for the stargazing course she'd organised to take place over the next six weeks, was just finishing setting up a screen in front of them all and then he'd be ready to go. The first session, tonight, was taking place at Pennycress Inn after Laura had come to the rescue when Polly had realised the meadow at the reserve had been double-booked amidst a flurry of rewilding activity.

She grinned as she glanced back towards the inn which had become her and Zac's temporary home. In a way, it felt fitting to be hosting the first event she'd planned as project manager here, where her new adventure had begun and at the heart of the community which had supported her so much.

'Are they here yet?' Zac rubbed Polly's shoulder as he looked around the large garden.

Polly shook her head. She knew exactly who he was talking about – Stacey and Freddie. Polly had been so excited when Stacey had promised to come down for this event, and equally disappointed when her friend had rung to tell her they were stuck in traffic. She glanced at the time on her mobile. If they didn't hurry, they'd miss it altogether.

'Oh look, is that them?' Zac pointed behind them towards a couple walking down the steps of the decking surrounding the inn.

Grinning, Polly jumped to her feet and held out her hand to Zac. Once he was standing beside her, she stepped over their blanket and hurried across to Stacey and Freddie. 'You made it!'

'Of course we made it. You didn't think I was going to miss my bestie's first big event as the boss, did you?' Stacey flung her arms around Polly before stepping back and looking Zac up and down. 'Glad to hear you're treating my girl right.'

Dipping his head, Zac ran his fingers through his hair. 'I try my best.'

'Course you do! Only kidding! Polly tells me everything and I know how much you mean to her.' Drawing him in for a hug, Stacey laughed before introducing her partner, Freddie. 'Zac, this is Freddie. Freddie, Zac. I hope you two get along because you'll both be enduring many, many, many double dates. Plus, of course, we'll be coming and staying when you two finally get your own place.'

'Hello, mate.' Freddie clasped Zac's hand and patted him on the back.

'Good to meet you.' Zac grinned. 'And you'll both be more than welcome to visit.'

Glancing towards Brian, Polly grimaced. 'I think he's about to begin. Come and take your places. I've set you up a picnic blanket, telescope and flask of hot chocolate right by us.'

'Lead the way.' Looping her arm through Stacey's, she followed as Polly led the way towards the back of the group.

'Here you go.' Turning, Polly gave Stacey another hug. 'I really am happy you made it. It means a lot.'

'I'm glad we did too. And this place is gorgeous, the inn and what we saw of the village as we drove through. I can see why you want to settle here.' Stacey grinned before taking Freddie's hand and lowering herself to the checked picnic blanket.

Settling back on their blanket, Polly snuggled her back against Zac's chest as he wrapped his arms around her. Tonight promised to be good. Not only did she have Zac here but she had Stacey's support too.

'Yum, this hot chocolate is the best!' Nicola called softly from her and Charlie's rug a few feet away from Polly and Zac.

Turning to face her, Polly laughed before pointing to Jackson, who was sitting in front of them with Laura. 'I may have had a little help.'

'Haha, it's Jackson's hot chocolate.' Nicola took another sip. 'I thought I recognised it.'

Turning around, Jackson pulled a face. 'Did I hear my name?'

'I was just telling Polly how delicious her hot chocolate was.' Nicola grinned.

'Hey, I didn't take the credit.' Polly held her hands up, palms forward. 'Even though I was tempted.'

'I would have.' Zac chuckled beside her as he held up the flask in Jackson's direction. 'I can see why Laura is marrying you now.'

Twisting on the rug, Laura glanced in their direction. 'His famous hot chocolate isn't the only reason, you know. He makes that mean French toast too.'

'Oi! Charmed, I'm sure.' Jackson wrapped his arm around Laura, drawing her towards him and gently ruffling her hair. 'Well, I'm certainly not marrying you for your culinary skills.'

Squealing, Laura pulled away. 'I'm learning. I can make a tasty version of Vivienne's fruit cake, Nicola can back me up on that one. Even your mum said it was good, didn't she?'

'She did, yes.' Nicola smiled.

'When's she going to teach you, Nic?' Charlie joined in.

'Umm, or you. Why can't you learn to make my mum's fruit cake?' Nicola shook her head.

'Because I'm slaving away on the farm, planting and harvesting the crops so you have the ingredients for your fruit cake.' Charlie chuckled.

'And I'm working my fingers to the bone at the inn!' Nicola retorted.

Holding her hand against her chest, Laura looked at Nicola, mock-shock covering her face. 'I don't make you work that hard, do I?'

'Well...' Nicola broke first and burst out laughing. 'Hey, Polly, maybe you can organise some cooking classes at the reserve next time.'

'Now, that's not such a bad idea. You could take everyone foraging around the reserve first and then go back to the classroom and cook with whatever you've found.' Charlie raised an eyebrow.

'I actually like that idea. I might just steal that.' Polly grinned as Zac pulled the blanket over their knees and Brian began to introduce himself. The last few months had been a whirlwind, with the flat sale going through, Zac starting his new job and Declan awarding her the promotion. And spending her first Christmas together with Zac at Pennycress, which had been magical and everything she'd hoped for.

'And, in a moment, I'll ask you to use the telescopes in front of you, but this is what you're looking for, the star constellation of Taurus. This particular constellation from this particular location should be very clear at this time of the year. The joys of January.' Giving his audience a few moments to ingest the map of the stars from the screen, Brian then turned it off, plunging them into darkness, before talking them through how to pinpoint the constellation in the sky.

Leaning forward on her knees, Polly closed one eye and peered through the telescope. Frowning, she moved the end of the telescope around a little, trying and failing to find Taurus. Sitting back, she shook her head. 'I'm actually terrible at this. I can't tell one star from the other.'

'Sure you can.' Resting on his knees, Zac looked through her telescope and repositioned it before turning to her and ushering her forward. 'Here, come take a look now. Just keep the telescope super still.'

Doing as she was instructed, Polly once again closed one eye and looked through the lens. Nothing had changed. She still couldn't find the star pattern Brian had instructed them to look for. 'I still can't see it.'

'Do you see a cluster of stars which look like a V?'

She could feel Zac's breath against her hair as he spoke softly next to her, and she resisted the urge to giggle. Instead, she squinted again, this time looking for a V shape. 'Yes! I see it. I see the V.'

'That's great, that's the Hyades star cluster, the head of the bull. Now, kind of in the middle of the V, do you see a really bright star?' He brought his hand to her face, gently tucking her hair behind her ear as he spoke. 'It'll be brighter than the ones surrounding it, so it should stand out.'

Polly grinned. 'I see it.'

'That bright star is called Aldebaran. Now if you pan out slightly, you'll be able to see the whole constellation, the bull.'

Polly widened her open eye. She could see it. For the first time in her life, she'd been able to spot a constellation. Leaning back, she looked at him. 'Wow, how do you know all that?'

Zac shrugged. 'Every weekend I stayed at my grandparents' place, my grandad would pack up the car on a Friday night and we'd drive into the middle of nowhere. During the day, he'd teach me how to fish and, come the night, he'd teach me about the stars.'

'Wow, how didn't I know this about you?' There was so much she needed to learn about him, so much she wanted to share with him too.

'I don't know.' Zac grinned.

'You know what?' Polly leaned back against him as he wrapped his arms around her. 'I can't wait to move in with you, to spend every moment of every day together.'

Zac chuckled. 'We basically do anyway, what with working in the same office and staying at Pennycress.'

'That's true, but still, I can't wait to get our own place.' Polly looked through the telescope again, focusing once more on the constellation.

'Maybe the one we're going to view tomorrow will be the place where we decide to put our roots down.'

Quickly leaning back on her haunches, Polly whacked her eye against the lens of the telescope. Rubbing it, she looked at him. They'd been searching for somewhere to rent for a few weeks now, but every time they found somewhere they liked the look of, they rang up and were told it had already been let. 'Which one? Which house?'

Zac grinned. 'Not a house. A cottage.'

'You got a viewing for a cottage? How?' She'd thought the rental market was quick and the properties sparse back in Featherford, but here, in Meadowfield, they were like gold dust. No, rarer than gold dust.

'I have my contacts.' Zac tapped the side of his nose with his index finger.

'Aw, no, you've got to tell me now!' She slumped her shoulders. 'You know what will happen, don't you? We'll get a call in the morning cancelling the viewing and telling us it's already been let.'

Shaking his head, Zac chuckled. 'Not with this one. It's the cottage Nicola used to rent down The Twistle. It's not even on the market yet. The tenants are moving out in two weeks' time and we've got first dibs.'

Polly let her mouth drop open. 'Seriously?'

'Seriously.' Leaning forward, Zac cupped her cheek. 'This is going to be our new start, Polly.'

Biting down on her bottom lip, Polly stifled an excited squeal. This was it. This was what she'd always dreamt about, moving to a village, falling in love and moving in together. She just hadn't guessed that the man she fell in love with would be one she'd known all along. 'I love you, Zac.'

'I love you too, Polly.'

* * *

MORE FROM SARAH HOPE

The next book in the Pennycress Inn series from Sarah Hope is available to order now here:

https://mybook.to/PennycressInnBook4

ACKNOWLEDGEMENTS

Thank you so much for reading *Fireworks at Pennycress Inn*. I hope you've enjoyed reading about Polly and Zac's path to finding true love in Meadowfield as much as I have enjoyed writing it.

A massive thank you to my wonderful children, Ciara and Leon, who motivate me to keep writing and working towards 'changing our stars' each and every day.

Also thank you to my lovely family for always being there, through the good times and the trickier ones.

And a huge thank you to my brilliant editor, Francesca Best – thank you! Thank you also to Jade Craddock for copy editing and to Shirley Khan for proofreading *Fireworks at Pennycress Inn*.

Thank you Team Boldwood!

ABOUT THE AUTHOR

Sarah Hope is the author of many successful romance novels, including the bestselling Cornish Bakery series. Sarah lives in Central England with her two children and an array of pets and enjoys escaping to the seaside at any opportunity.

Download your exclusive bonus content from Sarah Hope here:

Follow Sarah on social media here:

f facebook.com/HappinessHopeDreams
X x.com/sarahhope35
○ instagram.com/sarah_hope_writes
BB bookbub.com/authors/sarah-hope

ALSO BY SARAH HOPE

The Pennycress Inn Series

Welcome to Pennycress Inn

Falling in Love at Pennycress Inn

Fireworks at Pennycress Inn

The Cornish Village Series

Wagging Tails in the Cornish Village

Chasing Dreams in the Cornish Village

A Fresh Start in the Cornish Village

Happy Days Ahead in the Cornish Village

Escape to... Series

The Seaside Ice-Cream Parlour

The Little Beach Café

Christmas at Corner Cottage

Boldwood

Boldwood Books is an award-winning fiction publishing company seeking out the best stories from around the world.

Find out more at www.boldwoodbooks.com

Join our reader community for brilliant books, competitions and offers!

Follow us
@BoldwoodBooks
@TheBoldBookClub

Sign up to our weekly deals newsletter

https://bit.ly/BoldwoodBNewsletter

9 781806 560592